HALFWAY TO HELL

Peter Birkett Thompson

PBT publishing

Other books by this author include the Midas trilogy. Midas, Chiller and Viral. By Peter Birkett.

www.peterbirkettbooks.com

https://www.facebook.com/profile.php?id=100078507815773

1

Joe rubbed his bearded chin as he looked up to the top of the wooden pole. *Forty feet?* He called back to base.

"It's Joe again. Are you sure there are no cherry pickers available?"

"Nope. I can see two right here in front of me, but they're waiting for maintenance. We only got the one till...next Tuesday." replied Dean, the telecoms manager.

"Where's the mechanics?"

"One on holiday, one sick. What's the matter Joe, you forget your training?" Dean, who generally cooled his heels in the office, always had that snidey tone to his voice.

"No, I haven't forgotten, it's just been a while and this is pretty high."

"You developed a fear of heights in the last twenty years?"

"Not so much a fear of heights, but a fear of falling, particularly the hitting the ground part. I do the boxes. That's my thing, you know that. I don't do poles."

"Aw. Tell you what, if you feel you're getting too old, I'll send one of the younger lads out."

"I didn't say that."

"Just dust them boots off and get up there."

Joe ended the call. Dean had never been an engineer out in the field. The boots *had* been gathering dust at the back of the van for quite some time.

Technically, all he had to do was climb up the pole and re-attach just one wire that had come loose in last night's stormy weather. *Just one wire. Ok, I got this. Just don't look down. Don't...look... down.*

As he slid the van door open, Joe tried to remember the last time he'd scaled a pole of this height. *Ten years? Longer?* It was probably back when he was in his thirties and the difference between thirties to forties had felt a lot bigger than from twenties to thirties. *You are overthinking again.* He looked down at his slightly expanding pot belly and then breathed in. *Who was he kidding. He could do this in his sleep.* He'd breeze through it and then Dean would have shut his snidey little cake-eating mouth for a while.

He wiped some of the cobwebs off the boots, emptied whatever substances and items had accumulated inside them onto the ground and then pulled them on. Then he walked over to the case with any occupation."

"But, that will be me, dead on the ground?"

"You are not dead yet," Norman looked at his pocket watch, "But I must push you to make a decision. If you say no, then I have fulfilled my responsibility. You only have thirty seconds left to provide me with an answer, by the way."

"So, what you are saying is, if I don't accept, then that's it for me. Goodbye, Joe Briscoe."

Norman nodded and shrugged.

"Uh-huh. Everyone dies. Twenty seconds left."

"And that's it?"

"Yes sir, you will remember nothing of this conversation and your soul will pass on. Fifteen."

"My soul."

"Yes, not everyone has one, though it is a pre-requirement to be offered this *particular* role. It has to be worth our while. Eight seconds. I must press you for an answer."

"Not much of a choice is it."

Norman's image started to flicker and fade out.

"Three, two…"

"I accept." Joe said quickly.

"You cut that close. *Were you in time?"* Norman put a finger to his left ear as though he was awaiting a decision. His image stabilized a little, "Just. Just in time apparently," His image solidified, "You just need to sign here." He passed Joe an old worn-looking book bound in ...something similar to leather. Then he passed him a feather for some reason. Joe realised it was a quill, the kind that Shakespeare used to write with. He scribbled his name in the book. There was no ink on the quill and nothing showed up on the page. Norman closed the book with a slap. "You're in. Welcome to the team," He then passed Joe a small blank piece of parchment, "Place that somewhere safe." Joe placed it in his trouser pocket. *Sooner or later he was going to wake up*. "I'll answer any further questions when you get your first assignment. As for now, it's time for you to go back down there. Back to the grinder." Norman smiled and then turned around.

"Wait a moment..." Joe said, and then he opened his eyes.

"He's coming around," Becky, the female paramedic at the scene said. Joe looked up. The bird was back on the wire. The paramedic held the pads of the defibrillator above his chest, "Stay where you are for a minute." Joe had no intentions of getting up just yet. *That was a weird dream he'd had whilst unconscious.*

"You most likely have a concussion," Steven, the male paramedic said, "We will help you get to your feet and then take you to the hospital. You've had a bad fall and knocked your head." He didn't tell Joe that his heart had stopped for a short time. Joe looked at his dented yellow helmet that was a few feet away on the ground; he'd broken one procedure by not using the rope support, but at least he'd had the helmet on. *Probably what saved him.* He saw a few onlookers with relieved faces. His agoraphobic neighbour had seen enough and retreated to the safety of her own home. Joe got to his feet with some assistance. "We have to take you in with concussion, just for an assessment," Steven said, "What is your name?"

"Norman.... sorry not Norman. It's Joe. Joe Briscoe."

"Ok, Joe," Becky said, "Just lie down in the back for a while and we'll take you in."

Joe led down and looked out of the window. The blackbird flew off into the distance.

"I need to call in to work and tell them what happened." Joe said.

"Don't worry about that." Becky said.

"I left the van open. There are a lot of expensive tools inside."

"Where is the van?" Steven asked.

"Just around the corner," Joe said. Steven asked the ambulance driver to make a quick turn and then he locked the telecoms van remotely with the key fob. "You know, I feel fine. I will be ok to carry on working." Joe said.

"Nope," Becky said, "You are probably still in shock. You need to be assessed by a doctor. We wouldn't be doing *our* job if we just sent you on your way, would we?"

Joe sat back.

"All right." He did feel a bit different. Something felt off. Perhaps he did have a concussion. *After a clash of heads, footballers weren't allowed back on the pitch.* He briefly wondered what Dean back in the office would make of this. No doubt he would have some sarcastic comment ready to spew out under his breath. At least the van was now locked and he wouldn't get into trouble for all the tools being stolen.

2

Joe waited fifty-three minutes and then a doctor saw him. According to some others in the waiting room, that was a quick turnaround and it was not a typical day in A & E. The doctor shone a light into his pupils and was satisfied with what he saw. The medical team did the standard tests and then they sat him down in a little booth, where he waited for a further two hours before a nurse told him that he was ok to leave. They asked him to call if he felt any nausea or headaches or had blurred vision. He told them that he would do and then he decided to walk home as the hospital wasn't far. At the entrance, he saw the same two paramedics who had treated him at the pole.

"Glad you're ok," Becky said, "You were lucky."

Joe smiled and the paramedic duo carried on with their next call. He checked his phone. There were no calls: no one had missed him in the three hours that had passed since the pole climb. Technically speaking he *had* fixed the issue with the line and that job was completed. Maybe he wouldn't even bother telling work about the fall and the trip to the hospital. He'd probably save himself a lot of stick from certain people in the office. The doctor had advised him not to drive for twenty-four hours. The van would be ok where it was, but after thirty minutes of walking, he decided to make the brief detour back to the van. They wouldn't like it if he left it where it was and he wanted to be certain it was secured. It occurred to him as he started the engine that, if he felt inclined to, he could do one *hell* of a good job of taking his foot off the gas at work. Most of the work was done by just a handful of people and the rest just rode along on their coat-tails. The ones at the top and in the office were so off the ball that they wouldn't even notice. *That wasn't his style.* It would just mean extra pressure on the ones that actually pulled their weight and it would probably take more effort trying to dodge work than actually getting on and doing it.

The adrenaline burst the fall caused had now completely worn off and he was starting to feel a little shaken up, although less so than was to be expected. When he got back home, the first thing he did was pick out a can of beer from the fridge. They'd been sat in there for a few days and were nice and chilled. The main reason that they had survived in the fridge for over a week was that they were an *acquired taste*, made by a trendy microbrewery. Good marketing, decidedly average product.

"Why do you bother drinking that stuff?" his brother, Derek asked him, "Tastes like dishwater."

"It was on offer. Have you ever tasted dishwater?"

"No, but if you chilled it in the fridge, it would be very similar. Fancy looking cans though. All that glitters is not Heineken."

"At least it means you won't be drinking any."

"Well, there's a logical concept*: drink crap beer so that your brother won't steal any,*" Derek said. Joe nodded. His brother had moved in with him, *temporarily*, after splitting with his wife. Just a couple of weeks. That was two months ago. But, he *was* paying his way without having to chase him up for it. "Late back today bro. Work busy?"

"I've been at the hospital." Joe said. Derek looked genuinely concerned.

"What for?"

"Fell off a pole." Joe said, as a matter of fact.

"Bloody hell. How far?"

"I don't know, I didn't measure it.'

"But you are ok? You look ok."

"Yeah, they kept me in for a couple of hours, just to make sure."

"No broken bones then. Do you want me to go out and get some proper beers?"

"Na, this will do. I might go and soak in the bath for a while."

"Ok, bud."

Joe went upstairs and turned on the taps. He went to the bedroom and pulled his boots off. He *was* very lucky not to have broken anything. He took off the hi-vis jacket and then his cargo pants, emptying their contents onto the bedside table: notes, coins, pieces of paper, fuel receipts, and toffee wrappers. He didn't often take a bath as showers were a lot more *energy efficient*, though money wasn't tight as Derek was splitting all the bills down the middle.

Joe and Derek had always been pretty close. Their father had left and never returned decades ago and the death of their mother five years previously had brought them together even closer. Derek had always seemed like the charmed one. A bit flashy, some might say. His recent split with his wife hadn't seemed to affect him too much, at least not on the surface. This had been the first occasion that Joe could remember he had needed a favour from his younger sibling.

Joe led in the hot bath for about half an hour, with the can of beer on the side, which he left half full. He submerged his head and then got out and walked over to the mirror to trim his beard. He wiped the condensation off the mirror and saw something *unrecognizable*, just for a split second and then it was his familiar forty-three-year-old face staring back. He wrapped himself in another towel and then climbed into bed for a nap.

◆◆◆

“Don’t think much of your parking,” Derek said as he passed Joe some tea the next morning. Joe looked across at the telecoms van outside his house. It was halfway onto the curb, “Were you drunk?”

“No, course not. I probably shouldn’t have driven the van back. They did say not to drive for a bit.”

“I’ve seen worse. How are you feeling today?”

“All right. Slept like a baby,” The tea was spot on, his brother always did make the best brews of tea, though Joe had never told him this.

“A baby. You woke up crying?” Derek asked.

“A baby that sleeps in. Not like I did, or so I’m told.”

“No, I could lie and say that you used to wake me up, but I was only four at the time myself. Your eyes are nice and clear today. Are you going in to work?”

“Na, they told me to take the rest of the week off.”

“That would be generous if today wasn’t Friday. Still, *my* boss wouldn’t have done that for me.”

“You are self-employed.”

“I know, but I’m still the toughest employer I ever had.”

"You want to lighten up on yourself then. Life's too short."

"I'm kidding. I have it easy; *too* easy some might say."

Joe took the tea upstairs and then wondered what to do with the rest of the day. He stared through his bedroom window and he remembered the dream and chuckled to himself. He sat down on the edge of the bed and gathered his money together. He stacked the notes together and then stacked all the coins on top of the bedside cabinet. There was a small scrap of yellowing paper mixed in with the notes that looked about as old as a piece of Egyptian parchment. It had a number written on it, quite a long number. His glasses for reading were downstairs, but he could make out what was written on the paper. It was odd, there was a long number that was blurred, as expected without glasses, but it appeared to be changing at random every few seconds. *That could wait.* He lay down on the bed and hoped this symptom was only a temporary thing.

Derek was struggling, underneath, to get through a difficult time. Joe's divorce, by comparison, had been a walk in the park. They had no kids. His ex-wife, Charlie, had woken up one day and decided that she liked women. It probably hadn't happened as swiftly as that, but that's how she'd portrayed it to him. Joe felt that her explanation was both good and bad. Firstly, she hadn't run off with another man. because that would have been the hardest scenario to take and also the biggest insult. He understood the whole *concept* of being attracted to women and he could understand it. He'd never expected his wife to understand it in the same way, but what the hell. Had he been so appallingly bad as a husband that his wife had swapped gender preferences? Probably not.

Derek's wife and Joe's sister-in-law, *Joy*, was hardly a bundle of it. She was a different kettle of fish: a social climber. At least that was one of the cleaner-sounding and less profanity laden phrases that Derek used to describe her. He seemed fine on the outside, since the split, but as Joe's older brother, Derek had *always* seemed fine, even when severely tested at their father's funeral. Derek and Joy had produced one child, Ian, who occupied the third bedroom at Joe's every second weekend.

You should have kicked her out. You shouldn't have been the one to go. Joe had told Derek. Though he didn't know all the complexities of the story as he only received Derek's inevitably weighted side. On the rare occasion that Joe had spoken to Joy since the split, he only received guarded, short-sentence answers; almost like she had military captive training. *Just name and number.* Derek had responded, *I'm away too much with the job. There's*

Ian to think about.

It meant, as is the case with most divorces, they had the dubious pleasure of splitting everything down the middle. The solicitors were on the case but seemed in about as much of a rush as a turtle race competitor. Joe was ok with his brother staying with him, for now, but he hoped it wasn't a situation that would go on for *too* much longer, even if his brother was away on business for the majority of the time.

Joe got dressed idly as he planned to walk down to the nearest supermarket to get something for lunch. Derek declined his offer of food and began loading up his Audi estate in preparation for the three-day meeting he had scheduled. He needed to set off around sunset to arrive in decent time to settle in and be fresh to begin the next day's corporate meeting.

Joe walked downstairs, flipped open the kitchen bin and attempted to throw in the faded piece of paper that had been in his pocket. The lid closed again, just as the paper arrived. He tried again, this time he held the lid open and *placed* the paper inside. Somehow it drifted onto the edge and fell on the kitchen floor. He picked it up once more and screwed it up tight in his fist, held the bin lid open and then put his whole fist inside the bin. He let go of the paper and it unwrinkled itself and lay flat on top of the other waste. On it, Joe could see a number in faded-looking ink, it was definitely not written in biro. It would have been easy enough to close the bin lid, but he didn't, instead he just stared at the number for a few seconds. Then he picked it out again, made a mental note of the last four digits, 7..4..3..9..and placed the paper down on the kitchen worktop. It could sit there for a while, at least until he got back from the shops.

He set off. It was only a ten-minute walk, but that was long enough for him to warrant getting his earphones out so that he could listen to a few tunes on the way. He selected *shuffle*, and his phone selected *The Whole of the Moon*, by the Waterboys. As he closed the front door behind himself, he noticed that the works van *was* parked at an untidy angle. *Man, that parking.* What the hell, if it got clipped by something on the way past, it was no big deal. It wasn't his van. He walked past it.

He arrived at the large red supermarket sign, he walked inside, picked up a basket and headed down an aisle. *Fruit, pizza, ice cream*: his nephew was staying over in a few days, and beer. *Not the microbrewery stuff*. He picked a six-pack out of the refrigerated cabinet. As he picked up the Heineken, he noticed something written in the condensation on the glass door of the cabinet. *Call the number*. It looked like someone had done it with their finger, but there was no number to call.

He paid for the shopping and set off back home. This was to be his exercise for the day, which was marginally better than nothing at all. *Live and let die* came through his earphones as he passed by a campervan that had been parked in the same spot for several weeks. *Don't forget,* was written on the grimy back window.

When he arrived back home, the first thing he did was pull the ring on one of the Heinekens. It was nice and cold. He looked around the kitchen as he drank it. Derek had tidied up. Not just that, he'd arranged every mug by size and colour. He'd done the same with the kitchen cloths and towels. In the drawer, every piece of cutlery was in its correct place. The only thing that was out of place was the paper that had been given a reprieve from the waste bin. Joe walked over to it. The numbers that he'd made a mental note of were still on it and hadn't changed since he last looked. *Twelve numbers.* Mobile phone numbers were eleven, so if he called the number, as the messages on the supermarket trip had suggested that he do, that was one too many. At any rate, it didn't start with zero. *Was this all part of the concussion?* He picked the paper up again and stared at it for a few moments. Then he got his mobile phone and decided to call the number, out of plain curiosity, just to see what would happen. Then, when nothing did, he would put it back in the bin and take the whole black sack outside and put it in the main wheeled bin. Out of sight, out of mind. Just as he was on number 8, his phone rang. It was Derek.

"Yep." Joe answered.

"Hi, bud. Listen, I've forgotten something I need. Please look on the dining table for a folder, blue I think it is, with a pen drive in it." Joe walked to the table and, sure enough, there was a blue A4-sized folder on it, containing just a few sheets of paper.

"Got it."

"Aw, man. Is the pen drive in it?" Joe shook the folder, tipped it up and the pen drive fell out.

"Yes, it's here. Have you set off already?"

"I'll come back and get it." Derek ended the call. Joe went over to where the piece of paper was. He couldn't see it. *Where the hell did that go?* No matter. If Norman *had* written the little prompts and wanted to contact *him* again, he would do. *Did Joe want him to do that?* No. Norman was just a dream from a bad day at the office.

Four hours later.

Joe's neighbour, directly to his left, heard some commotion as he watered the plants in his small patioed backyard. He peered over the five-foot-high separating wall to see Joe on his knees; his waste bin was upended and he was unceremoniously sifting through the contents.

"You ok there?" the neighbour asked.

Joe looked around to see his blank-faced

neighbour.

"Yeah. Lost a receipt."

"We've all done it. Expensive was it, whatever it is you need to return?"

"Very. Well, no, not really. I don't know really."

"Oh." His neighbour thought it odd, but who was he to speculate? Joe's angular parking had been the topic of conversation earlier in the day, "Hope you find it, whatever it is you've lost."

Joe ignored him and kept on looking. He went through everything. *To hell with it. It's gone.* He threw everything back into the bin and uprighted it. Then he put his hand in his pocket and pulled out something. It was the old piece of paper. He didn't remember placing it back in his pocket. He dialled the long number. It rang three times before being answered.

"Hello there." Norman answered. *He wasn't just part of a dream.*

"What on earth is going on?"

"Aw, don't worry. We are just trying out a new method of contacting agents. The Boss wasn't very enthusiastic about trying new methods. He's what you might call ...old school."

"Mobile phone numbers aren't really *old school.*"

"Try telling him that. Anyway, we aren't taking it on permanently, just trialling it out. He won't want to move with the times. Believe me."

"Ok. So, I was supposed to ring you? Those

messages on the shopping trip. I assume that was you?"

"Yes. Your first mission."

"I was sort of hoping either you'd forget or that I'd dreamt it all."

"Nope, we never forget our clients, actually, that's the wrong term...*employees*? No, that's not quite right either. *Members...*?"

"Well, whatever I am, I'm being lined up for one of these red flag jobs you were on about?" Joe was hoping that this strange business with Norman would fade away and disappear, but for some reason, he felt compelled to go along with it, for now.

"*Agents*! I like that. Sort of a secret agent vibe going on. Indeed. I do have the details right here."

"Fire away then, if you must."

"Have you already read the case notes?" Norman seemed surprised.

"No, how could I have?"

"It's just that you said *fire away*. No matter, it's one of those *coincidences* that occur all the time. This is a small mission involving a junior employee at a branch of a large company. At first glance, it appears to be some kind of disgruntled employee type of thing. That's what the notes say."

"Ok."

"Now, the young man in question has a bright future. He's a decent sort, but he makes a mistake, just one stupid error of judgement that acts as a catalyst for quite an *alarming* downfall in fortune. You see what I did there?!"

"No, I don't. What does he do? I suppose I'm to stop him from doing whatever it is that he does?"

"He sets off the fire alarm at his place of work because, well, I don't know why, it isn't in the notes. This singular act is the catalyst for being bypassed for promotion, eventually getting himself fired from the job, and then developing a drinking problem. For him, it all goes downhill rather steadily from that moment onwards, until he ends up a dishevelled wreck, sipping wine from a brown paper bag on the high street."

"And he deserves saving?"

"He is entitled to a red flag warning. If he wasn't, we wouldn't be having this conversation."

"Oh. What does he look like?"

"About *so* big. Skinny little tyke looks like he should still be in school, you can't miss him. Mission one always takes a little bit of getting used to. Just do what you can to stop him from setting the alarm off. It's scheduled to happen at 5:08 pm tomorrow," Norman continued, "It's at the building society with the red & blue sign on the high street."

"What's it called?" Joe wondered.

"We can't divulge brand names, it's against company policy. It's the one with the red & blue sign ...next to the wagering shop."

"Ok. *Policy. Wagering*?" Joe smirked for a split second and then Norman was gone.

Derek entered the room to see Joe deep in thought, toying with his phone. He wondered whether his brother was feeling any negative after-effects from the fall.

"You sure you are ok?" he asked. Joe nodded, "You haven't had any blurred vision or headaches since falling off that pole?" Joe looked up, shook his head and pursed his lips, "Any hallucinations?"

"Nope." Joe answered, though the whole *Norman* thing may well have been a giant one.

"I'm going again soon, had to come back for the folder."

"You doing some housework, was that real or just a hallucination?"

"Yes, real. I know I like things in a certain order. It's just a temporary measure."

"Your OCD, or you helping out?

"No, me being here."

"I know."

"I know I said that three months ago. Listen, bro, I do appreciate what you are doing, I really do. I'm going to set off again now. I'll see you when I get back."

"Where are you staying?"

"Birmingham travel lodge, as per usual."

"Why don't you stay somewhere a bit nicer?"

"You know me. All I need is a bed.

Would rather spend the extra money saved on something else."

"Don't drink the mini-bar then!"

"Noted." Derek said and then he left to begin the three-hour drive to where the conference was being held. As soon as the door clunked shut behind him, Joe's phone rang.

"Norman?"

"Yes. I have your phone number now. It's sort of in the rules that you have to call us first. In the fine print somewhere along with the other stuff we don't want you to be able to read. I hung up when you got company. There was some more to tell you...*wasn't there?* Ah yes, your first assignment. Actually, that's everything you need; just stop him from setting off the fire alarm. His name is...Karl, with a 'K'."

"Are you sure that's it? It does sound a bit... trivial."

"You wouldn't think so if you were in the fire brigade and not the...whatever it is that you do. Anyway, we always start new admissions with something simple. There'll be plenty of time for more advanced missions. Plenty of time to make *amends.*"

"Ok. Is that it then?"

"Indeed yes. Au revoir." Norman ended the call.

Joe sat down. He had the house to himself. He ordered a pizza delivery, sat down on the sofa and aimlessly channel-hopped until the time reached 11:00 pm. Then he went upstairs, peeled off his clothes and flopped into bed.

3

On the next morning, Saturday, Joe still got out of bed when the alarm sounded, even though he didn't have to. It would have been a work day, but policy on concussions meant that he had to stay off for at least three days, because his employer had to, not because they cared about his well-being. Some outside agency telecoms techno wannabe was probably already botching up a job that he would have been assigned to. *Those agency staff simply weren't worth the hassle.* He said it out loud they irked him that much. He wasn't on his own in that opinion.

He had some time to kill before five pm. He thought it a good idea to go and do a recon mission on the building society that was pencilled in for his first assignment. As bizarre as this new situation was, Joe felt that he had no other option but to go along with it, for now at least. It wasn't as if he was being asked to do anything nefarious, and he was beginning to get more than a little curious.

After a pointless wander around the town centre, he loitered outside the building society with the red & blue sign. It was five stories high and covered a lot of ground. *Built with other people's money.* Joe took a brief look into the reception area. Norman hadn't stated which floor the fire alarm in question was on. He pushed the door open and walked inside. He looked at the name badges on every visible male member of staff. None of them fitted the bill. Then, a young trainee came walking through the foyer. Joe didn't see a badge, but he knew instinctively that this was the lad, Karl, the target of the mission. He took a moment and assessed the situation. Security looked on point: the internal doors were secure and opened only by keycode. If this event was scheduled to happen at 5:08 pm, then there was no obvious way for Joe to be in the right place at the right time. The branch opening hours were 9-5 pm, he couldn't loiter around till six. He was no master burglar or Tom Cruise impersonator. He called out to the lad walking past.

"Hey, excuse me." Karl stopped, surprised. He guessed that it was probably just a customer wanting to be directed to someone important. The young man looked a little down-trodden. His hair was a little untidy and his attempts at growing a beard were largely unsuccessful, "Could you tell me where I could open an account, please?" That was all Joe could think of saying.

"Just see them at the counter. They will guide you through the process. Or pick up a leaflet," The young man answered with a smile that struggled to get past pursed lips, "Is there anything else?" he asked, as Joe had not diverted his gaze.

"Just one thing," Joe took a step nearer and spoke more softly, "Karl, isn't it? If…if you get the idea of doing something …rash, later today… don't do it. Just wait. Everything will work out here given time."

Karl wondered how this person might know his name. He looked back at Joe as though he might have been reading his mind, somehow. He didn't know how to respond to this *odd* comment.

"Ok." Was all he said in response. Joe smiled at him and then slowly turned and made his way out of the building. *Had he done this right? Or was that just a cop-out?* It was nowhere near 5:08 pm, but that would have to do. Norman would just have to accept that as his effort. *Was it his best effort?* To hell with it. That was all he was going to do. If the kid still decided to set off the fire alarm, it was down to him.

Joe walked around the town centre a little more. He bought nothing but did a lot of window shopping. In some of the windows he half expected to see Norman's reflection alongside his own. *Was Norman up there somewhere watching and judging his efforts …or lack of them?* Joe had a strong feeling that he would find out soon enough.

◆ ◆ ◆

Derek put his bag down on the over-firm mattress of the travel lodge hotel. Eight-thirty. He'd made it in just over three hours. He didn't find driving distances a chore as some do. He tended to speed as far as he could push the boundaries and he'd tipped 100 mph a couple of times on the way here, though he wasn't in a rush and wouldn't be able to explain, if asked, why he felt the need to drive that fast.

His wife had never appreciated all the travelling. At least, not at first. Later on, she found it more of a blessing.

He set his laptop up on the table and did his necessary searches. He was all set for tomorrow's meeting, but with a few hours to kill, he decided that he would drive around for a bit. Twenty minutes after checking in and in total contrast to how he arrived at this city, he was now driving very slowly. When he reached a specific spot, he stopped and wound down his passenger window.

◆ ◆ ◆

Joe picked up his toothbrush. There had been no new messages, written on window panes or otherwise. 5:08 pm had come and gone the previous night. Then, as he descended the stairs, a figure materialized at the bottom.

"Norman."

"Good morning. Well done for yesterday."

"Well done?"

"Yep. *Mission accomplished*, as they used to say during the war."

"Oh, right. That kid didn't set the alarm off then?"

"Nope."

"All I did was…"

Norman cut him short.

"No, we don't require any details. You did it and that's it. That's all we need to know."

"Good. So, did you just come to congratulate me or are you here with another one?" Joe asked as he brushed past Norman's insubstantial form.

"Am I that transparent?" Norman replied, as he held up his right arm and gazed through it.

"I'd offer you a coffee but…."

"I don't drink liquid. Please, carry on though. Don't let me disturb you getting your fix."

"Did you drink coffee before, I mean, before you became…?"

"The messenger, slash, intermediator, slash, *whatever it is* I am now? Nope. Wasn't even a thing. Neither was the potato. No coffee and no chips."

"Let me make one to help wake me up and you

can tell me why you're here."

"Be my guest. There is plenty of time. The next one is not till tomorrow evening."

"I got a day off then."

"Oh yes. We don't work you too hard or too often. Sometimes a whole month can go by before your services are required."

"Not like it's work if that first one was anything to go by." Joe made the coffee whilst Norman waited and faded in and out of view, "So, you don't call on the phone every time?"

"No. I could, but I don't. Mobile phones aren't my favorite. You can't see the other person's face as you are giving them the bad news. To be brutally honest, I liked my last position better. It was far simpler. Have you ever seen one of those black & white WW2 films where they push things around a giant-sized map with sticks?"

"Err…yeah."

"I was on that for 300 years or so. I enjoyed that, though I did make the odd error here and there. I once manoeuvred some *Captain or other* to Penzance by mistake. The pirates got them in the end. Walked the plank. Ce la vie. Then with the big one. The whole escapade was a cock up. Plenty of red flags, bucket loads of them, but did anyone spot any of them or act upon them? It's not so much the spotting, but the acting on them that's the deal breaker you see. Well, they did … eventually, but not enough. Too little too late."

This character was mildly amusing if just slightly annoying.

"What are you talking about?"

"*World war two*. You must've heard of it. Far too many missed opportunities to stop it from starting in the first place, and that was no mean feat, let me tell you. That's why all of the new recruits are vetted more carefully. When we have the time or the inclination."

"*I'm* a new recruit. And that's where you come in. You're vetting me. I get it. What is it then?"

"There weren't any of these issues when it was just dinosaurs and plants, or so the boss says, my memory is a little foggy. It was his big idea to give a species the power of speech and free will. A mistake some might say, but here we are. There have been so many wars and armies and battles that I've lost count. Mind ..." he whispered, "*I did start a few of them*. Back to the matter at hand; *not* a world war, thankfully not on mission two. You simply have to save a young man from himself. Again."

"There is a point to your rambling then."

"Yes. I do ramble, yet I do eventually get to the point. Do you want to know what it is? Mission two?"

"Please don't let me stop you," Joe said. The coffee was already half drunk, "But if first, though, you could make a bit more sense of all this ...this whole scenario, I would be grateful."

"Very well, I will shed some more light on the matter. It appears that you are not yet convinced. So, it was decided, many thousands of years ago, that human beings, such as yourself, should be entitled to a little help. *Why you ask?* Because you aren't always very good to each other. *An understatement to be sure*. Does a Lion catch and kill an antelope because it is acting unreasonably? Of course not, it's just doing what a Lion does, what it has been put here to do. It does not awaken on the savannah plains one morning and think, *I'm going to be a right bastard today*? Of course not. Only people do that. So, with that concept in mind, the concept of humans acting with free will, the Boss has allocated each *deserving* person his or her red flag provider. This is only an afterthought. If he hadn't given people free will in the first place, then there would be no need for this measure. If you ask me, it's applying a band-aid after the event, however ...here we are. He thinks that it is the least he can do. And it probably is the *least*."

"So, God is a *he*, then?"

"In a manner of speaking, but he can use either bathroom."

"So, this isn't a dream and I'm stuck with it?"

"Dream, reality it's all pretty much the same. This for that. Tit for tat."

"And you can just beam down, like on Star Trek, or I can call you, and you can ring me on an ever-changing phone number?"

"*Nothing* in life is ever constant. It's *all* continuously changing. And please don't mention Star Trek or William Shatner either. Awful, awful man. Thinks he's a god himself."

"The universe is expanding, I saw that on TV." Joe said.

"Don't get me started on *that* subject. As if I didn't already have enough to do."

"So, I would have died the other day. If I'd refused all this?"

"I'm not at liberty to answer that," Norman faded out a little more. Joe didn't speak for a while, "Come outside, there is something else I need to let you in on." Joe didn't argue. He took the mug of coffee with him. Norman stopped under a tree twenty meters from Joe's house. Joe looked around at life passing by. People, cars, birds. It didn't feel like a dream. "Something else for your future assignments. Some extra tools for your toolbox. Part of being an *Angel* is that you have a trick or two up your sleeve. Makes the tasks easier, if you use them wisely and to your advantage." Joe looked around again. He was a little concerned about speaking out loud to Norman, as he was now invisible. Also, he was standing outside in his dressing gown and slippers, to the slight amusement of a couple of teenagers walking past. He shrugged his shoulders to ask for more of an explanation. "You can control any animal or creature, except humans, who are sometimes some of the filthiest animals, for up to five seconds. With a little practice."

"Why not humans?" Joe whispered.

"The free will thing. The boss is pretty hot on that one, it's non-negotiable."

"So, cats, dogs, birds, goldfish and so on." Joe said.

"Good, you are getting the jist of it. Though I fail to see what use a goldfish might be in any situation," Norman paused and then referred Joe to a lady who was walking a medium-sized, tan-coloured dog, "See that woman over there?"

Joe looked over at the woman around thirty meters away. Norman was still completely invisible.

"Yeah. You sure you're still here?"

"Yes, I can tell you the pattern on your slippers if you like, now, focus on, not the woman, but the dog."

"Ok."

"What is it doing?"

"Just doing what dogs do; walking at its owner's side."

"What else?"

"Sniffing, panting."

"Ok, now. Make the dog sit up and beg."

"And what if it can't do that?"

"Humour me please, would you? Just make it sit and beg."

"And if I can't, you'll quit hassling me?"

"Deal. But you have to try with your best effort and no less."

Joe couldn't see Norman and wondered whether or not he still had visuals on the situation. He did nothing for twenty seconds except pace up and down. Then he said,

"You see, nothing happened. I'm obviously not the right man for you. May as well call it quits." As he said that, Norman shimmered back into view for a couple of seconds.

"You are *exactly* the right man. You didn't even attempt the task did you?"

"Ok, no …I didn't. This is just taking things to another level of stupidity."

"It's a skill you might need. Try again and focus on making a connection with the beast." Came a voice out of thin air.

Joe sighed. He focused his attention on the dog, which was slowly moving out of the picture, even though the old hound was in no rush to get anywhere. *Sit and beg.* Joe thought about the dog doing just that and he tried to plant that idea in the dog from a distance. Nothing happened.

"Pointless." Joe whispered. He tried a little longer. A little harder. Then, suddenly, the tan-coloured dog stopped in its tracks. It sat down and turned to its owner and with great surprise, to all except Norman, it offered out its left paw. The dog's lady owner had never taught him to do that. She stared at him, wondering how on earth he could have learnt this new trick. After a few seconds, the dog retracted its paw, turned and then carried on walking.

"There you go. Now do you believe?" Norman said.

Joe did believe. He replayed the scene of the pole climb, the blackbird, the fall and then the ambulance ride.

"So, I can control animals. *Doctor bloody Doolittle.*"

"Let me re-affirm. Non-humans, 2-5 seconds. When you get to be an expert, much longer than that. All this is in the notes. Objects, well, they vary. You need to get past tier one first. Now, this brings us to your second assignment. Your second assignment is to send a red flag, *surprise surprise,* to a twenty-year-old man. He's about to become involved with a woman of a similar age who will prove in time to be highly toxic to him. *Narcissists,* I think some of you more cerebral humans have coined the phrase, not you *specifically*, but the ones you have that are trying to unravel all of your complexities. A virtually impossible task, I must say."

"You mean psychologists."

"Freud. He was a dark horse. Anyway, I digress."

Joe whispered,

"Not for the first time."

"I'll ignore that. Anyway, send him the red flag, he is entitled to and then it's up to him what he does with it. I will text message the details to your phone. Goodness, I'd rather just say them to you, but this way you can refer back to them if needed. They will automatically delete themselves once the correct amount of time has passed."

"Just like mission impossible."

"Quite so. But don't get me on the subject of Tom Cruise, now *there's* a story and a half. Bye for now!"

Joe walked back to the house. The lady with the dog would never see it sit and beg again.

4

7:00 pm, Gino's Italian restaurant, Sunday the 12th, table by the fireplace. That's what the text message from Norman read. Joe attempted to add the long phone number to his contacts. His Samsung reported that it couldn't complete this simple task. Joe knew Gino's quite well, although he hadn't actually stepped foot inside the building for over a decade. He'd taken his former wife there just after they had started dating; just a few months into whatever it was that they'd had. *Some young man is about to get involved with a toxic member of the opposite sex.* A familiar scenario, though, no doubt, his ex-wife looked back and thought the same in reverse. The reasonably good terms they'd parted on had soured quite dramatically when it came to the house and the finances.

Sunday was quite dull, in terms of the grey-skyed weather and also general levels of interest. Derek was due to return from his business travels around lunchtime. Joe had the good idea to book in at Gino's sooner rather than later in the day, specifically, a table for two near the fire. The nearest available time to what he wanted was 6:30 pm. They'd have to linger and not rush proceedings.

As the day panned out, he wondered how difficult this job would turn out to be. He also wondered whether or not Derek would have eaten by then. He decided to and then forgot to send a text message telling him the plan. There was no black-or-white outcome with this second mission. The last time, the fire alarm either went off or it didn't. This scenario would play out over time. *What was so bad about this girl?* He didn't need to know.

He sat and drank coffee. His mind drifted back in time to a random occasion when he and his wife had visited the same restaurant. A time when they were in love, or at least they had each acted out the part. Gazing at each other by candlelight. Sharing their dessert with two spoons. Happier days ...or *were they?* Today, life wasn't earth-shatteringly great, but at least it was real. But then with Norman now on the scene, reality had taken a holiday. He sat flicking through tv channels and let time pass by as it pleased.

Around 4:00 pm he heard the front door opening. Derek had returned.

"Hi buddy." Derek said as he dropped his overnight bag down in the hallway.

"How was your journey?" Joe asked.

"Fine, fine. Just one congested bit. Speed cameras, you know the one's that average out your speed. Do you think they actually do that?"

"I don't know. I've never heard anyone say that they have been done by one of them. Maybe it's a con."

"Still, with five points, *already*, I wasn't going to risk it."

"You eaten yet?"

"No. Probably just get a takeaway or throw something in the oven." Derek said as he flipped his leather shoes off.

"Nope, I've booked a table at Gino's, my shout."

"Gino's? What's the occasion, don't tell me I forgot something? If I did, man I'm sorry."

"No, you didn't forget anything, my birthday is July. I just thought it would be a nice change and I fancied Italian food. It's booked for 6:30."

"6:30 ...pretty early?"

"All they had left. We probably won't eat till 7:00."

"Ok, thanks, I'll go and have a quick shower, then get changed." Derek headed upstairs to the spare room. He'd had a shower already that morning, perhaps the long drive had left him feeling *grubby*.

◆ ◆ ◆

At 6:20 pm, Joe parked the works van in Gino's small car park. He left it at an angle that would prevent him from being blocked in when it filled up later on.

His brother had changed into a white short-sleeved shirt, his hair still a little wet from the shower.

"Isn't that a work shirt?" Joe asked.

"Yeah. Couldn't be arsed ironing anything. Looks too formal?"

"No. It's fine, just that you might be mistaken for a waiter."

"Good. I'll enjoy telling people to go and screw themselves if they ask me for the wine list."

"Please don't do that. You can have a few drinks. I'll just have the one." Joe said as they were getting out.

"You could always leave the van here and have a few as well? I don't like drinking alone."

"Na. Do you know that sticker on the van that says, *no tools left in this vehicle overnight?* It's a blatant lie; there's about a grand's worth in tools. It's too remote out here to risk it. Statistically, vehicles left in car parks are more at risk. Anyway, I'm not in a drinking mood." he added, as he opened the main door. He told the girl behind reception that they had a table booked and she bade them go through to the bar area and wait as they were just preparing it for them.

In the bar, there were a few couples; *potential red flag recipients.* None of them looked to be in their late teens or early twenties. Still, it was early yet. Derek ordered drinks at the bar and the barman set up a pint of lager and a small glass.

"What's that?" Joe asked as he took a sip of the lager.

"Whiskey."

"Whiskey? Is it a double?" Joe asked. His brother shrugged and nodded, "You on a mission to get plastered? That latest meeting you went to was stressful then?"

"Kinda. I did leave the min-bar alone, so this is now my reward."

Before long, a front-of-house staff member showed them to their table in the main room, by the fireplace, as requested. There were three tables around the fire, which wasn't lit. The person that took the booking thought it odd someone actually requesting a table by the fire in the *summertime.* There was their vacant table, a table for four and one other table for two, all with occupants who looked to be in their mid-forties.

"Not them," Joe said, quietly. He noticed that the couple on the small table were too busy chatting to finish the desserts they had in front of them, "Get a move on." he whispered.

"You say something?" Derek asked, he'd

already drunk most of the double scotch.

"No."

"Oh, I'm going back to the bar. You sure you don't want another one?"

Joe looked at his glass, which was still ¾ full,

"No thanks," He then looked at his watch, it was now 6:40 pm. He still had no idea how he would proceed in this situation, he would just wait and see how it unfolded. His brother returned with a strong lager for himself and sat down, agitated. "You ok? Try and relax now. Forget about business meetings and chill out for a bit."

"Yeah, yeah."

A waitress brought over two menus. On first impressions, it looked like the food hadn't changed much in the last decade. *Why fix something that isn't broken*?

"What are you having?" Joe asked. There was still no sign of another set of diners at the next table.

"You're paying right?"

"Yeah...but."

"I'm joking. I'm in a steak mood. I'll have the rump steak with a nice pepper sauce. It's not the *most* expensive one. Have you decided yet?" Joe looked at the items on the menu in terms of how long things might take to eat. He needed this scene to pan out for a while in case the other table was late. He stalled the waitress when she politely asked if they were ready to order, though he knew what he wanted, and so did Derek. The second time she appeared, ten minutes later, he again stalled the order. The other table was now empty, and the two forty-somethings had moved on with their quiet ritual into the bar area. It was now 6:55 pm. Joe toyed with his fork, turning it over and over. "What's the matter, you starving hungry?" Derek asked him.

"Yeah. A few empty tables tonight."

Derek took a look around,

"Just one or two." Just as he said that, the same waitress who had led them to their table ushered through a young couple who sat down at the small table near the fireplace. The young woman was very pretty. *All that glitters.* Facing her was a young man who looked like a good-natured type. *Decency* just radiated off him. Her looks were so beguiling that he was probably smitten. *Why would he need a red flag with this beauty? A green one,* maybe, but then *...all that glitters.*

This second assignment seemed about as strange as Norman looked. There didn't seem to be any valid reason for Joe being there.

"Aren't you even looking at the menu?" Derek asked. He'd noticed his brother's gaze was elsewhere.

"No, I know what I'm getting. Spaghetti."

"Ten years since you came here and you're

playing it safe."

"I know what I like."

"Fair enough, me too. Half the fun is looking at the menu."

"Yeah. Get whatever you want."

"It's steak, I'm not going to change my mind." Derek noticed that his brother was preoccupied with the adjacent table. "Pretty girl huh?" he whispered.

Joe noticed that his brother had noticed his distraction.

"Yeah. I thought I knew them. It's someone else."

"Too young for you."

"I know that, that's not why I was looking."

They both turned and looked at the young man whose hand had just been clasped by the girl.

"Young love. Remember that?" Derek asked.

"Yes. Vaguely. Very vaguely."

They were interrupted by a serious looking front-of-house member of staff who proceeded to uncork a bottle of red wine. He placed the bottle on the table and then left. Derek told his brother that he'd ordered it at the bar. He poured himself a large glass and then hovered the neck over Joe's glass. Joe nodded and then held his hand up to say *stop* when the glass was just half full. Joe took a sip.

"Not bad. Aren't they supposed to pour it and let you taste it before they disappear?" Joe said.

Derek had already taken a bigger gulp and had not bothered to comment on it.

"I think if it's expensive they still do that," Finally, without any further need to delay, they gave their food orders to the waitress who had stopped smiling at them after her second wasted visit to the table, "This is cool," Derek said, "Spending some quality time with my brother," He took a look around the entire restaurant, which by now had no empty tables, "You realise though, that we probably look like a gay couple?"

"I never thought of that."

"Who cares, so what. Did you see the game yesterday…?" Joe was picking up snippets of conversation from the other table, "Are you listening? …The game?"

"Yeah, the game. V.A.R messed up again didn't they." Joe spoke without breaking his concentration from the adjacent table's conversation. Derek realized that his brother was not fully invested and decided to do a bit of people-watching for himself.

"Dark in here isn't it," he stated, "Is that so you can't see what you're eating? I suppose if they turned a big light on, then it would lose all the atmosphere. Perhaps if they served us naked? Hello, earth to Joe..."

"Sorry, yeah, I was miles away. Naked servers might put people off their pizzas."

"You were half-listening then. The house red

is always nice in these Italians. Anything more expensive is wasted on me anyway."

"Yeah. It doesn't touch the sides. You are mixing drinks tonight, by the way."

The girl had her phone strategically placed, not intrusive, but accessible. Napoleon himself couldn't have placed it any more skillfully. To Joe, it appeared that she wanted to see the whole moon, not just the crescent.

Before the food came to either table, the young man got up and went to the restroom. She took this opportunity to check her phone. She started to text a message. Derek noticed his brother's interest in this simple action but declined to make any further comments. Her date returned to the table and she quickly returned the phone to her bag, which was hung over the back of her chair.

Twenty minutes after ordering, the food arrived. It did look appetizing under the dim candlelight. Derek's steak looked a decent size. The plate of spaghetti was very generous. *Good.* Neither of the two brothers said anything else and they started to eat. Joe began to make inroads into the steaming plate. After half a dozen fork-loads, he asked,

"How is your steak?"

Derek nodded. When he'd finished chewing, all he said was,

"Good." Then he rested his fork and knife on

the plate, "It said eight ounces on the menu and it looks like it actually is that."

"Even though you had it *well done*. I never have steak past *medium*."

"Each to their own taste. I don't like the sight of blood." Derek said.

"Yeah. Italians do a decent steak, but I always order Italian food. Pizza or pasta."

"You know, pizza isn't an Italian thing. It comes from America."

"Leaning tower of pizza?"

"Not related. The Italian restaurants ran with it and made it their own. Not authentically Italian though," Derek said, in between chewing, "Basically, it's just cheese on toast." Derek took another swig of red wine. Joe took a sip of his.

Twenty minutes later, they had both finished their food. Joe looked up at the old wooden ceiling. It was ornately carved and looked original. In this dim lighting, it was hardly noticeable, but it must have taken a colossal amount of work from a master craftsman. His gaze lowered again. He needed the restroom himself. By comparison, his brother seemed like a camel, particularly taking into account all the alcohol he knocked back. As he pushed his chair back, Joe accidentally knocked off the bag belonging to the young lady on the next table. The contents spilt out onto the floor, they included some underwear and a packet of condoms. Her phone also fell out and the screen illuminated with an unsent text message. Her date looked at the items as she scurried them back into place. Joe apologized profusely, it was clumsiness on his behalf. She took it good-naturedly. Nothing had broken.

As he relieved himself, Joe wondered whether he had become completely delusional. *Had that knock on the head caused these complex hallucinations?* He wondered just what the hell he was doing on this night, studying other people's dating habits. He made an agreement with himself to contact his doctor in the morning. *They wouldn't cart him away for having these delusions? Would they? Surely not. That dog with the tricks ...*he let out a chuckle as he sat back down.

"What's tickled your fancy?" Derek asked.

"You ...wouldn't believe me even if I told you." Derek shrugged and poured the last of the wine. Joe would let the doctor do his job. Stress and trauma could be a real bitch of a thing and he felt like this whack on the head and escaping what could have been a fatal accident, had probably caused him more mental harm than was initially apparent. Here he was, sitting in a restaurant, on some crazy *re-con red flag mission*. At least the food had been good. "We should do this more often," Joe stated. Derek was a little surprised at this comment, as his brother had hardly been in *conversational mode* for the last hour and a half.

Nevertheless, he replied.

"Sure. Don't you see enough of me already? With me living with you at the moment."

"Ok. Maybe after you've moved out, we will. Once a year." Joe smiled. Derek sat back and sipped the last of the red.

"Look, I know I haven't said much about you letting me stop at yours and all that, but you've helped me since the split and I want you to know that I appreciate it. I really do. You've been a real angel."

"Grapes loosened your tongue?"

"I guess so. You know how it is. Stoic. Like Dad was."

"*Angel.*" Joe chuckled again.

"You know what I mean. I don't know what I'd have done. Especially with the lad."

"Family is family." Joe glanced at the couple to his right. He felt he noticed a change in the young man's demeanour. Nothing drastic. *Perhaps he was anticipating the bill.*

"We're splitting this." Derek insisted, as their bill was presented on the table.

"I said it was my treat."

"Nope. I had steak and I drank ¾ of the wine, so I insist."

"Ok. I won't argue." Joe said.

"You see, I feel totally relaxed now. If we were sat on the sofa with a takeaway, I'd still be mulling stuff over."

"Change of scenery. It's a tonic. I'll pay next time then."

"Next year."

"We better move soon; they probably want the table back."

To Joe, Derek had always seemed like the one who had his shit together. The one who would go through his entire life with no setbacks. He never saw him as vulnerable. Perhaps he wasn't now, but there was just a slim chink in his armour, just like everyone else's.

◆ ◆ ◆

On Monday morning Joe woke with the dawn chorus. He got up and looked out of the bedroom window. If he wanted a realistic chance of seeing a doctor today, he would have to call as early as possible. He watched his brother drive away and wondered whether he would be over the drink-drive limit. Then he saw a reflection in the window. He turned around.

"Didn't mean to startle you." Norman said.

"What the hell."

Norman chuckled.

"What the hell indeed."

"Where did you come from? Have you been here the whole time?"

"Goodness, no. I don't have the time to shadow a single member all day long; way too busy for that. Just dropped in to say *well done* on the last assignment."

"Well done? I didn't do anything..."

"Subtle, very subtle. I like it. Just knocking the bag off the chair and letting it tell its own story. Like the opening of Pandora's box."

"That? That was just an accident. Anyway, I'm getting an appointment to see the GP today, hopefully, to stop these hallucinations."

"Still not convinced? I've been called many things over the years, mostly deserved, but never a *hallucination*. Should I feel flattered?"

"What was knocking a bag over going to prove?"

"He will get another two red flags, provided by another agent. Then it is up to him. You fulfilled your role quite admirably, once again."

"Me being clumsy is hardly some achievement."

"In the great scheme, it is small, yet significant. Anyway, I have to go. Many pressing matters to attend to. I'll be in touch again soon with your third mission. Bye for now."

With that, Norman faded out again. Joe walked over to the mirror on the dresser. He looked fine, but then mental problems wouldn't be visible on the surface. He sat downstairs with his phone at the ready for when the Doctor's appointment booking window opened.

5

Joe had been lucky and successful in booking an appointment for the very same day. The receptionist was not unaware of her position of great power. For some reason she granted Joe the gift of someone else's cancelled appointment. Doctor Sloane was from Ireland and blessed with a soothing accent. He spoke with genuine concern.

"Do you take a break once in a while?" he asked Joe.

"Now and then. Actually, no, not really."

"You should. This could well be stress related, though falling off a telegraph pole won't have done you any good either."

"No. So, these hallucinations are nothing too bad then?"

"I think they are a cause for *some* concern. Did you take any time off after the accident?"

"Just the three days. That's what they said I could have. I'm due to return the day after tomorrow. I'm back on the rota on Wednesday morning."

The doctor did not look up from his keyboard as he typed. He'd stopped being surprised by an employer's lack of concern for their employees a long time ago. It also often worked both ways.

"I'm going to sign you off work for two weeks. Starting today."

"They'll love that."

"Don't be overly concerned about what they will think. You need time to rest. Also, we need time to see whether or not these visions you've been having persist. It would be unwise for you to carry on working under the present circumstances and don't drive."

Joe nodded. He felt like he was being guided down the right path.

"Ok."

"Stay off the strong painkillers with codeine, they might affect you negatively. Do you get headaches? Or, have you been getting any recently?"

"Not really."

"No blurred vision?" Joe shook his head, "Ok. The hospital scan showed no irregularities, so we should just wait and see. We can't do anything else at the moment. Just rest. Stay away from alcohol and strenuous exercise."

"Ok. As long as I haven't gone nuts."

"No more than the rest of us. But, rest and

more rest. You are lucky to be walking around, fairly unscathed, after that fall."

"I am. The more I think about it."

"Well, don't think about it too much. You came through it and that's all you need to know. See me again in two weeks."

Joe thanked the doctor and then left. He walked through the waiting room full of patients muttering about the waiting times, and then out under a clear blue sky. *Two weeks off. That'll bug the hell out of them.*

Norman hadn't made another appearance or contacted him by phone since the morning. Perhaps seeing the doctor had banished the visions as their source had now been brought out into the light. He hadn't told the doctor exactly what he'd seen, or the part with the begging dog, just the basic premise of what he'd been experiencing. *Two weeks off.* What was he going to do with that time? *Rest.* His brother was back & forth a lot, so he would have some time to do just that.

As he walked back from the surgery, he decided to make a detour and go into the town centre. There was a music shop that had a few guitars in the window that he liked to look at.

The closer he got to the town centre, the more pigeons came into view. Some flying, some on the ground searching for scraps. As he saw one do a running takeoff, he noticed smoke in the sky. He turned a corner and saw a fire engine, ladder extended, shooting water over the...it was the building society that he'd visited a few days previously; the same one where he'd given the red flag to Karl, the young employee. *Coincidence.* The blaze was under control, but it did look like a lot of damage had been done. Hopefully, no one had been hurt.

That part of the Town Centre had been cordoned off, so Joe took another route to the music shop. He stood at the window and looked in at the same two acoustic guitars that had been there for the last six months. He didn't like the shop owner too much: a sulky, miserable soul. *If he got one, would he play it enough to warrant the price tag?* If they ever had a sale then he'd reconsider. If he bought one, then perhaps the other would have been the better option. The guy behind the counter was so unfriendly that Joe didn't like to ask to try them both out. Joe had done that once before and he'd reacted like he had asked for one of his kidneys. That was five years ago and he probably wouldn't remember. Neither guitar was at the pinnacle of instrument building, so there would be always something better to play out there, unless he got one of the premium brands on the shop's back wall. But, *spend a couple of grand?* It seemed better to have zero guitars rather than something that wasn't the best. This logic didn't make sense when applied to other things. His car, for example, was not a premium BMW, Range Rover or Audi. His motoring use didn't warrant spending that much money. He didn't *have* huge amounts of money. His choice of house followed that same rule. He could though, if he really wanted to, buy a premium brand acoustic guitar. Even if he didn't play it much, just the sound of the strum of one chord could not be bettered by any rock star or millionaire. There was a degree of logic to this idea, but because this wasn't an essential item, he'd never felt like pulling the trigger.

As he mused and procrastinated, the fire engine retracted its ladder. The fire was now out, though the smell of it was still very much present. He turned and walked back home. There were no cryptic messages written on car windows or anywhere else. It was just him and his own thoughts as he turned the key in the lock. Once inside, he switched the kettle on and picked out a peppermint teabag*: perhaps too much caffeine wasn't helping with the visions.* Then he sat down with the brew at the kitchen table.

Weird coincidence about the fire. He hoped that the disgruntled young man hadn't been its cause. Then, sitting at the table facing him, Norman appeared.

"I thought you had gone." Joe said, flatly.

"Hoping more like?"

"Yes, to be honest."

"The doctor doesn't have a cure for this I'm afraid."

"You know that I've been then. He's given me something to relax me. I haven't taken any yet."

"I'll still be here when you have. I do feel rather unwanted, by the way, and remember, you did agree to this in a signed statement." Norman's smile lessened.

"Not enforceable through the courts?" Joe offered.

"Not significant in the great scheme. *Your* courts I mean. Do you have any idea how many people are in prison for crimes they didn't commit? Or walking around as free as birds for ones that they did? Shocking statistics. I know the exact number, if you are interested," then he whispered, "Because I put a lot of them in there. Not all mind."

"I can imagine. Well, you're back," Joe took a slurp of tea, "I'm guessing you have another thing for me to do?"

"Indeed. I wish I had the time to make purely social visits, but if you saw my schedule.... unbelievable. Shocking in fact."

"Don't take this the wrong way, but I was hoping that might be it for these missions." Joe said.

"A deal is a deal. Don't worry, this isn't going to go on indefinitely and who knows, you may end up enjoying these little...*missions* that I send you on. And remember, you are making a difference."

"Who knows," Joe stood up, "I'd offer you a drink, but..."

"As I said, I can't ingest matter, or even take corporeal form. Well, not without sacrificing livestock. Though maybe that's a good thing, considering that awful stuff you're drinking at the moment."

"Supposed to be good for you."

"Marketing. Manipulative and purely marketing. Those advertising men are evil. Anyway, we digress. I must press on. This next matter is a little trickier, as mission three *always* is."

"Go on." This didn't concern Joe unduly as the first two had been so easy.

"There is a certain someone about to make a rather large mistake. His actions will lead him into the situation of an irretrievable morally compromised position."

"Ok. In English please."

"The oldest profession in the world, if you read the book that is. Perhaps the *second* oldest."

"You're talking about prostitution."

"Indeed. Some misguided or guided, I'm not one to judge, because, believe me, I'm in no position to do that, *character* has been acquiring the services of the ladies of the night." Joe looked puzzled, "He needs saving from himself.

Delivering back towards the path of righteousness. You know I almost believed that myself."

"And I am to do...?"

"Put him off. Do something or other to make him fear the consequences of his actions. If not, he will fall foul of the law, yours not mine, and his reputation will be destroyed. Gone for good."

"What's the plan?"

"All I will give you is a time and place. The rest is up to you." Norman said. As he did so, a piece of paper materialized on the table. Joe picked it up. There was a date, time and location, all written in perfect handwriting, "Just do what you do. Improvise." Norman said, just before fading out of view. Joe put the paper down again. He walked over to the sink and poured the rest of the peppermint tea down the plughole. He'd wait a week. If Norman kept on appearing, then he'd make another appointment with the doctor. Perhaps he had expected too much in hoping that the visions would stop straight away. He hadn't had the time to convalesce yet. Never-the-less, he picked the paper up once more. Whilst he waited for things to return to normal, he'd decided that he would follow the instructions and travel to Warner Street tomorrow at ...midnight.

◆ ◆ ◆

Joe's brother had returned home in the early

hours. He'd tried to make as little noise as possible, but Joe had still heard him arrive. In the morning Joe got up at 9:00 am. Derek had already left again. His briefcase and laptop on the table were the only signs that he had returned from his latest business trip. Joe didn't envy all that travelling. All those motorways and service stations probably didn't get any more attractive over time. As Joe made coffee, he mused that one way to make all the tedious travel interesting would be to ride to each destination on a Harley-Davidson motorcycle. Then stride into corporate meetings in full biker-gear. Kick over a few plastic cups. Upend a few folders. That would liven things up a little. Make those number-crunching meetings less dull.

The next *job* was scheduled for tonight. For now, as long as Norman kept on appearing to him, then he would carry out his tasks. He couldn't explain why that was, and why he didn't just ignore this apparition, but he would do them each in turn, quite possibly out of plain morbid curiosity. The doctor may have thought that he was having hallucinations, but Joe hadn't yet fully decided what they were. The jury was still out and they seemed far too real to just ignore. Plus, he had nothing else better to do at the moment.

The day passed by at a nice steady pace. Joe spent a good portion of it watching YouTube videos on various subjects, one of which was *afterlife experiences*; others were *hallucinations* and *angels*. Unsurprisingly, nothing in the videos matched *his* present circumstances.

◆ ◆ ◆

At 5:00 pm, Joe sat down at the kitchen table in front of a plate of food. Just before he started eating, his brother walked in.

"What's that?" Derek asked.

"Something I threw together. There's more in the pan if you want some?"

"It looks like Chinese …ish."

"That was the intention. Fried rice. It's not as simple to make as it looks."

"It's *halfway* there. I've already eaten, but thanks and …don't give up the day job." Derek made himself a coffee and then went straight upstairs to his room.

Despite the poor visual review, Joe ate the leftovers. He spent the rest of the day with one eye on the time. After sitting around with ants in his pants, the time reached 10:00 pm, and he started to focus more closely on the latest task at hand. He began to feel like some cut-price secret agent about to go on a mission. Part of the reason that he was actually going to go ahead and do it, was that he was now extremely curious about who it might be. Norman had a knack for providing just enough bait. *Some curb-crawler*. Hardly a glamorous mission. This was going to be a little more *bizarre* than the first two and he wondered how he might proceed. But, the success of the first two missions, without him really trying, had bolstered his confidence. Perhaps he was a natural. *Or*...perhaps his easily achieved success was based on the strong possibility that these *missions* were merely delusions brought on by the recent head trauma.

11:40 pm. It had started to rain lightly. As he readied to leave, Joe considered shouting upstairs to tell Derek that he was going out but then decided not to bother. He hadn't heard a peep from his brother and he may well have been sleeping. The front door clunked shut behind him. Warner Street was about a twenty-minute walk away. He'd never been there after dark. It was a quiet part of the town full of industrial units and former mills that had been converted to office and storage space after the industrial revolution had been and gone. The rain increased and it altered his decision to walk. He got in the van and sat there for ten minutes before turning the key and setting off.

When he arrived at Warner Street, he parked his small van behind an old white Ford van. The whole area was meagerly lit by just three streetlights.

How accurate were Norman's schedules? It

seemed a big coincidence that the mission time was to be midnight exactly. Hopefully, he could get this one done quickly and get back home before it got too late.

The rain fell on the cobbles of the street and bounced back up. There wasn't much to see, except for two women who were taking shelter under the canopy of a bus shelter down at the other end. *Were buses running this late?* It hardly seemed viable. Then it dawned on Joe that those two were, more than likely, the ladies of the night that Norman had spoken of.

A police car ambled by. Joe checked his rear-view mirror and then his phone. 11:48 pm. He again wondered who this person that needed saving from himself might be. He created a picture in his mind of a fifty-year-old politician in a suit and tie. He imagined his face on the front of the local newspaper.

Warner Street must have been known for this type of nefarious activity. Joe had only crossed paths with a working girl once before. He had been walking back home from a late-night party when a random girl asked him if he *wanted any business.* He was eighteen years old at the time and had no idea what that meant. She hadn't looked much like a business advisor.

Car headlights appeared in the rear-view mirror. There was also a blue light. Joe slumped down in the seat: he didn't want to get a caution himself. They'd never have believed the *Norman* story. The patrol car passed by. Soon after, another car slowly approached the bus shelter and then stopped. Joe could see its passenger window roll down and one of the two women approached it. A few words were exchanged and then she got in. The car set off again, leaving just one mini-skirted lady sheltering from the now persistent rain. It was now 11:57 pm. Joe decided that he needed to drive closer, right up to the other end of the street. As he set off, the girl moved from the bus shelter to a doorway that was only half illuminated by the nearest street lamp and out of view from the police car that passed by once again. If the police car followed the same pattern, it wouldn't return for around ten minutes. 11:59 pm. Joe parked up and got out of the van. He pulled the hood of his jacket over his head and walked towards the doorway with the girl sheltering in it. As he'd been parking, another car had arrived on the scene and crawled up alongside her. Joe walked on a path that would lead him between the car and the girl. Midnight. He stopped. The girl looked at him. Hard. Irritated. Barely out of her teens. Joe ignored her and turned towards the driver. He pulled back his hood as he stuck his head in the open passenger window.

"......Derek?" Derek looked shocked. White. The girl asked Joe to move. He ignored the request, "...What...what are you doing?"

"...I'm lost. I was just going to ask for directions. What are you doing here?" Joe didn't answer. He wasn't doing what his brother was doing. In the distance, the lights of another car approached, "I've just remembered where I am. Stupid of me. See you back at home." Derek said, before setting off again.

Is that the best you could come up with? Joe whispered. He stood there for several minutes, motionless, out in the rain and ended up quite drenched.

◆ ◆ ◆

"I can explain," Derek suggested, with just a hint of authenticity, "I know what it must have looked like, but it wasn't that."

"Don't lie to me as well. I'd appreciate that." Joe said as he pulled his hooded top off. He went over to the fridge and pulled out a can of beer.

"I was just..."

"Please don't." Joe insisted. Derek knew that his younger brother had long since passed naivety. He also felt himself slipping headfirst out of Joe's respect zone. He thought it best to say nothing else for the moment. Nothing incriminating. Joe also said nothing for a minute, then, "You're taking a big risk, using those women. You could catch all sorts of stuff,"

"I don't *use* them."

"You could have fooled me. Unless of course, you were just offering her your umbrella."

Derek tip-tapped his fingers on the table. He knew that he'd been caught red-handed. He opted for honesty.

"I...I don't make a habit of it."

"Not your first time though," Joe stated. Derek shook his head, "How often? Whilst you were with Joy?" Derek gave the affirmative answer with his body language, "God man. Did she find out? Is that why you moved out?"

Derek stared at the floor.

"One of the reasons."

Joe didn't ask what the others might be; he knew enough for now.

"You have a kid." He didn't want or need to say anymore.

"I wasn't planning on telling him."

"These things have a way of coming out. The damage...Kids in the playground, all that shit."

"I know."

"You don't know. Obviously, you don't or you wouldn't be picking up prostitutes in the street," Derek couldn't argue, "This needs to stop *today*."

"Ok."

"Look, Im not gonna say any *holier than thou* bullshit, but promise me man."

"Ok." Derek nodded. Joe didn't say anything else, he just went upstairs with the beer and dried himself off. Norman had been right. He had done his job once again, but in the process, his opinion of his brother had been tarnished forever.

6

The next morning Joe woke early. His brother had already left. Joe wasn't sure whether he was out on business or just wanted to be out of the way. He didn't care which one it was and he felt relieved that he didn't have to face him.

He walked slowly downstairs, his feet in the slippers that Derek had gotten him for Christmas. He sat at the table and took one of the tablets the doctor had prescribed for him, just the second one of 28. He wondered how many he would have to take to make a difference and whether or not these would get rid of Norman eventually. As of right now, they hadn't. Norman's image appeared again in the kitchen; his face complete with a sardonic smile.

"Well done once again!"

"Well done? Did you not think it might be an idea to tell me that it was my own brother?"

"Must have slipped my mind."

"You knew then."

"I know everything. Scratch that, not quite everything. You seem a little perturbed?"

"Wouldn't you be?"

"I can't say for sure, I don't have a brother," Joe now felt that, whatever Norman was, he wasn't genuine or decent. That idea hit home all at once, "*Miss* communication, but *mission* success."

"That doesn't help. Mission success or not. I'll never look at my brother in the same way again."

"Delightful isn't it."

"What?"

"You prevented him from getting into serious trouble in the future, wasn't that worth it?"

"I'm not looking at this as a *win*. As you might have guessed, I'm not *feeling* these missions anymore."

"But you have a talent for them. You're a natural."

"That first one with the fire alarm, do you know the damn place burnt down two days later?"

"Most unfortunate…"

"Unfortunate?"

"Just a coincidence …no doubt."

"I'm not liking it. This weird deal thing. I want out."

"There's still a great deal more to do I'm afraid. You haven't even used the animal control skill yet. Now that's a good one." Joe had no intention of doing so. Not now. Norman noticed

Joe's sudden complete lack of engagement with the *project*, "Unfortunately you can't leave the system, not just yet. It's all in the small print. Look, this next one, there's no rush, no rush at all. Take your time with it. Not *too* long mind you, but relax."

Joe didn't speak for a while. At length, he asked,

"What is it?"

"This is a good one. Well worth doing. It's a *level one*, which are usually reserved for the more experienced operatives. You've done so well that the boss wants you to have it," Joe showed little interest. Norman continued regardless, "All that you have to do is travel to the capital city and stop someone from doing something, using your undoubted wits and guile. However you see fit … as long as you stop them."

"Stop who?"

"Some lab rat in a white coat. Bloody do-gooder. You need to throw a spanner in the works."

Joe didn't answer. Norman felt that he had said as much as was needed and a piece of paper with a place and time written on it appeared on the table, just as before. Norman didn't say goodbye this time, he just faded out to nothing, his sardonic grin being the last thing visible. He left Joe alone with his thoughts and the piece of paper. Joe's opinion of Norman had altered, but, *if he ignored Norman's missions and went back on the deal, would he end up back where he was after the fall ...dead on the ground?*

◆ ◆ ◆

Joe thought about contacting the doctors' surgery once again. Though he realised that if these visions *were* just a passing thing, an after-effect from the accident, then Norman could not have known about Derek's nocturnal activities. If these visitations were just hallucinations, then surely all that Norman could know would be identical to what *he* knew. He sat and thought about his next move. Nothing presented itself. It felt like a one-way street. There was no guidance book or YouTube video for his situation. He looked up to the heavens and wondered when or where help might come from.

An hour later, he was standing behind someone with an obvious drink problem or perhaps his own bar, in the queue at the supermarket checkout. Joe hadn't really needed any shopping and only had four items in the basket. When it was his turn, the lady on the fast checkout till looked up at him and broke into a smile. Joe smiled back through pursed lips. She said nothing as she scanned the four items. Then she quietly advised him that it would be a lot faster to use the self-service checkout with just these few items. He nodded as he placed the items into a bag. He declined to mention that this was *supposed* to be the fast, ten items or less, checkout. Then, out of the blue, she said,

"You're carrying something around with you, aren't you." It wasn't a question.

Joe stopped in his tracks.

"What do you mean?" There were only two people behind him in the queue.

"A weight, I can sense it from here. A large burden."

Joe looked around.

"What?"

The next customer in the line started to get a little twitchy. She was in a rush. Joe looked down at her basket. She had at least fifteen items in there.

"Here," The woman on the till scribbled down her phone number and handed it to him, covertly, "Better to call sooner rather than later..." she whispered. Joe took his bag and walked out of the shop. *What was it with all these pieces of paper that he was accumulating? And how did she know he was burdened? Was it written all over his face?* He'd seen the same lady on the checkout several times before. She always had a smile on her face. *How on earth could she tell he was troubled by Norman?*

When Joe got home, he made yet another cup of coffee, perhaps hoping the extra caffeine might snap him out of this dream-like situation.

He sat down and picked out the latest piece of paper with the number on it. It also said "Ada", he already knew her name as it was on her badge. *Who are you, Ada?* Was she one of those con artists who pretend to read tea leaves and the like? *Cross my palm with silver.* She had seemed to spot something within him. *Did he look that miserable?* He probably did, because he *was* that miserable.

He now had, on the table in front of him, two pieces of paper; one was from Norman, the other from Ada. Norman could wait a while, but he *could* ring the other number, *sooner rather than later.* Three hours had gone by since their chance encounter and she had him intrigued at the very least. He picked up his phone. Pushed Norman's paper to the side and then called the eleven digits on the other one.

"Hi. You gave your number to me earlier."

"Yes! You called. Good timing, I've just gone on my break."

"Erm, do you mind me asking *why* you gave me your number?"

"Well, you needed it…*need* it. I've seen a little glimpse of what burdens you."

"How…I mean, could you explain please?"

She talked quietly,

"I'm in the staff room at the moment, so I have to whisper. It's clear to me that you have a troublesome spirit weighing down on you. As plain as the nose on your face."

"A spirit?"

"Yes. By the way, they don't look like what you see on *Dr Who*."

"I don't get how you got to that conclusion from me buying a packet of crisps, milk and bananas."

"And yoghurt, you had four items if I remember rightly."

"And yoghurt."

"Long story short, as my break ends in ten minutes, I'm a psychic. I do readings like some of the others, but mine are for real. I identified your problem straight away. Most people have layers and try to conceal it, but you were like an open book."

Joe didn't see any point in trying to deny anything.

"Ok."

"And, you need my help it would seem. My fees are very reasonable."

"Fees?"

"Yes. Each of us has a gift to use, and remember, if you are good at something, never do it for free. They don't pay me a fortune at this place."

"So, say I did have something that you could help me with..."

"We'll discuss it tomorrow morning if you are free and if you aren't then I strongly suggest you make yourself free. Meet me at 10:00 am in the supermarket café."

"Your supermarket?"

"Yes. I get a staff discount of 20%. See you then."

With that, Ada ended the call. Joe felt like there was, at least, something else to think about. Whether she could help him deal with the visitations or not was another matter entirely.

◆ ◆ ◆

Joe didn't see his brother that evening; the spare bedroom door remained closed shut all night. That was probably for the best. Only after being given enough time would the negative feelings start to disperse.

The next day, Joe walked into the supermarket café at two minutes to 10:00 am. Ada was already sitting at a table in the far corner. She held up a coffee cup to signal that she already had a drink. Joe ordered a cappuccino, stared at the menu on the wall and tried to collect his thoughts whilst he waited for it to be ready. When he sat down, Ada gave him a warm smile. *God only knew what she was going to say.*

"Coffee's good in here," That is what she started with. Joe merely looked at his own cup, "Try it." she said. He gave it a stir and then took a sip.

"About these fees you mentioned?"

"Don't worry about that yet. Anyway, it's a no-win no-fee deal. Just like it is on the adverts on telly," She smiled. He didn't, "As you've probably guessed by now, you are under the spell of something rather unpleasant. Do you want to tell me about it?"

"Ok. Here, in public?" Ada nodded, "Where do you want me to start?"

"Start where you feel you need to start. The beginning is always a good rule of thumb." Ada said.

"Ok. I fell off a telegraph pole. This black bird flew into me and I knocked myself out. Whilst I was out cold, I had this strange experience, like a dream."

Ada nodded.

"What happened in this dream?"

"Well, this guy, Norman, appeared and offered me this deal."

"A deal."

"Yes. It wasn't much of a deal, to be honest."

"What did it involve?"

"I could either act as some sort of *red flag angel* or.... not wake up again."

"*Red flag angel*?"

"That's probably the best way to describe it. *Someone who warns others.* According to him, we all get these red flag warnings and I was to become one of those that give them out."

"To whom?"

"Anyone and everyone, I assume."

"And have you actually given any of these warnings?"

"Yes."

"Tell me what they were," Ada closed her eyes as he began to tell her the stories of Karl and the fire alarm, the couple in the restaurant and then, lastly, his brother and the prostitute. When he'd finished telling her the scaled-down versions, she asked, "Just those three?" then she opened her eyes.

"So far. I have another one booked in, but I have been given twelve days to complete that one." Joe took a bigger sip of coffee as another member of staff came over and chatted to Ada. It was more of a whisper in her ear. Then she left them alone again.

"Hmm. Red flags indeed." Ada said with a crooked smile.

"What do you think?"

"The building burnt down, the one where you stopped the young employee from setting off the alarm. If he *had* done that, then they would have realized that it was faulty and didn't work properly and perhaps then the blaze would have been avoided," She closed her eyes again for a few seconds, "The young man *was* put off by seeing the contents of the young lady's purse. It *was* enough to sow a seed of doubt and discourage him and they will split up very soon."

"What difference does that make?"

"*If* they stay together, in the future they would have a child that would go on to do great and useful things. Now he'll never get born."

"And the third one?"

"That's obvious. You and your brother's relationship has been irretrievably damaged," Ada said with a frown. Joe shrugged, "It would appear your new *friend* has got you working under false pretences. What did he look like, this *Norman*? What age?"

"Tall, skinny. Sharp features. Anywhere between forty and seventy. What can I do about him?"

"Simply tell him, the next time he appears, that you are not taking part in his little schemes as he is using you to do bad and not good."

"I did say as much, but he says I have to continue."

"No, you don't. You are under no obligation. These things are usually cowards. He/it will forget the idea and move on to someone else if you stand up to him."

"The thing is, I signed something. Some sort of contract. So that I wouldn't die."

"Contract? I've never heard that one before. Hmmm." Ada closed her eyes again and then went deep into thought.

"What are you doing? Like, going into the zone?"

"I *live* in the spirit world," Ada replied, eyes still closed, "Well, one foot in one foot out."

He'd asked for help and the very same day Ada had appeared from out of nowhere…. or, more accurately, the ten items or less local supermarket checkout. Who or what had she been sent by? Nothing seemed real any longer. Joe sipped his coffee and looked out of the café window. After five minutes, Ada opened her eyes again.

"Are you all right? You had your eyes closed for a while." Joe asked.

"Yep. Fine. Dandy," She looked a little exhausted by wherever it was she'd been to, "I get it, I think."

"What is it?"

"It's not exactly what I thought initially. The first instinct is *usually* right isn't it."

"Please tell."

"Rather than it just being a mischievous spirit, you have a rather malevolent demon thing that has honed in on you. It's got you in a headlock. It's using you to wreak havoc."

"You say malevolent?"

"It will get worse if left unchecked. It's just toying with you at the moment."

"How do I get rid of it?"

"I'm not certain, yet."

"You've done this before right?"

"Not exactly, no."

"Oh shit."

"But…I know someone who has. Once."

"That's good, who?"

Ada whispered,

"It's one of the members of a group that I'm part of. Janice, lovely lady."

"And she's done this before? What's the group?

"Just a coven really, we meet up every other Thursday."

"A coven? Is that witches?"

"Yes. Good witches in our case. Though, technically I'm a psychic not a witch, I still go to the meetings."

"They're the good ones?"

"Yes of course, hence the prefix *good*."

"I suppose so. Can you contact her as soon as possible please?"

"Yes, I will speak to her at the next meeting."

"When is that?"

"A couple of days. This next Thursday."

"That's too far away; I need this Norman gone as soon as possible."

"I thought you had twelve days? Ok then," Ada could sense a sudden burst of Joe's desperation, "I will ring her pronto," Joe screwed up his face, *when was pronto?* "Ok, I'll do it now then," Ada took her phone out of her bag. It was a model from the pre-smartphone era, kept in a pristine case. Joe sat back whilst the two ladies talked. It sounded like they were discussing the latest episode of a soap opera, the tone of the conversation was so light-hearted. After about ten minutes Ada said her goodbyes and her attention was back on him. Joe was wide-eyed in anticipation, "She's got a new kitten."

"That's great. What about my *problem*?"

"Yes, she knew something about the subject. She has come across it once before."

"And she knows what to do?"

"Yes, she does. More or less."

"I thought *you* knew about how to deal with these things? Can we go and see her?"

"These are big league. Yes. I asked her to meet us tonight."

"Great. Whereabouts?"

"It's a pub out in the sticks." Ada said.

"A pub?" Ada nodded. Joe shrugged, "Ok, doesn't matter where."

Ada stood up and then went over to talk to a work friend for a few minutes. She came back all smiles as though all Joe had wrong was a bad cold.

"I'll drive us there at 7:00 pm." Ada suggested. Joe nodded. Norman had given him more time to complete this latest task and, with any luck, he wouldn't show up again for a while.

◆ ◆ ◆

At 6:45 pm, Joe waited at the end of the street for Ada's arrival. Soon, a red mini with a *Union*

Jack bonnet pulled up alongside him. Joe saw that it was Ada in the driver's seat and he got in.

"Nice." He commented. The theme inside was similar to the outside. Ada hadn't struck him as the type to be a royalist, but even the air freshener was in the shape of a crown, as were the seat covers. The car made some *interesting* clunking and whirring noises, "What year is it?"

Ada's concentration was targeted at driving. She didn't process the question for three minutes, after which she answered,

"2008."

"How far away is this pub?" Joe hoped that the vehicle would actually make it there.

"Only a few miles." Ada answered after five minutes.

Before much longer, the mini pulled into the car park of the Fox & Hounds, the country pub where they were meeting Janice. The yellow glow from its original period windows looked both welcoming and comforting.

"This is it?" Joe said. Ada did not answer until the engine stopped running. She turned and gave him a warm smile.

"Let's go and meet Janice."

"Is she here already?" Joe asked. They were a little early.

"Yes, she is inside."

"Is that like a psychic thing ...you *know* that she's here?"

"No. I parked next to her car."

Inside the pub was as rustic as the exterior promised. A few people were sitting at the small bar and a few others were scattered around, sitting at the wooden tables. Even though it wasn't particularly cold outside, a fire blazed away under an old hearth. There were several stuffed animal heads above it as well as plenty of old pictures and books.

"I've never been in here before." Joe stated. Janice saw Ada and came over. The two embraced. Then Janice took a measured look at Joe. The same look a father might give his daughter's boyfriend upon meeting him for the first time. The two went over to the bar and ordered drinks. Ada beckoned for Joe to sit at one of the tables near the fire. He did so. *At least this white witch had driven here and not come by broomstick. Or perhaps that was a bad sign; perhaps it would have been more impressive.* The two ladies chatted as they ordered the drinks and then they brought them over to the table. Ada had a glass of Guinness beer in both hands, one-half pint for herself and one full pint for Joe.

"There you are." Ada placed it down in front of him.

"How did you know I like Guinness?" he asked. She smiled and he remembered her gifts. *Guessing people's drinks was not the issue tonight.*

Janice looked a similar age to Ada: late fifties

to mid-sixties. *Or, maybe they were older and used witchcraft.* Janice spoke with a slightly hoarse voice.

"You have a bit of a problem then?" Joe nodded.

"You could say that."

"Don't worry, we shall see what we can do for you." She said and then she took a sip of her peach schnapps. Joe wasn't sure if they had come here to help him or get drunk. "Don't worry," Janice said, "We are only having the one drink. It's not the done thing to go into a pub and not buy anything." Joe smiled. She was perfectly correct of course. When the drinks had gone down a little, Janice stood up, "Ok then, follow me." She walked out of the back door and into the outside beer garden. There were a few benches out here that people used more often in spring and summertime. As it was now October and just a little chilly, they were all vacant. The moon shone down, as did a million stars.

"Why have we come outside?" Joe asked. Janice urged him, gently, to *be quiet*. Ada whispered in his ear.

"Out the back is exactly on a ley line."

"Ley line?"

"Shhh," Prompted Janice. Then she produced some items from her bag and placed them into what looked like a metallic or pewter vessel of some sort. She mixed them and then crushed them using the butt end of her cigarette lighter. "Come over here," She beckoned to Joe. He looked at Ada and then walked over to the bench with the vessel on it, "I'm going to light this and you must breathe it in. You'll have to have your head over it when I say *go*."

"Ok."

"You ready?" Janice was on standby with the lighter. Joe tilted his head and gave the thumbs up. "Go!" She lit the concoction and Joe did his best to breathe in as much as he could. Whatever it was, it went up at once with a green tinge of colour. Joe coughed a little and then the smoke dispersed. Nothing happened for a few seconds and then, around ten feet away, Norman's image flickered into view. He didn't speak and was even more ethereal than in previous times as the moon's light shone through him. He merely looked displeased and then he disappeared once more, shaking his head as he did so.

"There he was." Joe said.

"Hmm. Looks can be deceiving." Janice said.

"You saw him?" Joe asked.

"Yes." Janice said.

"Me too." added Ada.

"I've now got a clearer idea of what we're dealing with, but, it's not a low-grade one that we can dispel with a few chants." Janice said.

"Oh shit." Joe said quietly.

"Well, there's good news and bad news."

Janice surmised.

"What's the good news?" Joe asked.

"We know more about what we are dealing with."

"And the bad?" Joe wondered.

"I haven't got the foggiest idea what to do next. Come on, let's go and finish our drinks." Janice said and then she led them back inside.

7

The next morning Joe did see his brother in passing in the kitchen. Derek offered Joe a tight-lipped smile. The smile where you hold something back. Joe mirrored the gesture. He didn't know what to say, so said nothing. *Nothing*, could not make the situation any worse. He sat at the table and he ate some cereal with a banana. Derek also briefly sat at the table with his laptop open. He thought that letting some time pass whilst they were in close proximity might mend the situation a little. It didn't do anything. Joe got up and took his coffee upstairs. Half an hour later Derek drove off. He'd made up an excuse and cancelled his son staying over for the weekend, as it had just seemed like the right thing to do. He had a lot of soul-searching to do. He felt like an alcoholic who had just been *made* to realise that he had a problem.

When Joe went back downstairs, there was a note, folded, on the kitchen table. It was from

Derek, not Norman or Ada. It read*: I'm sorry I really messed up didn't I. think it's probably best I move out as soon as. Make a bit of breathing space. And once again, Thanks for all that you've done. Derek.*

This was yet *another* note on the table that Joe didn't want. He scrunched up the paper and threw it back down.

Joe wondered whether or not he was overreacting to his brother's wayward behaviour. After all, it wasn't like he'd murdered someone. The effect had, no doubt, been multiplied by Norman's unwanted involvement and also the fact that it was Derek, the brother he had always looked up to. He had nothing to do now until 5:00 pm; that was when the next meeting with the ladies was scheduled. At least Norman hadn't shown up again yet, though Joe's blessings seemed few and far between.

◆ ◆ ◆

The second meeting took place at Janice's home. Joe drove, as Ada's mini wouldn't move. He was tempted to ask her why she hadn't seen that coming but thought better of it. When they arrived at a semi-detached house, Joe remarked that, for a witch's house, it looked just the same as all the others on the street, from the outside. That all changed when they went inside. Three motionless cats greeted them in the hallway. *Taxidermist's work.* Three *live* cats were roaming around the house, just one of which was black in colour. Janice later explained that the *Black cat thing was just a cliché.*

All the floors were bare wood, with several patterned rugs placed here and there. Joe wondered if Janice actually *had* an electricity supply, as there were so many candles scattered around. *Every* room downstairs was dark and dingy. Herbs and flowers filled the kitchen, hung down from the ceiling and gathered together next to the old pot sink.

Janice bade them sit down at an old and rustic pine table that was dotted by candle wax and burn marks. There was something slowly cooking on the stove. It smelt like nothing else.

"Nettle tea?" Janice asked.

"Yes please." Ada replied.

"Thanks." Joe said, his mind suggested that he say *no thanks*, but he thought he had better try some. Before long, three cups of freshly made nettle tea were on the table.

"I grow my own, of course. What do you think?" Janice asked.

"Lovely." Ada said. Joe took a sip and found that it was a lot more palatable than he had expected. He smiled.

"That will cure you of a lot of things," Janice said. She aimed this specifically at Joe, "Do you have to get up in the night to pee?"

"Erm. Sometimes."

"Nettle tea will shrink your prostate back down to size and stop all those nightly visits. Mind you, you aren't quite at that age yet where you get that problem."

"Ok. Could we talk about my problem please?"

Janice nodded thoughtfully and then moved on to the subject.

"Excuse the untidiness, I have been up all night reading."

"Me too. Did you find much out?" Ada asked.

"Yes. Well, enough to know that we need to be fairly worried."

"Great." Joe whispered. Janice continued.

"This demon that has selected you of all people, is quite a big hitter. He's been responsible for some pretty large-scale events throughout history."

"Where did you read this?" Joe wondered. He saw no evidence of any computers or laptops. He supposed it wasn't a subject to just *Google*. Janice gestured behind herself to a large oak bookshelf, filled with thick volumes with several bindings and spines in disrepair.

"Plus," she added, "I asked certain helpful spirits. And Ada, of course."

"With a Ouija board?" Joe asked.

"Good grief, no. Far too random and unreliable. Anyway, here's just a short list of

Norman's handy work that might be familiar to you: In 1066, he was the one that manoeuvred the two armies to attack King Harold at the same time. Harold was being protected at the time by good spirits, hence he was blessed with a speedy journey and good fortune. He got a virtual walkover against the Norwegians up in Northumberland. His luck ran out at the battle of Hastings against William, the Duke of Normandy, who had the backing of *Norman* and some of his cronies. It appears that the demon visiting you took the name he is currently using from this episode. Evil, yet not without a sense of humour. In World War 1, he was behind the assassination of Franz Ferdinand, knowing full well that all the mini-alliances between countries would spark a global conflict. Oh, and going back a little further, he was also the one who persuaded Roman Governor Pontius Pilate to wash his hands and release Barabbas, therefore condemning Jesus to death. That sort of backfired because Jesus, well, you know the story. And lastly, he was the one behind the lighting of the match that started the great fire of London."

"And you got all that from those books?" Joe asked.

"Not just the books, Ada helped and so did the rest of the coven."

"So," Ada said, "He comes back every thousand years or so."

"I don't think he has a tight schedule that he follows; rather he just turns up every so often." Janice said.

"And he picked me, of all people." Joe sighed.

"Perhaps he's scaling down. He is getting on a bit." Ada offered.

"Or," Janice said, "He's got something big planned for Joe further down the road and is just testing him out."

"Kind of a compliment," Ada said, "Sort of."

"So," Joe asked, "The big question is, what can I do to get rid of him?"

"What can *we* do," Ada corrected, "You have us on your team now."

One of Janice's cats, the black one, jumped up onto the table.

"Have you something to offer Smudge?" Janice asked it. The cat looked at each of them in turn and lastly at Joe. It held his gaze for several seconds before jumping back down and trotting off into another room. *Even the cat seemed to know he was in big trouble.*

"Why Smudge?" Joe asked, "It's pure black?"

"Why not?" answered Janice.

Through the doorway, Joe noticed Smudge sidle up to a ginger cat and it was almost like it was telling it something. Both cats then looked at Joe and then wandered off.

"I have something else from what I've been doing." Ada said.

"You ladies stay up all night? Pro-plus?" Joe wondered.

"No no, not that rubbish. Sleep can be deferred for days if you know what you are doing," Ada clarified, "We have two options, so far. Option one is to use witchcraft, that is where Janice and the others come in. Option two is to somehow acquire a religious artefact to use against the demon. But, we'd need to get hold of one of them. Hopefully, that would banish Norman to, well, wherever he comes from."

"So, I'm guessing option one is the easier one." Joe said.

"Yes," Ada replied, "It's not like religious artefacts are available in your local antique shop."

"It would have to be genuine. Something that had actually been touched by Christ would be ideal." Janice added.

"Why would option two work? Do you believe all the Jesus stuff, all the stories and that?" Joe asked.

"Never been surer about anything." Ada said, without a smile for once.

"No doubting any of that," Janice added. Joe was slightly surprised. He'd never given Jesus much thought. Perhaps that was because he'd been force-fed the idea, whilst his mother and aunts and uncles had never set foot in the church themselves, except for weddings and funerals. "I've already started laying the foundations of the spell that we would need."

"Is this something you can do?" Joe asked.

"No. It will take the whole coven." Janice replied.

"How many are there?" Joe asked.

"One hundred and twenty ...ish. That's throughout the country." Janice said, as she left the table and opened some tins of food for the cats who ambled their way in.

"That's a healthy number of witches. All good ones I take it?"

"All good. No doubt there are bad one's out there as well, but their help would probably do more harm than good." Janice said.

Joe turned to Ada.

"So, you are not a witch, not even a part-witch?"

"No. Just a psychic."

"A very strong one." Janice assured.

"Can you tell me why Norman singled me out of all the people that he could have chosen?" Joe asked Ada.

"That's hazy. Unclear. Something is blocking it, just like a roadblock. I'll have to see if I can swerve around, but that might take time," Ada said, "All I can get so far is that there *is* a definite specific reason for choosing you."

"Doesn't feel like a compliment." Joe sighed.

"I suppose not," Janice added, "But there are several *Normans* out there, with numerous different reasons for doing things. In time, his reason for singling you out will be exposed."

8

The next day Joe received a call from a work friend, Mark, who wanted to check up on how he was doing. Joe felt reassured to hear a voice from the recent past and it helped him put into perspective the most recent strange events. Just seven days earlier, Joe was worrying about all the day-to-day crap that seems more relevant than it actually is. Mark told him not to bother rushing back to work as it was the same old bull. Nothing had miraculously changed overnight, i.e. there were still only a few *actual* engineers and still more people spending all day in the office doing as little as possible. He went on to tell Joe that he had applied for a job in the office himself. *If you can't beat em, join em.* Agency staff were still as unreliable as ever. Joe reminded Mark that he had only been missing, *officially,* for three working days.

"Feels longer." Mark replied. He knew that Joe was one of the few grafters that got stuff done.

Joe didn't want any interruptions at the minute, particularly from turncoats who casually slipped into the conversation that they had designs on being a cake-eater. He cut short the conversation after just a few minutes.

At 5:00 pm, Derek turned up again looking very downbeat. He and Joe passed each other in the hallway.

"You don't *have* to move out you know," Joe told him.

"I know. I've got somewhere though. A guy from work has a spare room. I lied a bit and told him that you needed the space. He's letting me stop there for a couple of weeks till I'm sorted. The other thing is, I only said *two weeks* to you at the beginning and now it's been months. I feel like I'm taking advantage of your good nature."

It wasn't the *physical* space that Joe needed, but he supposed the two went hand in hand.

"Ok. But if it goes sour then you can come back here, you know that."

Derek nodded and then carried on getting his belongings together. As he left, Joe placed a hand on Derek's shoulder; their first physical contact since the prostitute thing. When the front door closed behind Derek, Joe bowed his head for a few seconds before levelling up again. He had things to deal with.

◆ ◆ ◆

Ada was on the fast track till again when Joe walked into the supermarket. She smiled when she saw him. He bought a bar of chocolate and a drink he didn't want and then joined the queue.

"I called Janice in my break and she's organizing a gathering of the coven." Ada whispered to him. She took as long as possible to scan the two items, to the slight annoyance of the builder on his lunch break directly behind Joe.

"Cool. Does she know what to do?" Joe asked.

"Do you want a carrier bag?"

"Err...no. Just two things."

"She thinks so. I'll keep you posted." Ada said as she handed his change over. Joe thanked her and left. On the way out it started to rain quite heavily. He stayed under the cover of the supermarket canopy. It had turned into a mini torrent and the raindrops were bouncing high into the air, they were hitting the ground with such force. Several other shoppers followed suit, took cover and waited out the flash downpour. The sky was dark grey, almost black in places and mist rose above the black asphalt of the car park. Then what looked like mist from the rain started to form into a shape. Only Joe could see it.

"Joseph," Norman said. Joe did not reply, "Now what on planet earth are you up to? I'm not so sure I'm overly fond of the company you are keeping." Joe tried to keep his face as expressionless as possible.

"Well." he said. Neither a statement nor an answer nor a question.

"*Well* indeed. Play around with these vagabonds if you must, as long as the next task is completed," Norman clasped his hands together, "But remember Joseph.... the clock is ticking..." Then Norman faded away, just as the torrential rain stopped.

"Flash storm," another shopper said. Joe looked up as the clouds dispersed. The sky was blue and white again, "Never seen that around here though."

"Probably caused by all this global warming." Another shopper offered. Joe pulled his hood down and walked slowly back home.

◆ ◆ ◆

"I have to say, I don't have a clue what I'm doing." Janice said. Not surprisingly, this did not instil any confidence in anyone present.

"This spell won't work then?" Joe asked as he drove to the Fox & Hounds. Ada and Janice were both in the back of his car.

"Oh, the spell should work," Janice said as he parked up. "It's the other bit I might struggle with."

"They have Wi-Fi, I've seen it before." Ada offered. Joe was still completely in the dark about what was going to happen. All Janice had said was to wear waterproof warm clothes. They went inside and bought the same drinks as before and sat down at the same table. After a short time, Janice looked at the old wooden clock that told them it was five minutes to six.

"Let's go." Janice led them outside once again.

"He visited me again earlier, just after we spoke." Joe said to Ada.

"What did he say?" Janice asked.

"Well, he called you two vagabonds. At least I think he must've been referring to you." Joe said.

"Downright cheek," Janice said, "Hopefully we can take him out of the equation here and now." she added as she opened her leather bag and produced a very well-used looking *I-Pad* tablet.

"What's the plan then?" Joe wondered. They had rushed to get here for six pm and hadn't told him much.

"We are going to gather the coven." Ada informed him, as Janice entered the pub's Wi-Fi password into the iPad.

"What, here?" Joe wondered. It seemed very short notice.

"Yes," said Janice, "But I really don't know what I'm doing."

She pressed various icons on the device's screen. Luckily, though cold, it was only raining a little.

"What are you trying to do?" Joe asked.

"Zoom. We are meeting over the interweb using Zoom," Ada clarified, "Janice has never done it before."

Joe stepped in and gave a little guidance. At least it was the *technology* bit that she didn't know about.

"Between six pm to seven pm, on this ley line, there is a lot of power just waiting to be tapped into. It is at its highest concentration at this time of the year and hopefully it will be enough to get rid of old Norman." Janice said.

Joe's expectations were suddenly boosted. Within a few minutes the Zoom meeting was set up and one by one, other witches joined the proceedings electronically. They each had surprisingly normal names.

"We are lucky," Ada said, "After next week, the energy flowing through this area wanes for three months. I think you need this sooner rather than later." Ada smiled at Joe as Janice finished the preparations. The wind picked up a little and bit into their hands and faces.

"Nearly there," Janice said. Twenty-two of the country-wide coven were now in the Zoom group meeting, "Just two more. If two dozen isn't enough, then it isn't enough, but that's the best I could do on short notice." Joe was fairly impressed at how fast Janice had mobilized her allies. Whether this idea would work, God only knew. "Also, I don't know if them not being physically here in person will negatively affect the spell, though they are all here in spirit. That should suffice." She left the I-Pad screen propped up on a bench, facing them. They didn't have to worry about being disturbed as the pub was quiet, and no one else was daft enough to go outside in the now howling wind. One older gentleman did keep one eye on proceedings from his table near an outside window. He was accompanied by Rex, his golden retriever, who seemed more interested in the events outside than he did.

Janice produced the spell in the form of a written incantation that she had earlier e-mailed to all the others. A light rain had started to fall. Janice had laminated the spell to protect it from the elements. She then produced a pewter vessel and placed it down on the table. Next, she took some ingredients out of a sealed plastic kitchen container and placed them in the vessel. In one hand she held a box of wooden matches.

"Has to be lit with *proper* fire," she said. Luckily, it was only a very light rain shower. "Right. Everyone ready?" She asked the Zoom group. The plan was to read the incantation in unison, "I'll countdown, in three...two...one." Then, together, they chanted a strange verse that sounded like it came straight out of a 1970s Hammer Horror film. It was Latin, mostly, and comprised of just one long verse. As the final syllable was uttered by all, Janice tossed a lit match into the pewter vessel. It sparked a burst of orange flame. Then it smoked and wisps of complex-smelling vapour filled the air. The dog looked suitably impressed: it looked a lot more fun out there than *inside* the pub.

All three stood in silence in the wind and rain for a short time, as though speaking might spoil the spell. Then, Janice thanked her online companions before bidding the ensemble farewell. One by one the other witches left the Zoom meeting, like lights going out in an office building at 5:02 pm on a Friday.

Eventually, Joe broke the silence.

"Did it work, do you think?"

"Time will tell." Janice said.

"I feel as though it has." Ada offered.

Janice collected her things and placed the I-Pad back into her bag.

"Now a hundred years ago, that would have been impossible," she said. Then she set off back inside, "Come on, there's no point being out here in the rain any longer. Let's go and finish our drinks."

The pub's landlord had also half-watched the proceedings from behind his bar. It all looked a bit odd, but paying customers were paying customers. He'd known Janice since school days and she had always seemed more interested in the school band and badminton than any form of academic studies. In fact, the two had kissed in the fourth year, after someone had poured vodka into the fruit punch at the school disco. Neither had mentioned it since.

9

A few more days passed by slowly but without incident. Every time Joe had looked in the mirror, he had half expected to see Norman's unwanted visage materialize behind him. Thankfully, it hadn't. He still had made zero progress towards completing the latest task he'd been given. After repeatedly thinking about it and after much deliberation, he picked the piece of paper Norman had left out of the kitchen drawer and placed it down on the table. He read through it once again:

28th October. London. Get on the 09:15 Euston to Westminster train. Go to carriage B. In seat number 45, there will be a bald man, aged fifty-three. Spill his drink or a drink (optional) over the laptop device that he is working on (suggestion) or sabotage it in some other way. Bon voyage! Norman provided a little more information to go with this one. More than likely, his task was to destroy whatever this *bald man* had been working on though, whoever he was, he must have been crazy not to have made a backup, particularly so if it was super important material. Joe wondered who this man might be. At any rate, the task would not be completed, not by him at least. Today was the 22nd of October. No doubt he would be getting a visit from Norman again on the 29th if the spell *hadn't* worked and he could still make an appearance. Ada had called him three times per day, just to check on any changes. Janice was quietly confident that the spell would hold Norman at bay, but not *overly* confident. She visited him and told him her reservations, which didn't help matters any.

◆ ◆ ◆

To Joe's pleasant surprise, the next few days also passed without incident. He'd taken the passive position of just letting the hours pass by as they pleased and the hours turned into days. Then it all got monumentally tense. Joe went to bed on the 27th of October knowing full well that he was nowhere near London and would be still in the same place the following morning. If Norman was going to show up, it would be after the deadline of 9:15 tomorrow morning. He went to sleep with one eye open.

He woke with a start. His phone displayed 3:38 am. There was no one else in the bedroom, ethereal or solid. The rain was driving hard against the window; perhaps that noise had woken him. *Dare he set foot outside the bedroom?* He did need to use the toilet. He tentatively set foot outside and then his feet were the landing. A few more paces and he was at the toilet bowl. This was when he felt the most vulnerable. He looked around once again. There was nothing to see except ...written in the light condensation on the bathroom mirror were the four words *...now you've done it...* They distinctly had not been there when he had gone to bed, he would have seen them whilst he was brushing his teeth. Derek wasn't living there at present, so it couldn't have been him, not that he would have cause to write that. Perhaps the spell *had* worked. *This was Norman's handy work*. It had to have been. Joe hoped it was to be the last form of communication from him, a sort of *final* comment. If Norman *was* able to appear to him, Joe was sure that he would have done so by now. He was hardly the shy and low-key type. All Joe could do was get back into bed and try to go back to sleep.

He woke again at 9:21 am. Past the latest task deadline. No sign of Norman and certainly no bald men with laptops on trains. He wandered into the bathroom. On the mirror were some smudges but no legible writing. *Had he dreamt that bit?* He wished that he'd dreamt the whole damned episode. Unfortunately he realized that wasn't the case when Ada called him.

"Any news?" she asked, excitedly.

"I haven't seen anything," Joe replied, cautiously, "Although there was something written on the mirror."

"In blood?"

"No, no, just condensation. A warning, I think. *Now you're in it*, or something like that."

"Ooh. I wonder what that means ..."

"I was hoping that you might be able to tell me, you being the psychic."

"I'm not getting a clear message from that or anything else. Perhaps that's a good sign."

"Hopefully," Joe wanted to call it all a *freak show*, but didn't want to tempt fate or Karma, "I hope that's the end of all this ...crap."

"Janice wants to meet up again at the pub. I think, if all has gone to plan, that she wants a celebratory drink. She doesn't usually need much of an excuse for a celebratory drink or any other kind for that matter."

"I'm up for that. I'll breathe a huge sigh of relief if he's gone. Tell you what, I'll drive, leave the car in the car park and get a taxi home."

"Oh, good plan. Pick me up at 7:00?"

"7:00 sounds good. I'll see you then."

◆ ◆ ◆

Ada had made an effort to look smart. She

answered the door wearing a beret style hat, but also a serious expression.

"Everything ok?" Joe asked her.

"Not really. I'm getting bad vibes and they just increased tenfold when you stepped closer."

"Oh. I haven't heard from or seen Norman...?"

"I know. That's good, but there *is* something niggling me." She broke into a smile as she opened the car door, just to appease him a little. She didn't say much else as Joe drove to collect Janice. He wondered, briefly, what Derek would think about his new friends.

Janice opened the door dressed in black. It wasn't a funeral that they were attending; unless it was the death of Norman.

When they got to the pub, *The Fox & Hounds*, this was the first occasion that Joe had noticed the sign outside, it had quite a few cars in the car park and several patrons were dining and drinking.

"Oh, I'm ready for this." Janice said in anticipation. She rarely got *drunk*, but did enjoy a few glasses of wine on occasions that were usually not too far apart. The same was true for Ada.

This time at the bar Joe ordered a bottle of Sauvignon Blanc, at their request, and a pint of lager for himself. He paid. This was to be his treat for all the effort his new allies had put in. There was an unoccupied table in the bar area and so they all sat down, just a nice distance away from the fire.

"So, you've not seen him then?" Janice asked.

"Not since the last time, no. Though there was a message written on the mirror. At least I *think* there was."

"That's great news," Janice said, "An arrogant nuisance like him would probably have shown up by now if he was able to." She raised a wine glass, "Here's to a job well done." They all clinked glasses and said *cheers*.

"What a week," Joe said, "What a week."

"It's done now. We are back to normal." Janice comforted. Ada did not comment, she was relatively quiet and less *smiley* than usual.

"Nice in here." Joe commented.

"Good aura." Janice added.

Ada wasn't paying much attention to what her friends were saying, hers was fixed upon a black Labrador that was sitting with a couple of locals at the next table. When they had walked in, it had been wagging its tail on and off. Now it sat still, staring directly at Joe. As she watched it, a snarl manifested on its mouth revealing surprisingly long teeth. Then it growled and started barking at Joe before suddenly leaping at him in an attempt to bite. Luckily, its owner still had hold of the leash and he managed to pull it back and prevent it from getting too close. The whole pub looked around to see the commotion. Its owner couldn't calm the dog, it strained on the leash as if its life depended on it, teeth bared and ready. The owner was a country dweller and didn't bother apologizing to anyone, he just downed his double brandy and then led the dog, still very agitated, out of the pub. Someone at a nearby table said,

"He's been bringing that dog in for ten years. Never seen it do that before."

"Maybe it didn't like the peanuts he was giving it." Another patron said. Within two minutes, the tranquility had returned. Ada looked very carefully at Joe for a moment. Then she asked him,

"Have you…ever gotten that reaction before?"

"No, never. I'm not really a dog person, but no," He noticed her concentration, "What is it?"

"Nothing. Probably nothing."

"You don't think it could sense Norman?" Joe asked her.

"No." Was her flat answer.

Two drinks later, the conversation and atmosphere had perked up. Ada spoke quite a lot about the strange customers and shoplifters they'd had in the supermarket store recently. One particular customer had brought back several rounds of cheese, complaining that *his* customers didn't like it. He'd been serving supermarket-branded cheeses and passing them off as speciality produce in the little bar that he ran. He also had a habit of *accidentally* miscounting the items in his trolley.

"He said I've got five of these camembert rounds, when I looked in the trolley, there were at least ten." Ada said.

"Did you know *psychically* that he was lying?" Joe wondered.

"No. I don't need to be psychic to spot the wrong uns like him." Ada added.

Janice enjoyed half of the bottle of wine. She giggled and laughed at Ada's funny stories. Then, when the wine was finished, the age-old question arose *...do we get another bottle?* Joe had just started on his third, and probably last, pint of ale. The ladies decided on another single glass of wine each.

The atmosphere was nice and relaxed. Thursday always brought out a decent crowd, some of whom liked to start the weekend early. Some didn't draw a line between weekdays and weekends. Joe looked around; there probably wasn't anyone in there under thirty-five.

When the last round of drinks was getting finished, Joe suggested that he ring for a taxi and he also insisted that he would pay for it out of gratitude for what the two ladies had done. Neither Ada nor Janice argued, they *had* done their bit after all. Then Joe remembered something. He said to Ada,

"You did say that there was a fee."

"Usually. Janice has done a lot of the work.

Let's call this one on the house. Or, we could class that wine as payment."

"I appreciate that. Thank you." Joe said.

In ten minutes, the taxi driver appeared at the bar and nodded towards Joe; he'd used the same guy for many years. The three companions got up from their seats.

"What a pleasant evening." Janice said. She felt a little light-headed.

"We must do it again." Ada said. She felt a little...*merry*. Joe wasn't too sure that they would be going out for drinks *very* often, though he was extremely grateful for both these ladies' timely assistance.

It was very dark outside and cool rather than cold. The taxi was parked in the car park rather than right outside the entrance, so it meant a short walk. After five steps, Joe heard the distinct *caw* call of a crow. Then another. As they walked, Joe and the driver exchanged pleasantries; but the noise from birds interrupted them as they got louder. It became almost deafening. Then, at around six paces away from the taxi, several large black birds began to swoop down. They seemed to be targeting Joe and not the others. Joe ducked down and frantically tried to fend them off as he quickly opened the taxi's front passenger door and then got in. The birds noisily circled above the taxi. Ada and Janice looked at each other and then got in the back.

"Don't like you much do they," The taxi driver said, "Remind me not to get the same aftershave."

"You don't usually have this effect on animals, do you?" Ada asked Joe.

"My cats liked him." Janice offered.

"No." Joe said.

"Something isn't right." Ada said. That was glaringly obvious.

The taxi moved off. The birds followed it for a while before dispersing just as quickly as they had gathered.

The two ladies were dropped off first and then Joe, who gingerly got out of the car and then quick-stepped it to his front door without pausing for breath. The key was in the lock of the door and then it was out again, he'd dropped it in his haste to turn it. He quickly snatched it off the ground and then he focused more closely on the lock. Once inside, he sat at the table and kicked his shoes off. Norman may not have shown up again, but something weird was going on. *It had to be linked.* He remembered the *controlling the dog* trick. *Was this out of the frying pan into the fire?* He headed upstairs. He'd get some sleep and then maybe tomorrow would be a better day. The last thing that heard before drifting off, was a rustling, scraping sound. It sounded like pigeons had nested in the roof gutter. He'd worry about that later

Not long after he'd drifted off, he awoke

suddenly to a shooting pain in his left big toe. *What was that, a splinter?* He must've stepped on something. Boy did it hurt. He swung his legs out of bed and switched the bedside lamp on. *What was that?* There was an ant on the carpet; but not just one, several were crawling over his feet, legs and body. He leapt up, almost breaking the bedside lamp and then briskly walked into the bathroom. He flicked the shower on as he peeled off his boxer shorts. The water was still stone cold as he jumped underneath it. He took the shower head and aimed it at the crawling black insects. A spider fell out of his hair and he tried his best to remain calm. He didn't normally kill any bugs, but he had no issue watching all the tiny creatures that had been on his body flowing down the plug hole. The water came warm and then hot. He stayed underneath for twenty minutes and well past the moment when every intruder had been rinsed away.

10

Joe woke up to the faint sound of gnawing and immediately looked at his body, brushing imaginary creatures off himself as he did so. *He was clear.* There wasn't anything on him. He looked up at the blue-tinged light coming through the window and he remembered pitching the tent in his bedroom. It had an insect-proof sleeping compartment. He could see the shapes of some little critters on the outside of it. Nothing had got through this defence, though he ruffled his hands through his hair, just to make sure. The gnawing sound came from two rats that were trying to chew their way through the tent's outer barrier. His phone was next to the bed and he found a way to shimmy over to it whilst still inside the tent. He positioned it near the zipper and quickly unzipped and grabbed the phone. Just two ants took this window of opportunity and got inside; they were mercilessly crushed. Ada accepted his call as she walked down the high street.

"You're what?" she asked.

"Stuck inside a tent. I woke up in the middle of the night covered in insects."

"Oh, dear. Let me see what I can get from this, don't hang up," she said and then she stopped next to a tree and sat down on the wooden bench underneath it. She closed her eyes and, oblivious to anyone else walking past, she reached out with her feelings. Her eyelids flickered for a moment and then her eyes opened again. "You still there?"

"Yeah, I can't do much else." Joe said, flabbergasted.

"I get what is happening to you. Norman cannot re-appear; in other words, the spell must have worked. Instead, he, or something, has mobilized every possible creature to become hostile towards you."

"Not sure that's a good trade-off."

"Hardly an upgrade is it. I sense that something bigger has stepped in. Bigger than Norman."

"Oh, great."

"I know, these really bad spirits don't pull their punches." Ada sounded quite serious.

"Spirits? I thought it was demons? What can I do? I can't stay in this tent forever."

"Similar things, bad spirits and demons. Do you like camping? We used to go twice a year when my husband was still alive. We Loved it.

Nothing like the great outdoors."

"Could we get back on track please?"

"Sorry. Don't worry, I'm thinking as I talk," Ada reassured him, "How big are the holes in that mesh would you say?"

"I don't know ...a millimetre...or less. What are you thinking?"

"I was thinking about making you a face and head covering so you can get out of the tent. You could wear something on your body with no gaps that the crawlies couldn't get in through. Just as a temporary measure."

"That would be a start at least."

"I'll get the material. I'm off today and I'll dust off the sewing machine. Is your front door open?"

"I don't think so. I'll have to try and crawl downstairs and open it."

"Good. Be careful though. Give me an hour or two and when it's ready I'll bring it around."

"Thanks, Ada, oh, and there's a rat or two." Joe said and then he moved the tent, which pretty much collapsed.

"Rats? Oh, I hate rats." Ada ended the call.

Slowly and awkwardly, Joe manoeuvred the whole tent to the top of the stairs. Lots of people met their end by falling downstairs. He supposed that if he went tumbling down and became another statistic, he would be the only one to have done so whilst inside a tent. A few minutes later, with plenty of contortion and effort, he arrived at the bottom step and then he started moving the tent towards the front door. The paintwork was being scraped and scratched, but that wasn't an issue. Luckily, the key was in the door and with a swift *smash and grasp*, he turned the key and then brought his hand back in, free of insects. Now all that he had to do was wait for Ada.

Ada had bought some suitable material a few years ago which would be suitable and then had never done anything with it. Though her sewing machine skills weren't brilliant, they were adequate enough. She fastened the length of the mesh fabric over one of her supermarket baseball caps. This would give him some breathing room. She called Joe again, who wasn't exactly going anywhere anytime soon.

"Do you have waterproof pants and a jacket?" she asked.

"There is a drawer full of stuff. I have work boots. I should be able to make myself pretty safe from the bottom down."

When Ada arrived at Joe's house, the front door was closed but not locked. Wasps and flies buzzed around the windows, which were, thankfully, all closed. A row of birds sat on the telephone wire that fed into Joe's house. She also had to shoo away two angry-looking dogs from the front gate. Once inside, she saw fewer creatures on the floor than she was expecting. She held a stiff brush, ready to fend off any rodents and then she passed the makeshift hat through the zipper, before heading upstairs to go through Joe's wardrobe to find suitable clothes. Five minutes later, Joe emerged from the tent looking like a five-year-old kid's attempt to look like an astronaut.

"Two dogs were snarling at the front gate, but no sign of any rats." Ada said.

"No cats?"

"Nope. I guess not even the Devil can get a cat to do something it doesn't want to." Ada said.

"The Devil?"

"Figure of speech," then she whispered, "I hope."

The clothing worked. Nothing got past the hat, clothes, golf gloves and two pairs of socks wrapped around the bottom of waterproof walking pants, with duct tape holding the whole look together. He couldn't realistically go out walking around like that and he needed more protection from airborne threats, but it did the job for now.

Ada called Janice and filled her in on the latest news. Janice adapted to the current situation quickly, like it was the most natural thing in the world. *"It needed another spell,"* she advised. One which she would get to work on immediately.

"I could do with a cup of tea," Joe said, "I'm parched." Ada had an idea.

"I'll make the tea, you go and stand in the bath tub and when I bring it up, you can take the hat off briefly." She suggested. A line of ants was circling Joe like Indians on a wagon train in an old black-and-white cowboy film.

The idea worked. Joe stood in the bath for half an hour until Janice turned up at the front door. Ada let her in. The first thing she asked Ada was about the rats. Ada shook her head, though she wasn't sure that there were none. Janice let out a snort of laughter when she saw Joe, but quickly let her face go serious again.

"Not exactly Dr Doolittle are you." Janice said.

"Not exactly." Joe echoed from behind the mesh.

"Give me five minutes." Janice said. She went downstairs and prepared some ingredients which she produced from a plastic food pouch and then compounded using a pestle and mortar. This spell was a variation on something that she had done before. When she was ready, she took the potion upstairs and told Joe to remove his makeshift protective clothing. He was hesitant to do so, but only a few insects had gotten into the bath. Janice yanked a bed sheet from the wardrobe and covered Joe with it as he knelt with his head down. She asked him to ready himself and then placed the granite mortar under the sheet, before producing a box of matches.

"Why do you need to set fire to everything?"

Joe asked as he crouched down and brushed the odd ant off his body.

"Fire is one of the elemental basics of the universe," Janice said as she lit the concoction. Blue smoke filled the sheet Joe was under, and then it turned to grey. She bade him stay underneath for at least ten seconds, and then she whipped the sheet away, leaving him exposed. "That should do it," she said, with a hint of self-approval.

"What did you do?" Joe asked.

"Similar to what we did with Norman. Cloaking spell. Makes you invisible to creatures … *ish*."

"How long does it last?" Joe asked.

"I have no idea. I've never done this before. Not exactly. I did do something similar for a girl who was sick of unwanted attention from leery blokes. Made her invisible to them, at least till she'd had a break and finished her exams."

Sure enough, Joe no longer seemed to attract the attention of the ants, who lost interest and filed off in an orderly fashion to wherever they had come from. Joe then got dressed in his usual clothes. The bugs seemed to have all *bugged out*.

"Thanks," Joe said, "What the hell next."

"Shh," warned Ada, "Don't tempt fate."

"You're right." Joe agreed.

Whilst Janice was performing the latest spell, Ada had been trying to focus on why Joe had been the focus of these demonic attacks and unwanted creature attention. She had come up with an answer.

"I have been using my psychic powers to try and find out why you have been singled out for all this," Ada said, "And if it's right, you are the great, great, great, great, great...how many was that? Anyway, it doesn't matter ...you are the direct descendant of someone who rather pissed off Norman and some of his cronies."

"Fantastic. That's just awesome. What did he do?" Joe asked.

"The sins of the Father." Janice whispered.

"I don't know exactly, not yet, but it will come to me. At the moment it's rather vague," said Ada, "What Joe's ancestor did was rather good. It made just a relatively small difference of some kind but, in the process, it angered certain demons."

"And just now they decide to get revenge on *me*? What did I do to them?" Joe asked.

"These things are eternal and as such, time has not much meaning to them." Janice added. Ada nodded in agreement.

"So, what can I do?" Joe wondered, "To get out from under this...*curse*?"

"I'm...working on that," Janice reassured, "For now, at least, you are ok."

"Why is it just animals and bugs attacking me and not people?"

"They have free will," Ada said, "God gave

them free will and so they can't be used or manipulated.... not directly."

"Just as well." Janice said.

"That's what Norman told me with those missions he had me doing. I suppose that's one good thing, otherwise, I really would be screwed." Joe surmised. Ada added.

"With a capitol...*S*. All we have to do now is find a way to get things back to normal."

"This last attempt just made things worse. How many spells do you have left in your locker, Janice?" Joe lamented.

"Well, I still have a few. I do like a challenge," Janice said, "I'll gather the clan and put together a smoke screen spell that will last for good if we can."

"Won't this guy just get fed up with me and move on to someone else?" Joe wondered.

"Possibly," said Ada, "But I don't think so, somehow. I need to try and find out just who it is that you are descended from," She turned to Janice, "It's so shrouded that I might need an antenna or something to boost the signal so it's strong enough to go way back into the past. Could you help?"

"Couldn't we just go to the records place?" Joe offered, "Like on TV, where they trace your ancestors through the record books?"

"I have the distinct feeling that they won't go far back enough." Ada said.

"All right," Joe said. He was now relying completely on these two ladies who, three days ago, he didn't know from Adam or Eve, "I'm going on Amazon to buy some things."

"That's good," Ada commented, "Try and keep things as normal as possible."

"What are you thinking of buying?" Janice asked.

"Insect repellants and a beekeeping suit."

11

Derek had thought it best to let a few days pass with zero contact with his brother. Tonight, he sat in a bar, alone, sipping a pint of strong lager. Out of the blue, by chance or necessity, he'd made the connection between his drinking habits and his *questionable* behaviour. *But everybody drank?* Well, no, not everyone did. He thought of all the people that he knew who were no longer around. The ones that were the friendly and familiar faces in the pub, day after day, night after night. Just from his one local bar, there were several *missing persons*. One had fallen down the stairs whilst drunk. Another had drunk himself to death before the age of fifty. Liver failure; the ambulance had been outside his house one day as Derek was driving past. Another *regular* had also died young, alone in his flat, surrounded by empty vodka bottles ...and then another and another. For the first time in his life, Derek looked down and saw the drink in front of him for what it was ...ethanol... *poison*. If he was going to get his life back on track and not end up like all those other hapless people he had just thought of, from that one local bar, he was going to have to do the unthinkable and quit drinking alcohol. *This pint of beer would be his last.*

Back at home, whilst he was searching for a beekeeper's suit to use as a backup should the spell wear off, Joe had a sudden realisation. If he indeed was the direct descendant of someone who had angered demons, then so too was Derek. That was logical amid an insane series of events. *Should he warn him? Was the prostitute addiction down to these demons playing with him and trying to bring him down and destroy him*? If that *was* the case then it instantly made Derek more easily forgivable. At present, there were still so many unanswered questions. *But, how do you warn someone that they've been targeted by demons without looking like you've lost the plot?*

Got to love Amazon. It may be responsible for killing off the high street but there it was on the screen, a full beekeeper's suit, available for delivery tomorrow if he ordered within the next three hours. He was super relieved at that moment that he'd forgotten to cancel his *Prime membership*. Potentially, it was the best £89 he'd ever spent.

As the day moved on, the more he thought

about it and the more he wanted to know about this ancestor who was at the heart of all this *non-divine* retribution. He called Ada and her phone gave him the engaged tone, she called him back to say that she had been talking on the phone with Janice and also that they had devised a *theoretical* method for boosting Ada's psychic abilities, temporarily, using a form of amplifier. Sort of like a Wi-Fi booster signal. Ada told Joe that once they knew who his ancestor was, they would have a better chance of combatting the negative effects and attacks coming his way. Her instructions were that he was to head over, once again, to the pub on the lay line at 8:00 pm. She also advised him to wrap up warm as it was cold outside and rain had been predicted. He'd responded that was almost a given for October.

Joe passed the time, with one eye on the clock and a mind full of questions, until 7:30 pm and then he got changed into warmer clothes topped off with a light waterproof raincoat. This time he was meeting both ladies *at* the pub. He hoped that these meetings at the Fox & Hounds were not just a convoluted excuse to get drunk. Trying to keep a reign on his negative thoughts was becoming increasingly difficult.

When he arrived, the pub car park was almost full. It was Friday night and the place was rocking, as much as an old country pub does ever *rock*. When Joe walked in, he immediately saw

Ada and Janice, accompanied by two other ladies, sitting at the same table near the middle of the pub. Some *reasonably* talented pianist was letting some standard, non-offensive tunes fill the room and the atmosphere was pleasantly chilled out. In challenging financial times, these patrons were the ones with money. These well-established country locals with their own properties and pension plans and everything that they needed. Recessions and rising prices didn't make a dent in this lot; the car park was a testament to that, it was full of premium branded vehicles. Joe had parked between a Range Rover and an Audi. He wondered how many would be driven home or would be still there in the morning.

He got himself a drink and then sat at the table with the four women. The barman recognized him from his recent visits and wondered to himself why Joe, who looked to be in his late thirties, was hanging out with these slightly eccentric ladies closer to retirement age. He didn't come across as some sort of gigolo. It was rather unusual, but he saw many *unusual* things whilst sober behind the bar.

The two unknowns greeted him as they sang along to the music in quiet voices. Janice seemed in no rush to perform what they had talked about earlier. Eventually, without wanting to waste any more time, Joe brought the subject up in between songs. He said to Ada.

"So, you have a plan?"

"Yes," she answered. "At exactly 9:13 pm, we are going to go outside again."

"Why 9:13?" he asked.

"That's when the power through the ley line is at its peak." Ada answered.

"How do you know all this?" he wondered out loud.

"I haven't a clue; it's Janice that knows that sort of stuff."

Joe nodded. They all sat smiling and singing and chatting, just like it was any other normal Friday night, then, when the old clock's minute hand clicked onto the twelfth segment, everyone at the table got up and, like prisoners who had just finished their exercise in the yard, trooped outside in orderly fashion. Ada asked someone at the next table to watch their seats and their bags. All the rest of the pub assumed they were leaving on mass for a cigarette, but only Janice smoked and they had another agenda. There were drops of rain falling as they all sat down at a circular bench. Ada told Joe that he had to sit in the middle of it, whilst the four Ladies sat in a circle and joined hands.

"We moved this bench, so it's exactly on the ley line." Janice said.

"How do you know where that is? It's invisible right?" Joe asked.

"It's like a water divider. A stick that vibrates

when it passes over something, with a bit of witchcraft thrown in." Janice briefly explained.

"This should, in theory anyway, boost my reach into the past." Ada said. Luckily all the pub windows were misted up by the heat from the fire inside, otherwise, the other patrons would have thought what they were seeing through the window was more than a little odd.

The process began. The three good witches began to chant and channel as much power as they could muster up. Then they tried to manifest this energy into the body of Ada. Ada closed her eyes and let her mind reach out. Joe felt a bit of a pratt, sitting in the middle, but if they had asked him to run around the pub car-park naked he would have done it. A few minutes went by. All had their eyes shut. Then, Ada started to speak.

"I'm going back. Further. Further. Further. I can see London, with chimneys and black smoke. There is no barrier on the river, just sailboats. Further back. The sky is blue. There are peasants everywhere. Pigs, goats, chickens, a lot of chickens for some reason. Further back. Horses. Knights on horses. Metal shining. Spears and axes and swords. Mud and fields. Further. Further. Romans. The red colour of their uniforms. Hadrian's Wall is being built. Further. It's breaking up a bit. Ships sailing across the English Channel. Kings and Queens. Not in England anymore. It's hot, very hot. Like Crete when I went on holiday. It is too hot. More Roman soldiers, but not in England this time. A man is walking in front. He's struggling. There's a crowd of people shouting. Throwing rocks. Some flowers. Thorns. I'm helping the man. It's heavy, very heavy. Made of wood. There are splinters in my hands. There's a way to go. I'm not sure if I can do it. It's heavy. Heavy." Ada took a deep breath and then opened her eyes. No one spoke for a minute or two until Ada said. "Now I know who it is."

12

Derek sipped his coffee a lot more slowly than he drank beer or wine, as he sat at a table in the local Hospice shop café. Joe had asked to meet him there at 11:00 am. He'd told him that he had something important to tell him. Derek hoped to God that it wasn't the news that he didn't want any further contact with him. *Why had he chosen neutral ground on which to meet?* All he could do was hope for the best.

His right hand was trembling slightly and he didn't know whether that was nerves or early withdrawal symptoms. He hadn't drunk alcohol for two days, that was all, but it felt like an achievement. *Long way to go.*

Joe turned up right on time to see his brother sitting on his own. He took his coat off and sat facing him. He asked the server for tea and when it arrived, he started to speak.

"You alright?" he asked Derek.

"Yeah," Derek wondered about telling his

brother about quitting drinking and decided against it: it was too early in the campaign, "What is it you wanted to speak about?" He had intended to play it cooler, but needed to know right away.

"Something is happening," Joe stated. Derek nodded as though to urge Joe to continue, "It's kind of, well it's definitely...*out there.*"

"What do you mean...*out there*?"

"What would you say if I told you that the sins of the father came back to haunt the sons?"

"Is that something from the Bible? I'd like to know what the hell my father did."

"Well, I know that phrase is true. Have you had any strange occurrences lately?"

"Like what?"

"I don't know. Has anything weird happened?"

"Not really, why?"

Joe took a sip of tea and then a deep breath.

"Well, bear with me. I'll just get to the point. Our ancestor, great-grandfather times ten or whatever the number is, did something pretty... unique and good, at the time. The problem is ... some dark spirits are pissed off about it."

"Our ancestor...?"

"Yeah, you know...our father's ...father's father and so on."

"Ok," *Had his brother lost the plot?* "So, you think that...?"

"It's them getting reckoning or revenge. Some

really weird shit has happened to me in the last few days. Are you sure nothing has happened to you?"

"Did ...did that knock on the head, you know...?"

"It's not the knock on the head, at least I don't think so."

Derek paused and drank some more coffee before he spoke again.

"I'm not sure what you are on about here, but, and this wasn't the way I planned to tell you, but somebody should have done by now. I can't *not* tell you."

"Tell me what?"

"You know how Dad came back from the army and then bailed out on us?"

"Yeah. Mum said it was PTSD from combat in the gulf and he couldn't cope with slotting back into family life."

Derek nodded slowly.

"You know I was four years old when he came back home and you were...?"

"I wasn't born. I was born *after* he'd left for good."

"Yes, you were. Several months after he left for good."

"Several months?"

"Yeah, I worked it out when ...I actually can't remember when. But the dates added up. I confronted Mum about it and she didn't deny it."

"Mum ...was already pregnant with me when he got back?"

Derek didn't want to speak the word *yes*, so instead he nodded gently. After a while, he said,

"I'm afraid so."

Joe took some time to absorb that little bombshell. In a way, it vindicated his, well, Derek's father, but shed a poor light upon his mother, who had passed away five years previously without coming clean about this.

"So, we have different fathers," Derek didn't want to speak so nodded again, "All this time and different fathers." Joe said.

"I didn't think it my place to tell you." Derek sighed.

"If not yours then whose?"

"I didn't know how to say it and then, you know, things get brushed under the carpet. It wasn't an easy conversation to start."

"And you're sure about this, you didn't miscalculate the dates?"

"I went over it several times and as I say, I confronted Mum about it. She eventually admitted the brief affair and she also said that she would tell you herself and that she wanted to tell you when the time was right."

"But never did."

"It is a tough conversation to have."

Neither spoke for a full minute.

"So, we are half-brothers, not full." Joe stated.

"Full in my eyes. I know, it's a tough one to take and I know it is you that wanted to meet to tell *me* something. I just feel like I want to get everything out into the open ...be *transparent*."

Joe didn't say anything else for a while. He just stared at the teacup. It occurred to him that, if this was the case, his brother would be off the hook and so would his nephew. There was no need to further explain the *demon wanting revenge* story. *The sins of the father*. The question now remained ...*who the hell was his father?* Somehow or other, whoever he was, that man's DNA led right back to ..

Thirteen hours earlier...

"Simon of Cyrene." Ada said. Snowflakes landed on her head. No one at the gathering at the table recognized the name.

"Who?" Janice asked.

"Simon of Cyrene." Ada repeated.

"What did he do?" Joe wondered. He had been half expecting to hear the names of *John the Baptist* or *Moses* himself.

"He carried the cross for Jesus, along streets filled with..." Ada stopped; she could say no more for a moment. The vision had been too real-seeming. "He was a black man visiting Jerusalem on some sort of business. Some say that he was compelled to carry it by Roman soldiers and had no choice in the matter. But, if that were the case, then I suppose the demons wouldn't be seeking revenge on his ancestors."

"Just that one act of kindness," Joe said. "Would that be enough to anger these dark spirits?"

"Yes," said Ada, "They had contrived to destroy Jesus, a being of pure light. They hate that kind of purity. I felt the hate in the vision. They wanted ...they wanted him to suffer as much as possible. They had manoeuvred him carefully towards his cruel destination. Simon carrying the cross took some of the *shine* off their achievement. Even the crowd were jeering and spitting. Simon gave that day something pure and kind when everything else was wretched."

"And now they want revenge on me?" Joe asked.

"It looks that way." Ada said.

"After all this time." Joe added.

"Remember," cautioned Janice, "That these things are in no hurry. Human beings have been on the planet for about three million years. The time that has passed since Jesus's crucifixion is nothing by comparison and perhaps you are the last in the line."

"Let's go back inside." Ada said. Thick snowflakes had begun to fall and stick on the ground.

"How can I possibly defend myself against such things?" Joe said.

"You have us." Janice said. Ada smiled at him as did the two newcomers. They all mentally closed ranks against the impending evil. Joe looked at these ladies each in turn as they sat back down at the table. Then he looked into the roaring fire and watched red and yellow flames dance and devour.

13

The news that Joe's estranged father wasn't, in fact, his biological father came as a shock but one that paled into lesser significance when compared with recent events.

He'd seen just the one photograph of his *supposed* father; standing wearing combat gear and mirrored shades with some of his unit's men, over some defeated soldiers. He never did see his eyes. He supposed that his mother had destroyed all other photographic evidence in response to him up and leaving. Now Joe realized that the man dressed in khaki in the photo had a good and valid reason to disappear. He could have, perhaps, kept in touch with Derek, though it must have been an incredibly difficult decision to make.

Joe didn't now have a new mental image of his own father. That just didn't manifest itself. Somewhere down the line though, *someone* had gotten involved with his mother. He didn't want to know any more details about who this man was or how and when it happened. With his mother gone, he'd never be able to find out who he was or where they had met.

He sat with the TV on, unable to relax or concentrate on whichever channel he flicked on to. The conversation with his brother that had taken place just that very morning seemed like a thousand days ago.

The bee-keepers suit arrived in the afternoon. The Amazon delivery driver had no clue as to what was inside the package as he handed it over and he'd never have guessed correctly given a million tries. Joe thanked him and then took it out of the cardboard packaging, but not the cellophane wrapper. If they managed to resolve this, then he would return it. With all the crazy shit that was going on, he was still thinking cautiously and frugally. It was placed on the dining table, ready if needed. The big question was, *would he need it?* On the previous night, the same Labrador dog was again there in the Fox & Hounds, the same one that had lunged for him with teeth bared. This time it had just stared in his general direction as though there was something that it couldn't fathom out. He had no idea how long this cloaking spell would last and, more worryingly, neither did Janice, the one who cast it.

◆◆◆

Janice had gone to speak to Ada at the supermarket around the same time that Joe had met with his brother. Ada took a break and the two sat down in the staff canteen area. The manager briefly looked at Janice, who shouldn't have been in there with the staff-only rule and he couldn't care less. He was moving stores in three weeks and he couldn't wait to get out of this one. If some *armed* robber had turned up with a plastic gun demanding the takings, he'd have given it to them and also yesterday's takings for good measure.

"So," Janice started the conversation whilst Ada set down two coffees on the table, "We have only just met this man and we seem to have become very embroiled in what is quite a situation."

"I know. It has all happened very fast." She took a drink of coffee and screwed her face up in disapproval, "They give the staff the cheap stuff, not the stuff in the cafe."

"Tightwads."

"Wait here," Ada got up and came back with two cold drinks from the fridge cabinet, "I'll pour that stuff down the sink later."

Janice continued.

"To be brutally honest, Ada, I'm worried that we might be in over our heads." She watched closely for Ada's initial and probably accurate reaction. Ada's facial expression didn't alter much, "What do you think we should do?"

"Well, *technically* speaking, it isn't our responsibility to help this man," Ada said, "But *morally*, it is. He has found his way onto my path and yours, via me and I feel as though I have to follow this through and do what I can to help him. I'd never forgive myself if I didn't. But, you have to make that decision for yourself. Don't be swayed by me and my thoughts."

Janice smiled.

"I knew you would say that. We've come too far to abandon him now. I sense a lot of goodness in him; a rare quality in a lot of people. I suppose I'm with you. Whatever it takes. I just wanted to see you alone to make sure you felt the same way. Because it could be dangerous things that we are messing with. Dangerous to *us* I mean."

Ada nodded.

"I Know. What's our next step then? Do you think that shielding spell will hold?"

"To be honest? No. Not indefinitely. It's a bit flimsy, but it will have to do for now."

"So, what's the next plan then?" Ada wondered out loud.

"We don't have one."

"Let's make one, now, before I go back on the till. I'll feel better if we have a plan of some kind, then we aren't just probing around in the dark."

"Ok. What do we have to go on?" Janice

wondered.

"Well, Simon the...great...whatever it is, of Joe. He's going to be the key because he is the cause of all the problems. Unless you think that might *not* be the reason Joe has been targeted?"

"No. It is one hundred per cent the reason. Perhaps this *is* happening now, today in 2023 because Joe is going to be the last in the bloodline. It does seem a bit OTT though, carrying this grudge on for so long, just for what Simon of Cyrene did." Janice said.

"Well, these demonic spirits are not known for their reasonable actions or sense of fairness. I am a hundred per cent sure as well that they are behind all this for that reason. It could well be that he is the last one to take revenge on, so they are not letting it pass them by," Ada said. She also had a suggestion, "I was thinking earlier, seeing as this problem has quite a hefty religious slant to it, what about you going to visit the church and speaking to the vicar?"

"The church. Are you sure? Do they provide that kind of service?"

"Well, they might. Doing so can't make matters any worse and I do feel as though it will help."

"The church. Which one?"

"Well ...any I suppose."

"Catholic or...non-Catholic?

Ada thought for a moment and let her

instincts guide her choice.

"I'm not sure that it matters. Jesus and carrying the cross feature in both versions. What about the one behind the cinema?"

"Have you ever been in there?" Janice asked.

"No. But try that one. Go and speak to the Priest there. He's a man in his mid-fifties. I just got a mental image of him."

"And ask him what?"

"You will know what to ask when you get there." Ada said, and then her break was over.

◆ ◆ ◆

Janice didn't dress like a stereotypical witch in a pointed hat and cloak; she looked more like a Woodstock child transported into the 2020s, clad in bright colours, a comfortable cotton kaftan and tennis shoes.

As she walked up the path to the *Church of St Hubert*, she wondered whether or not people could tell there was something different about her, just from her external appearance. The priest certainly couldn't. Or at least if he could, he still greeted her with a nice warm smile. Janice wasn't too sure how a witch of any persuasion would be welcomed by the Catholic Church. She decided to leave that bit of information at home.

There was no service planned for that day and Father Jones had been kind enough to sit down and have a chat with one of the flock over a cup of tea. He was, as Ada had described, a man of fifty-six, just under six feet tall and lean looking.

"I don't recall seeing you at service. Forgive me, I'm not great at putting names to faces." Was the first thing Father Jones said. Janice didn't think it prudent to explain why that was the case.

"I sit at the back." she lied and then immediately felt bad about doing so.

"What can I help you with today?" *How did she start this one?* All she could say was,

"Erm."

"Come on child, don't be shy. You can tell me anything."

She was obviously troubled by something, but they weren't in the confessional booth. Janice could see the lines moving on his face. He called her *child*. She must have been a little older. She started speaking.

"We have a problem, Father." she'd forgotten his name even though it was *Jones,* the most common name in the whole country.

"Go on ..."

"Well. It goes like this; I'll start from the beginning. A friend of ours, well, a newish friend, is having trouble with, what you might call ...bad spirits."

"Spirits like vodka and whisky?" Father Jones commented. His eyes twinkled. Janice didn't expect a Priest to have a sense of humour.

"Not exactly," She paused for thought for a moment so as not to say all the wrong things, "I have come to see you today because he needs help ridding himself of demonic forces." *There, she said it out loud. Was that too ridiculous?*

Father Jones placed his teacup back on its saucer and the smile on his face faded away.

"Demonic forces you say. And how are these forces manifesting themselves?" At this point, Father Jones would have been entitled or inclined to think that this lady, whom he'd never seen before, was a complete nut job.

"Well, my friend who is very ...*spiritual* ... noticed he was carrying a burden. And as it turned out, he was being visited by a ghost of some kind."

"A ghost now?"

"No, not a ghost a ...thing. And then..." *Should she tell him about how they stopped Norman's appearances? Not yet,* "He was being attacked by ants..."

"Ants you say? You mean the little creatures, not his parents' siblings."

"No, the creatures."

"And are these ants still after him?"

"Not at present, but that could all change."

Father Jones smiled and pushed the teacup to one side.

"Janice. Tell me, Janice. Are you on any type of medication at all, at the moment?"

"Medication?"

Father Jones nodded. Janice realized.

"No. No, I know this must all sound daft, but we really need to help this person."

Father Jones stood up.

"Might I suggest coming to church this Sunday? Sit nearer the front so that I can see you." he said with a smile. Janice wasn't the first eccentric member of the flock he'd ever encountered. She wouldn't be the last.

"He's the direct descendant of Simon of Cyrene!" she blurted out.

This was a new one for Father Jones.

"Simon of Cyrene?" He knew exactly who that was.

"Yes. The demons have come to exact revenge on him. He's the last one in the long line of descendants."

This was a complex delusion.

"And you know this how, exactly?"

"We just do know it. It's down to my spiritual friend, Ada."

"Ada. I don't recognize the name. Does she attend Church?" Janice didn't know for sure but guessed not. She only shrugged her shoulders. She expected, now, that the priest would probably bid her goodbye and then go about his daily tasks. She waited for him to say so. All she could do was look down at the old wooden table and hope. "Simon of Cyrene," Father Jones said, in a strong voice, "One of the last men to help our lord and saviour. One last act of kindness. I suppose that the dark spirits didn't like that after they had contrived so hard to bring him down. They want all the world in darkness and Simon held up a small candle that day. Just enough to see by." Janice looked up. This man wasn't dismissing what she had said out of hand as the musings of some unstable/unhinged/menopausal woman. Her mouth opened, but she didn't say anything. Father Jones continued, "If this man is troubled, then bring him in with you. Let me see him and speak with him."

Janice was pleasantly surprised at this response. He could have said anything to her just to get rid of her. Whether or not he believed the story of Simon of Cyrene was debatable. This priest had not closed the door shut on their little band of refuge seekers. Janice thanked him for the tea and said that she would return at a mutually agreeable time, as soon as they possibly could. Father Jones suggested later that day at 4:00 pm. He could see her un-veiled desperation and, if he were being honest, she had his curiosity.

◆ ◆ ◆

At 4:00 pm, Janice walked down the path to the church doors again, this time sandwiched by Ada to her left and Joe to her right.

Father Jones smiled briefly at Ada, another one he hadn't seen previously, and then he fixed his curious gaze upon Joe. As he walked through the front doors of the church, the sunlight caught his frame in silhouette.

"Come through to the back into the vestry," Father Jones said, "I have made more tea. Though don't think I sit drinking tea all day," Father Jones closed the church doors behind them; they were never locked, not even at night. All four sat down at an old wooden table in the vestry. The room looked quite like any other vestry, apart from the table tennis table at one end, "I like to practice regularly. Father Michael and I have a little rivalry going and we have a game coming up," Father Jones poured some tea from a teapot with the word *Lourdes* written on it and then he placed it down upon the table. He set the ball rolling, "So, I believe you have a problem that you need help with?"

"Yes." All three answered at once.

"Tell me, if you would please, why have you come here to ask for help? Not that you aren't welcome of course."

Joe thought he'd better be the one to explain as it was all solidly upon his shoulders.

"It seems like I have angered some spirits or demons," He turned to Ada, "Ada thinks that I am descended from someone who helped Jesus carry, you know, carry the cross."

Father Jones's expression didn't alter.

"Indeed. How might Ada be aware of that wonderful piece of information?"

All three allies looked at each other. Tentatively, Ada offered,

"I am fortunate to be able to...see into the past." She waited for that bombshell to ignite some anti-heretic fueled response from the man dressed in black opposite them.

"Hmm. That is a rare gift indeed." Father Jones said.

Ada continued.

"And I was able to see that far back. Joe is related to that same man. Simon." Father Jones paused and drank more tea. If he followed the accepted Catholic Priest's policy on such matters, he might well request the removal of these guests from his building immediately. Ada continued, "And he's been visited by a spirit ...a not very nice one."

"And a plague of insects." Janice added.

"A plague indeed?" Father Jones exclaimed.

"Well, not exactly a plague, but a lot of them were crawling on him," Janice added, "How many would you say there were?"

"I didn't count them." Joe said.

"You didn't just leave some sugar in your pocket?" Father Jones asked.

"No. It was really weird, to say the least. And dogs and birds tried to attack me. We think that

Norman is behind all this and that he sent them." Joe added.

"And who, might I ask, is Norman?" Father Jones asked.

"This spirit that had been getting me to do these little tasks." Joe said, flatly.

Nothing in his or anyone else's priests' studies had prepared Father Jones for this situation. Twenty years ago, he might well have dismissed them out of hand. He had an idea. He asked Joe to join him in the main body of the church. They both stood up and walked the short distance. Then he bade Joe stand under the carving of Jesus at the front of the church, whilst he sat down on the front pew. Then he calmly studied this man. He watched the candlelight cast small shadows on his face. He saw the sunlight from the stained-glass filter onto his features. He looked up at the face of the carving and then back to Joe's. All at once he was filled with a feeling of some certainty. He stood up. With one hand on his shoulder, he guided Joe back to the vestry. They sat down again and Father Jones spoke in a calm and measured tone.

"What is it that you would like me to do?"

"You believe the story we just told you?" Joe asked.

"I don't *not* believe it ...if that makes sense. We all have our demons to battle. *All* of us. Let us see if we can help you conquer yours."

14

"We have two choices," Janice summed up, "We can either a) wait and see if the cloaking spell holds indefinitely or b) do something else." She sat on her favourite sofa, whilst Joe and Ada occupied the big leather Chesterfield at a right angle to it. Joe was still hidden from all the creatures that were straining against the hurriedly put-together spell, but Janice had said that she wasn't exactly over-confident about going up against these big hitters. She felt like an amateur in comparison, but then who wouldn't have? Father Jones had listened to their story with calm interest. He already knew, from his own experiences, that good and evil spirits existed. He wasn't one of those priests who were just going through the motions and doing what they did as a job with accommodation provided. He had not discounted anything that they had said to him. Not yet.

So far, there was no formal or informal plan

of action, just a diminutive list of options. Joe felt rather uneasy about the uncertainty of the spell's long-term effectiveness. At any moment it could break and a pack of rabid-like hounds, rats and insects might descend on him in an instant, or a flock of angry birds might swoop down and attack him. With this harrowing thought at the forefront of his mind, not surprisingly, he preferred to stay indoors as much as possible. Whenever outdoors, he carried a strong umbrella with him. His original idea was to carry a baseball bat, but then he realized that might look a bit odd or threatening to others, particularly without the accompanying bizarre explanation of why he had it. The umbrella could be used to ward off both dogs and birds and be particularly effective when opened. He'd practised the manoeuvre of opening the brolly quickly and then fending off imaginary adversaries like it was some strange new martial art. It wasn't a great or infallible plan, but it was better than nothing. At any rate, he had no desire to visit the zoo.

Several more hours passed by quietly, whilst the newly formed group pondered on the problem and possible solutions to it. Father Jones kept the issue on his mind, but not constantly like the others did. He was hoping that the problem might just go away in time if left to its own devices.

"Father Jones asked us to pray." Ada said.

"That isn't what I meant by a *plan b.* Not

really." Janice replied.

"So, something else other than just waiting around sounds good to me," Joe said, "And I'm not saying that I don't trust your spell skills by the way."

"I understand," agreed Janice, "I am a relative novice. I'm surprised it's held to be perfectly honest," She looked at Ada, "What do you think?"

Ada had been trying to look at all the angles.

"I think.... I think we need a plan b. At least *I* would if I was in Joe's shoes."

"Ok," Janice paused their conversation whilst she talked on the phone for five minutes to one of the other members of the coven. Then she said, "I still can't believe Father Jones took us seriously."

"Unless," offered Joe, "He *was* just humouring us."

"He did say he would think of something." Ada defended him.

"He did." Echoed Janice.

"I half expected him to dunk my head in the christening bowl." Joe said.

"Filled with *holy water*," Janice added, "Tell you what, that might not be too far off a solution."

"Should we suggest it?" Joe said, with more than a hint of desperation beginning to creep into his voice.

"I think that might be rude," Ada said, "If he thought that would work, then he would have suggested it himself. We don't want to *cliché* his whole way of life," The other two nodded, "He did pretend to be deaf in his left ear when I told him I was a psychic and that was how I knew about Joe's troubles."

"I don't think the Catholic church recognizes psychics as a bad thing," Joe said, "But then that's only a guess."

"Hopefully not," Ada smiled, "It's good that he is open-minded. Mind you, I knew he was, that's why I suggested that his was the church to go to."

"So then, who's hungry?" Janice pulled some freshly baked scones out of the oven. *Were they scones?* Joe bit into one and it was more like a rock cake. He was tempted to suggest that she use witchcraft the next time but felt it wiser to keep schtum.

◆ ◆ ◆

The next morning, Joe got a text message from a co-worker asking him how he was; possibly instigated by Dean, with the ulterior motive of gauging the timeline of his return. He also told him that the boss had saved several *carefully chosen* jobs for him on his return. By *carefully chosen*, he meant ones that involved the climbing of poles. Joe told him that two weeks was two weeks and not to expect him back any sooner. To Joe, the low-level and vindictive boss from work seemed toothless and irrelevant now. If he did get through the next several days unscathed, then he would be a cinch to deal with.

Joe had planned to try his best to relax at home until he heard from one of the others. That plan changed when Derek called him at 11:30 am, asking him to meet up in the town centre. When asked why, Derek didn't tell him that he wanted to buy him a gift. He'd received a tax-related bonus and he planned to buy his brother the best acoustic guitar in the music shop. He knew how much Joe had procrastinated on the decision. It would be more dramatic as a gesture of goodwill if it were a complete surprise.

Joe looked out of his living room window. Outside looked safe enough. No animals were waiting in the wings, none that were visible. The spell *had* held up until now. He looked at the bee-keepers suit, still in the cellophane. He could hardly turn up wearing that as a precaution. *Should he tell Janice or Ada about venturing outside?* As this was a short trip, he decided that it would be fine to not bother them. He put his shoes and jacket on and then his front door closed behind him with a *clunk*.

The walk into town was only a short ten-minute hike. Parking was difficult and expensive and so he rarely drove there. It felt good that his brother was reaching out and making an effort to build bridges. Perhaps their relationship would improve from now onwards. *Sometimes you have to hit the lowest point in order to be able to rise again.*

Derek was already waiting for him in the high street café. He offered as warm a smile as he could muster, and Joe reciprocated. They sat near the window.

"I was in town and I know you are off work for a while longer." Derek said.

"It's fine. Gets me out of the house for a bit. How are you?"

"I'm good." In truth, Derek was struggling a little with alcohol withdrawal symptoms. His hand was trembling slightly as he picked up his coffee cup, but it wasn't too severe or too noticeable.

They made some light chit-chat; nothing that could potentially lead towards any more serious subjects, like parentage. When they'd finished their drinks, Derek said he'd walk up the high street with his brother. It was all pleasant and low-key. The conversation had not gotten deep and it felt like the first foundation stone in re-building the bridge that had been washed away had been bedded in.

"This way." Derek suggested that they head up the street instead of down. Joe wasn't fussed about which route they took. Derek stopped at the music shop and looked in the window.

"I didn't know you were interested in instruments."

"Let's go in." Derek said. When they were inside the shop, they were greeted by a young man who was as far away from being a pushy salesman as you could imagine. The miserable owner was nowhere to be seen. On the wall were about a dozen electric guitars and also the same number of acoustic instruments. A whole host of wind instruments were on the opposite side of the shop, and then violins and larger stringed instruments were positioned in the centre. Derek asked Joe which acoustic guitar he would recommend and Joe went through the available selection and gave his brief opinion on each. "Which is the best one?" Derek asked him. Joe was a little surprised at his brother's interest. Perhaps he was trying to develop a shared interest or was thinking of buying his son one to learn on, "Which one would you get if money was not an object?"

"This," Joe pointed to the most expensive guitar on the wall, "It's all solid wood; spruce on the top and mahogany back and sides. Makes it sound better. Much richer."

Derek went over to talk to the sales assistant. Joe looked out of the shop window, *from the inside* for a change. Two dogs were staring back at him. Much to their owners' dismay, they had dragged them over to the window and were refusing to budge. Joe felt a sudden unease. When he turned back around, he saw the salesperson carefully picking the all-solid wood guitar off the wall.

"We only have one of these," he said as he placed the guitar into a black hard-shell case. Joe walked over as Derek put his bank card into the machine.

"You got it?" Joe said, with another glance behind him.

Once the payment was processed and the guitar case was in Derek's hand. He passed it to his brother.

"For you. You are far too careful with money to buy it for yourself."

"Me? The most expensive one in the shop. You didn't need to do that."

"No, I didn't *need* to. But hey, I got a nice tax refund. For once, they gave *me* something. This is just me saying thanks for letting me stay with you. Just make sure that you play the damned thing."

"Man, that's great. Thanks, I will do."

"Na, thank *you* for all you've done these last months."

The first support for the construction of the bridge to recovery was securely in place. Joe felt the weight of the case in his hand. Now all he had to do was get it home. He let his brother open the shop door for him. The two dogs were still sitting there looking at him. One was a small breed. Joe wasn't too concerned about that one. The other was a German Shepherd, possibly a crossbreed. Derek held the door whilst the two dog owners tried to pull their dogs away from the window. All at once, the German Shepherd's lip curled into a snarl. A deep growl emanated from it; so deep that it seemed unnatural. The small dog started yapping, barking and jumping up and down. Derek looked at Joe and then down at the dogs. The big dog lunged at Joe, pulling its lightweight owner off her feet. Joe had left the umbrella at home on the table. Instinctively, he held the guitar case in between himself and the dog. It was knocked out of his hands and went skidding across the pavement. Then he darted back inside the shop, leaving both dogs acting like angry wolves, barking and snarling and knocking into the glass of the door.

"I'm so sorry," The big dog owner said, "He's never done this before." Derek assessed the situation as quickly as he could. The dogs had no animosity or hostility towards him and for whatever reason his brother was the target of their aggression. He grabbed the lead of the German Shepherd and being much stronger than its owner, was able to pull it away from the door and then fasten it to the nearest lamppost. The dog looked pretty scary. It strained and pulled and barked, but it was secured. The small dog's owner simply picked it up and carried it off. Derek picked up the guitar case, which was now quite scraped and dusty. He looked up and saw a few birds of different species circling overhead. The world had just gone mad in an instant. With the big dog secure, Joe stepped back out onto the street.

"Did you drive here?" he asked Derek.

"Yes."

"Please, get the car and pick me up from here. I'm feeling a bit ...off."

Derek said that he would. He was more than a little puzzled, but he went and got the car and then parked outside the music shop so that Joe could dart in. When he sat in the back, the birds that had been circling started to fly down and divebomb the car.

"You sure everything is, ok? This is all very strange. These birds don't like you either, by the looks of it." Derek asked Joe.

"Yeah. Just feeling a bit queasy."

Derek dropped him off safely at home and carried the guitar in for him. He told Joe to ring him if needed but advised him to get his head down for a bit. Before he left, he said,

"You know when you were talking about that stuff yesterday ...demons and whatever. I'm worried that you might have some after-effects from the fall."

"I saw the doc."

"What did he say?"

"Just to give it a week or two. He gave me some pills."

Derek nodded. That was all well and good, but

did not explain why, and he'd seen it with his own two eyes, animals were acting hostile towards his brother. *He* hadn't had a blow to the head and dreamt that. He again advised Joe to rest. Joe said that he would and then he closed the front door behind his brother a little more quickly than was needed. Derek sat in his car and watched, his mind racing on muddy ground as his fingers tip-tapped on the steering wheel. The next thing that Joe did was go and unwrap the bee-keepers suit from its cellophane. It was going to have to be *plan b.*

◆◆◆

"It's broken." was how Joe explained the situation to Ada. He'd called her first, even though it was Janice and her friends who had cast the cloaking spell. The three of them agreed that it was time to start on plan b. This time the group would gather at his house and this time Janice and Ada would bring Father Jones with them.

"Is there any point in trying that spell again?" Janice asked Ada on the way, "It would only hold for so long, if at all."

"These forces are very strong," Ada said, "I'm surprised it held for as long as it did. Perhaps you could re-work it. Beef it up a little."

"As I suggested before, I think we might be in over our heads." Janice said as she rapped the door knocker.

They entered to see Joe standing there in the bee-keeper suit that was dotted here and there with a few ants and other crawlies.

"Greetings," Ada said, "Have you seen any rats?" As though the situation was the most normal thing in the world. Joe shook his head and then he waved them inside before any nearby creatures took a fancy to him.

Ada made some tea and they passed the time chatting about what had happened since they'd last met, whilst they waited for the newest member of the group to arrive. Twenty minutes later the door knocker sounded again; this time it was Father Jones who stood there on the doorstep under a black fedora hat. Ada let him in. He seemed remarkably unperturbed by the sight of Joe wearing the beekeeper's suit.

"Pestilence for one," Father Jones said, "I don't think that look will catch on," Joe would have laughed if he hadn't been so thoroughly and completely pissed off. Father Jones sat down and then got down to business. "It would appear," he made a sweeping gesture with his hand, "That you *are* being targeted by demonic entities. If indeed you *are*, as Ada here believes, a direct descendant of Simon of Cyrene, then perhaps these malevolent spirits are wanting to torment you, as in turn, Simon lessened Jesus's torment all those years ago. Not by much, it has to be said, but a little can go a long way."

"Is there a remedy for this?" Joe asked from behind the mesh.

"This torment comes from the Devil, or at least his minions, his demons," Father Jones said, "What we need, I think, and I am by no means an expert on this type of thing, is a powerful symbol of goodness to combat and banish these dark things that are hounding you. Of course, they may just get bored of tormenting you and move on to some other poor soul." This was just an estimated guess on his part.

"A crucifix?" Janice suggested. Father Jones stood up and placed the crucifix symbol from the chain around his neck against Joe's head.

"I don't think this will be enough," he said. Sure enough, when he moved the cross away the ants were still walking around on the outside of the suit. Father Jones looked outside the window and noticed the line of birds on the telephone wire directly outside the house. "Must be a little off-putting. At least these malevolent spirits can't control people. That's *something* to be grateful for."

Ada had been a little guarded about what she said in the company of Father Jones. She had no idea whether or not the church had pre-set rules about psychics and witches. Father Jones *seemed* to be fairly open-minded. He'd accepted Joe's predicament surprisingly easily.

"Have you come across this kind of thing before?" She asked. Father Jones pursed his lips and shook his head quickly. "What do you think we need to do?" She already had a mental image of a specific place, as yet unknown, that she felt might be the key to a solution.

"Visit the Pope?" Janice offered.

"Does it matter that I'm not a Catholic?" Joe said, rather muffled.

"Did you choose that path, or was it your parents' choice which church, if any, you frequented?" Father Jones answered. Joe didn't know how to respond, "Don't worry, it is a rhetorical question." Father Jones had another idea, "You have invoked the unwanted attention of some pretty diabolical demons. That's not to say there are any *good* ones knocking about. At least one of which called itself *Norman*, who seemed to be toying with you at first. Using you as an instrument for bad deeds wrapped up in false agendas. You said that you signed something in this dream-like state you were in?"

"Yes. It looked blank and there was no ink on the feather." Joe explained. Father Jones nodded.

"An open-ended agreement. What we need is purity. Purity and goodness will, in turn, dissolve their *badness*. It's physics and chemistry really if you think about it."

Ada smiled. She was starting to warm to this man and she let it show in her face.

"So what is the plan?" Joe asked, hopefully.

"A plan." Father Jones responded, "That is what we need to come up with. You can't stay in that suit indefinitely. And from now on, you can all call me "FJ" it's easier and saves time."

"Ok *FJ.* I'd rather not stay in this suit, if at all possible." Joe said.

"In the mean time, I will begin working on a new spell straight away." Janice said, "I'll gather some of the *others* and crack on with it."

"The sooner the better." Ada said. Joe nodded.

◆◆◆

Just an hour later, back at Joe's house, the new spell seemed to have worked. The insects that crawled on Joe's suit and the birds on the wire outside his back door had dispersed. How long this version of the spell would hold for was an *unknown variable*, and that meant time was of the essence.

Joe called Janice just after he watched the birds fly away. He took the headgear off.

"It worked, the spell did. Thanks, Janice."

"It worked?" Janice asked for confirmation.

"Yes, the ants have buggered off and the birds waiting for me outside have just flown away."

"Oh. That's odd, I wasn't expecting that at all."

"Hey, don't talk yourself down. You did great again."

"No, I didn't mean that. The thing is, we have only just finished preparing it, and we sure as *hell* haven't got around to casting it yet ..."

"Really?" Joe wondered.

"Really."

"Oh. Well, perhaps it's all over then," Joe sighed, "Maybe they've had their fun, got bored and moved on to someone else like Father Jones said they might. Thank God for that."

"That's good news. Not for the person that they've moved on to, but still." Janice said.

"I'll ring the Father and tell him the news."

"Good idea. Does Ada know?"

"Not yet. I'll call her right after I've finished speaking with you."

Joe ended the call and immediately called Ada, who was sitting watching the news.

"It's ended. The things hounding me have bugged out," There was no audible response from Ada, "Ada, you there?"

"Yeah, I'm here."

"That's good then isn't it?"

"Erm..."

"What is it?"

"I just got an overwhelming feeling." Ada said.

"About what?"

"I don't think we should celebrate, not just yet."

"Why not?"

"Because I feel that it isn't yet over. Something bigger is coming."

"Bigger, you mean bigger than a dog?" Joe asked.

"Bigger players. I think that something has really taken a dislike to you. I sense a more intense and ominous danger looming on the horizon."

"Like what?"

"I can't see it at the moment, it's too shrouded."

"Great. What can I do? You have been wrong before though, yes?"

"Not this century. Unfortunately, all we can do is wait till it shows up before we can face it and try to deal with it."

"Ok. Not exactly what I was hoping for." With that, Joe ended the call.

He sat alone on the sofa for a while and just mused. Nothing was crawling on the outside of the suit and Joe realised that he needed to use the toilet. He walked upstairs and looked around for hostile critters. He saw none. *Fantastic*. Joe peeled off the trousers from the suit and tossed them aside. Then he stopped in his tracks. On the big toe of his right foot was a mark about the size of a small coin. He touched it and it was numb. He called Ada back,

"Ada, there's something else happened." He didn't speak for a while as he studied the mark.

"You still there?" Ada asked.

"Yeah. It's a bite I think, on my toe. Must've been from one of the ants that got through earlier. It's *weird* though."

"Put some cream on it."

"I don't think I have any," Joe suspected that cream would not do much good with this, "Listen, I got to go. Will call you back."

"Keep me..." Ada was cut off mid-sentence. She switched the TV off and let her mind open up to this new looming threat.

◆ ◆ ◆

Joe opened the church doors in haste and then hurriedly made his way down the aisles until he had reached the font. He dropped the umbrella, the sound of which echoed around the church and then flipped the shoe off his right foot before splashing it with what he perceived to be holy water. FJ had been in the vestry and on hearing the sound of water splashing around, he came out into the church. He didn't panic when he saw Joe trying to bathe his foot in the font; instead, he walked over and put his hand on his shoulder. Joe said nothing but ceased his efforts to wash away the circle which seemed to have widened in the last thirty minutes. He sat down and FJ looked at the blemish with some concern.

"What caused this? Is it a blood blister?" he

asked.

"I don't know, but it's from where one of the ants bit me. It's getting bigger. I'm sorry, I lost my head for a moment there, but there's something *evil* about it."

FJ examined the mark more closely. It was black and blue but seemed to become less dense, then almost purple in colour and then darker again, continuously waning in and out. All he said was.

"Hmmm..." Though it looked like something very odd.

"Is it growing?" Joe asked for a second opinion.

"I...don't know."

"Are ants poisonous?"

FJ shook his head slightly.

"Painful, but not poisonous. Do you think it is getting bigger?"

"Yes. An hour ago, when I first noticed it, it was the size of a small coin."

"Now it is the size of a large coin," FJ put his reading glasses on and studied it for longer, "The insects and birds have left you alone now?"

"Yeah."

"Hmmm," FJ stood back up, "We need another opinion. Your friends perhaps." FJ didn't say their names, or name their abilities as though it might be pushing the envelope a little too much to mention them in the church building itself. He didn't mention to Joe that he had seen what looked like symbols or text on his toe.

"Ok."

FJ took one last look at the mark before Joe pulled his shoe back on. Then he looked up at Joe and smiled thinly.

◆ ◆ ◆

FJ drove Joe to Janice's house. Joe sat at the dining room table. Ada stared at his foot. Janice peered from behind her shoulder. Neither could identify what the mark on Joe's foot was. Janice's black cat came over and inspected it. It also had nothing to offer.

"It's not a normal insect bite." Janice said.

"It's not a bruise either," Ada added, "Was it definitely an ant?"

"I think so ...I don't know," Joe explained, "I think one might have got through, unless it was from the previous night."

"Is it getting bigger?" Janice wondered.

"It seems to be, slowly." Joe said. It was now nearly two inches in diameter.

"Do you have a magnifying glass, Janice?" FJ asked.

Janice looked around in the kitchen drawers and eventually produced an old magnifying glass, dusty but functional. FJ took it and focused on the mark.

Ada had closed her eyes briefly. She opened them with some unwanted news.

"There's something bad," she said, "And it's gotten in you. This is why the animals left before the spell was even cast. You have been poisoned and there is no longer any need for them to stalk you."

"Great," said Janice, "Frighten the poor man to death. We need cool heads, Ada." Ada looked back at Janice and replied.

"He needs to know. No point in sugarcoating anything is there."

"Indeed not," FJ said, "Take a look." He passed the magnifying glass to Janice, who observed the mark. Then she passed it on to Ada, who did likewise.

"What is so interesting?" Joe asked before putting his shoe back on again.

"So, you don't know anything else, other than you think it's serious Ada?" FJ asked. Ada nodded and then she added,

"I'm at a loss to explain any more, other than to say that this ties in with my earlier thoughts."

"That something worse is coming?" Joe asked.

"I'm afraid so."

"And there's nothing you can do Janice, no spell or anything?" Joe asked, with a stronger hint of desperation in his voice.

"I…I don't think so. This is beyond me." Janice said.

FJ had been wondering whether or not to tell Joe what they had seen. He decided it best to tell him.

"There are lines of script on the blemish. Very tiny, but they are there."

"Script?" Joe asked, "Saying what?"

"It is not in any language that I recognize." FJ stated.

"Let me see." Joe took his shoe off again and used the magnifying glass. He saw the strange text and symbols that formed a circle.

"This is something...ancient," Ada said, "And I genuinely *do not* want to frighten you, but it is something much bigger than we can sort out with a spell or two. I sense that quite strongly."

"What does it mean? I am going to turn black and blue? Is that it?" Joe asked.

"It's not the colour that will be the problem." Ada said.

"We need to decipher the meaning of this strange text." FJ said. He took out his iPhone, zoomed in as far as it would go and then took a couple of photos of the mark.

"What do you think it is?" Janice asked him.

"I wouldn't like to speculate." FJ said.

◆ ◆ ◆

FJ sent the pictures of Joe's strange blemish to both Janice and Ada via e-mail. Magnified, it was clear that it was text or symbols of some kind, starting at the centre and then spiralling out like a Catherine wheel. It looked like a mixture of Latin, and hieroglyphs and only God knew what else.

Janice suggested that Joe should stay with her so that she could keep an eye on him, whilst Ada and FJ were tasked with trawling the internet in search of answers to the symbols. Ada's psychic abilities had drawn a complete blank when trying to gain any insight into them. FJ had the strange, unwarranted, feeling that he'd seen the like of them before. It was as though something struck a chord somewhere in his memory.

Back in the vestry, he hit the Google search engine and tried every combination of words and phrases that he could think of. After four hours of searching with no positive result, he got up and then led out on the sofa for a power nap. Thirty minutes later, he resumed the search with a strong cup of coffee.

After lunchtime, when he opened his eyes again, his right hand pressed down on the laptop's keyboard and the screen came back on. He'd fallen asleep and the open web page confirmed his lack of searching success. It displayed some manga cartoon that was based on demons.

He walked into the kitchen and splashed his face with cold water. Then he opened the fridge door and built a simple cheese sandwich, spiced up by a spoonful of pickle. He took one large bite and then he walked into the bathroom and took a quick shower. He changed into clean civvy clothes and went back to finish off the sandwich. As he ate, he slowly paced up and down the kitchen. It dawned on him that the answer to the meaning of those strange markings was not going to be found on Google.

◆ ◆ ◆

Father Michael hadn't spoken with FJ for over a year. When, out of the blue, he heard his voice, he was briefly transported back in time thirty years to the small town in Ireland where they had met.

"Patrick Jones. To what do I owe this honour?"

"FM. How are you? Can't I call my old friend once in a while?" FJ said. It had been FM's idea to shorten their names to two letters for ease and speed of use when both were studying.

"Always a pleasure."

"Indeed it is."

"And how can I help you today?"

"How do you know I'm not calling to wish you a happy birthday?" FJ said.

"Two reasons. One, it isn't my birthday for another four months, and two, you never did remember when it was."

"Technically, that is only one reason, but, I do need a bit of advice."

"Go on."

"Well, I'll get straight down to brass tacks. I have someone within the parish with some strange marks on his person. Looks like a bit like a tattoo, but it's growing larger."

"A tattoo you say. Never liked them."

"No, it's not a tattoo. It's *text* of some kind."

"Why on earth has he had that done?"

"He hasn't had it done. It just appeared on his foot overnight."

"I see. That is odd. Text saying what?"

"It's just symbols and characters. Certainly not English, Latin or any language I know of."

"Sounds like devilment or witchcraft. You haven't been on the church wine have you?"

"No. It's very strange. I called you up because I know that you have an open mind. And, you've been around the block, like I have."

"Charming. Have you Googled it?"

"Nothing on there. He also says that dogs and birds were attacking him. It's almost like the Devil himself is after him."

Neither priest was judgemental, although many were underneath a façade.

"I've not heard anything like this. Nothing that comes to memory anyway."

"Me neither," FJ sighed, "Do you have any thoughts?"

"Lots of thoughts, probably none of any use. Why don't you take a photo of it and send it to me."

"Do you have an iPhone?"

"I'm only a year older than you. I'm not exactly a dinosaur. Yes, well a Samsung. Never got on with Apple that much."

"I'll send it over. Let me know if you have any ideas would you?"

The call went silent briefly, as FM studied the image that appeared in his inbox.

"Well, I've had a look. Can't make head nor tail of what it is. But, if there's any place that might shed a little light on this it is probably the old library where we trained and studied back in the 80s."

"The one at Chetham?"

"Yes. A trip there might just provide you with the answer." Chetham was the oldest library in the country and it was barely an hour's drive away. The two had studied there as young priests, "If there's anywhere that might have a record of this funny text, that's where it will be. Wear the dog collar when you go. You might get preferential treatment."

The Library dated back to 1653, but the building it was housed in was much older. Built in 1421 it was one of the most complete medieval complexes in the U.K. Way back in history, it had accommodated generations of Catholic priests.

Though it was still open to the public, visits had to be booked in advance. FM was right, it had a strong historical connection to the Catholic church and FJ hoped that might pull a few strings for him. He said goodbye to FM and then sent an e-mail to the library using the *official* church address. Then he sat looking at the laptop, trying to will a response from it. Sure enough, after ten minutes, he received a reply. It was an automated response. He called the number on the web page. The librarian answered and FJ began to state his case for needing immediate access. The Librarian, Darragh, informed him that the library was closed that day. FJ stressed that it really couldn't wait. Darragh's father had also been a priest. He relented and told FJ that he would meet him at the library in exactly one hour. He did this, largely, so that he didn't risk bad karma from saying *no* to a priest and also out of some loyalty to his now deceased parent.

FJ called Ada, who had nothing to report. She had called in at Janice's house and watched Joe fidget around on the sofa as she spoke. FJ didn't tell her where he was going, just that he would be *off grid* for a couple of hours. He left his accomodation with the keys to his ten-year-old VW golf in hand. He returned, picked up his dog collar and fixed it in place. Then he set off for Manchester.

◆ ◆ ◆

Ada was back on the checkout. She smiled instinctively at each customer and scanned each item on autopilot, but her mind was very much elsewhere. Once or twice she briefly closed her eyes and tried to allow in insight about the strange symbols on Joe's foot, but nothing came. It was a completely empty psychic storeroom and the first time she'd ever come up with nothing. It felt as if her psychic gift had disappeared. The door on this was closed airtight.

◆ ◆ ◆

FJ parked up in the visitors' car park and then just stood and looked at the old building in front of him. Of all the things that had changed in his life over the past thirty tears, this hadn't altered one iota. That does tend to happen with listed and protected buildings. He'd spent many hours of study here in his early twenties. He was tempted to think *happy* years, but were they? Back then he was aiming towards something he achieved a long time ago. *Life always seems better when you're aiming at something*. This wasn't the time for much reminiscing.

The medieval windows and doors were exactly as he remembered them. Inside the stone pillars, the cool serenity of the place hit him in a wave of nostalgia.

The building, as it still stood, was built in the 1420s to accommodate a college of priests. The site its foundations rested on was much older and was used as an easily defendable settlement by the Saxons, being ideally situated between two rivers. It became a library after wealthy benefactor Humphrey Chetham purchased the building and opened it up to the general public. Echoes of the past dripped off every smooth edge and angle. As FJ stepped towards the heavy rivetted door at the front entrance, he thought it might be of use to him that *the priests were here first*.

A small black arched door that looked like something from a Harry Potter film or Alice in Wonderland, had the word *Please Ring* over the top of what looked like the oldest doorbell in existence. FJ pressed the button, the same one that he'd pressed three decades previously. As then, there was no audible sound, but something happened somewhere and soon he heard footsteps on stone floor from the other side that grew steadily louder until the black door swung inwards.

"Hasn't changed a lot has it." FJ greeted the slightly portly forty-something-year-old man that stood there holding the door, "You are the librarian I take it?" The man nodded. He didn't invite FJ in with words but just gestured with a nod. *Man of few words. Unusual for a librarian.* FJ gave him a smile that wasn't returned as the door clunked shut behind them, "Thank you for opening up for me today."

The librarian offered a tight-lipped smile and then spoke.

"Is it information on something specific that you seek?"

"It is."

"You have the place to yourself." Darragh said as they walked slowly, *no one ever moved quickly inside this building,* towards the vast dark wood shelves that went from floor to ceiling. FJ stopped and looked around.

"I'm a bit rusty as to where things might be."

"That's not surprising; we had a major overhaul in 1999. Just tell me what you are interested in and I will point you in the right direction." Darragh wanted to get back to what he would have been doing, had FJ not been there, as quickly as possible and he didn't have to say it for it to be obvious.

"Well, it's symbols and texts that I need to research. Do you know anything about this subject at all?"

Darragh didn't answer. He walked a short distance to some wooden gates and then unlocked them with a brass key. He pushed one side open.

"In here are the language volumes." He made a sweeping gesture with his hand, which took in about two hundred books. FJ looked at all the volumes. He was hoping this *friendly* fellow might pick out one hardback book for him to look at.

"I feel I might be a little swamped by all these books. Do you have any knowledge *at all* of strange languages?"

"Can you be more specific?"

FJ got his phone out of his pocket. This modern device seemed way out of place in these surroundings. Darragh thought so too,

"We do ask that all visitors keep their mobile devices switched off and concealed when inside the building." *This guy sounded and acted like a robot.*

"Quite right, but there is a picture on here that I need to show you."

Darragh unenthusiastically took a look at the offending item. After ten seconds, he asked,

"What is it?"

"It's a mark, on somebody."

"A tattoo?"

"Not exactly, no. I was wondering if there was any way of deciphering what it means?"

"I'm not an expert in that field."

FJ took another look up and down the shelves that reached from top to bottom. Some books were even chained to prevent theft. Many were too high up to reach.

"Is there anyone who would know about this type of thing?"

"Emily, if anyone."

"Who is Emily?"

"She is the archivist. If anyone knows, it would be her."

"And is she available today?"

"Normally, I would say no, but she is coming in to do some work whilst we are closed to the public. Well, we *were* closed."

"And what time would Emily be coming?"

"I don't know. She has her own key." Darraghs irritance was steadily growing. This building may have been heavily linked to the Catholic church in the distant past. It wasn't now. Darragh's father had also been a priest. He used to beat him with a bamboo cane. "Can't it wait? You could book a proper appointment."

"Not really. It is fairly urgent."

Darragh broke his own rule and took his mobile phone out of his jacket pocket. He walked a few steps in the opposite direction, spoke a few words and then paced back over to FJ.

"She's is on her way." Then he pulled out a chair from a heavy wooden desk, "Take a seat." With that said, he paced off back in the direction he came from. The clunk of the heavy door closing echoed and confirmed his exit. FJ got up and paced up and down the shelves, stopping every so often and reading the titles on the spines that were still legible. Twenty minutes later, the sound of the door closing echoed down the corridor once again. This time, the softer sound of comfortable soles padding on stone and then wooden floors got louder until a woman in her early forties appeared at the wooden gate.

"Emily?" FJ asked. She nodded, with as much initial enthusiasm as the librarian had displayed, "I have something rather interesting to show you." Her facial expression suggested that she would be the judge of that. FJ opened his photo gallery on the picture of the symbols. All at once she became more animated. "Any idea what this is?"

She took the iPhone and studied the picture more closely.

"I've seen something like this." She said as she rubbed her palm up and down her forehead.

"You have?"

She did not answer, but went over to a particular section of books, removed three of them and placed them down on the desk, less carefully than FJ might have imagined she would. He didn't interrupt as she began flipping the pages of each open book. It was quite an impressive sight to see someone reading or studying three books simultaneously. He let her carry on in full flow. *This is something.* One particular book from the trio then took precedence and the other two were closed. She left the book open on page 326 and then looked up at FJ.

"Is this a tattoo?" she asked.

"No ...it just appeared overnight." This statement would have been ridiculed by most, but it didn't seem to faze Emily. She read more of the text and then looked up again.

"Appeared overnight?"

"Yes. I didn't think there was any point not telling you the truth, plus ..." he pointed to the dog collar. She asked to see the photo again, and then she said,

"There is another volume in the archives, not on display. Wait here please." She then got up and left more quickly than she had arrived. Quite soon after, she appeared again pushing what looked like a small tea trolley. On the trolley was just one book, its outer cover protected by cellophane. She parked the trolley at the desk and then carefully lifted the book onto the desk. She took a minuscule brush from her jacket pocket and gently gave the cover the once over. "We aren't supposed to move these." She said and then muttered under her breath, "But, there's no one to check up on us, we are the *checker uppers*."

FJ watched as she cracked the book open. It looked very delicate and nowhere near as robust as the other volumes on display. Some of the inside pages were protected by cellophane covers.

"Shouldn't that really be in a museum?" FJ said.

"This is a museum." She answered flatly, "Of sorts." She turned the pages slowly and stopped on one section that was in relatively good health. Her index finger hovered over the text and moved down the page. Then her finger stopped on one particular line. "Here it is. I knew it was in here somewhere."

"You've read this before?"

"I skimmed through a long time ago. You say that these symbols appeared on someone overnight?"

"More or less. The person only noticed it when it was the size of a very small coin."

"And what size is it now?"

"The size of a bigger coin, I suppose." She gently turned the book to face FJ and moved back in the chair. Halfway down the page, in a line rather than a circle, were the same markings that were on Joe's foot and in the picture. FJ put his phone next to the book to confirm. "It's the same." The rest of the book was in Latin, a subject that he'd always struggled with, "How old is this book?"

"Older than when the library was built. Probably quite a lot older."

"My Latin is a little rusty, what does it say? Assuming you can read Latin that is."

"Of course." She swallowed, "It relays a story

of a monk, circa 1206 A.D. He also had these strange markings on his body, his chest to be precise. It says that the writing appeared very small and then expanded outwards until it covered his entire body."

"Does it say what the marks are?"

"It's an ancient transcript, largely forgotten. There are no other records of it appearing and there weren't back in the 1300's either. Its closest relative is ancient Sumerian, circa 3100 B.C. It is about as close to that as English is to French, or Italian is to Latin."

Between them, they had discovered a match, but FJ still had no answers.

"Does it say *anywhere* in the book about what it all means?"

"Not exactly, but judging by the surrounding text, the monk, it does not mention his name clearly, the page is very worn …disappeared."

"The page has disappeared?"

"Not the page, the monk."

"Disappeared where?"

"If the other monks didn't know that at the time, I'm sure I wouldn't be able to tell you. The mark covered his whole body and then the next day he was gone. Left the monastery, never to be seen again."

"And you were able to remember this from reading this book years ago."

"It was quite an interesting story. Plus, it's my

job to remember these things, as the archivist."

"Quite. Nevertheless, it is remarkable. Does it say anything else about this unfortunate monk?" FJ asked. Her finger followed the text down the page and then onto the next one.

"No, just that he wasn't seen again. It does mention suspected witchcraft. That was quite a big deal back then. The order tried cleansing his spirit and praying for him. None of it worked, sadly."

"Poor soul."

"They wanted to take him to the Holy Land, apparently, but the journey was too long and too dangerous. Bandits, warring factions and the cost involved. Also, it seems like they ran out of time. The marks covered his entire body within a matter of three or four days. A journey like that, back then, would have taken weeks."

"And are there any other instances of this happening?"

"Not that I am aware of, but obviously I haven't read every book in existence."

"Three days."

"The text is a bit faded. When did your friend notice the mark?"

"Less than a day ago. Half a day, maybe."

"And it has grown in size?"

"Yes. A little."

Emily read a little more of the text and then she carefully closed the book.

"Just because this is written down, it doesn't mean for certain that it is the same situation or that it is real."

"What do you think?" FJ asked.

"Honestly?" FJ nodded, "I have no reason to doubt what happened to the monk. I've seen cases and read stories from the past that have *opened up my mind*, you might say."

"You say they wanted to take him to the Holy Land?"

"Yes. It seems the monks thought it the mark of Satan. They believed that when it covered his whole body, he would be transported to hell. Visiting Jerusalem, the place of Jesus, was the only chance of a cure."

"Hell, you say."

"Whatever they perceived hell to be."

"And he just disappeared. Vanished. Perhaps that is where he went." FJ said. Emily sat expressionless. As a historian and archivist, she had discovered a long time ago that the people from the past knew more than they were given credit for. After a lengthy pause, she asked,

"Is there anything else that I can help you with today?" She didn't often get visitors that took her enthusiasm level from one to a hundred. FJ shook his head.

"The Holy Land."

"Yes. To walk the path that Jesus walked. That is the translation from Latin. More or less."

FJ thanked Emily. He stared at the books and collected his thoughts. That information was all he was going to get. It was all that he needed. Further digging would eat up valuable time. He thanked Emily once more and then started towards the door. Emily wheeled the book back to where it came from. FJ could hear the squeaking of the trolley's wheels until the heavy door closed shut behind him.

15

“This is what I learned from the visit to the library; that *mark* could well be the doorway to another dimension. And, if and when it covers you completely, that’s where you’ll be transported to.” FJ said. He’d driven straight to Janice’s house to report his findings.

“According to an old book from the middle ages?” Joe asked.

“Yes. I saw the markings in the book with my own eyes. This woman, Emily, seemed to read Latin very well.”

“Another dimension?” Joe asked.

“I hate to use the word *hell*, but…” FJ said.

“Hell? Can I get back from there?”

“Not once you are there. I don’t think so.” Ada said.

“And the marks in the book matched the one on my foot exactly?” FJ nodded. Joe looked again at the mysterious mark and contemplated the awful legacy that his distant ancestor had left him.

"At least we have *something* to go on." Janice said, "Someone else had been in the same situation."

"And then they just ...*disappeared*." Joe said.

"The other monks wanted to take him to the Holy Land. They considered that an antidote." FJ said, " But back then, it was a very long and perilous journey. They simply ran out of time."

"I feel," Ada said, "I feel that this is all correct. There was a very kind-hearted monk many years ago with these same symptoms and this is, unfortunately, history repeating itself."

"If it is, then we must go on this journey. To have the best chance of success." Father Jones said.

"A journey?" Joe wondered, "To where?"

"Back to the roots of the matter. Going back to the roots of a problem is often the key to solving it. To the place where it all happened, all those years ago. We will visit the Holy Land, just as those monks wished to do all those many centuries ago."

"Where is that?" asked Joe.

"Jerusalem." FJ answered and Ada now had a name to give the place she'd envisioned in her imagination.

16

Travel to Jerusalem. It seemed a simple enough solution. It came with no guarantee of success, but Joe didn't have the luxury of several options to pick from. Without any other plan other than the one suggested by the trip to the library and the story of the unfortunate monk, *and* with the psychic approval of Ada, it looked like a trip to the Holy Land was Joe's only chance to get rid of the mark and return to normality. Ada had agreed with the decision and told the others that she already had the city in her imagination. Joe mused on what type of insects might be lurking in wait over there. *Did they have scorpions and tarantulas?* They had all agreed that, although Joe was presently unperturbed by hostile creatures, that situation could change again very quickly. Janice left to work on the newest version of the smoke screen spell, which never had been cast. This would have to be one that would work on a much larger scale, due to the vast distances involved. On the positive side, it only needed to work for 24 hours or so. After that, hopefully, they wouldn't need it.

Other preparations for the journey were already underway. Ada wasn't going: she wasn't due any holidays and would blow any savings she had on the journey without necessarily needing to go along. Janice had not given a definite answer …yet. FJ would have to cancel his planned trip to Lourdes to enable him to travel with Joe, but it was doable from his point of view. Jerusalem was somewhere he had never visited and the Church took surprisingly little persuading in helping fund his trip.

Being a priest does have its perks. Mused Joe, at the ease of FJ's travel sponsorship. Although the Catholic church was no travel agency, FJ had stressed the importance of the trip to the purse string holders and they had offered only limited resistance to the idea. Of course, it helped in no small measure that he'd known the decision-maker for more than twenty years and that they both came from the same small town in Ireland. He transferred the travel funds into FJ's account within the hour.

◆ ◆ ◆

After another collaboration with the coven, Janice managed to tweak and finalise the cloaking spell. FJ had turned a deaf ear, once again, to this aspect of her involvement. She had tried the first spell with limited and temporary success and perhaps the dark spirits were wise to that one *...perhaps they were fast learners.* She had stayed up all night and tweaked the first one here and there. She explained the process as being similar to her using two different mathematical methods to solve the same equation. Janice never was any good at mathematics, but that didn't matter. After some deliberation, with Janice at the helm, the coven came up with the revised blueprint for the cloaking spell mark 2. After one quick trip to the Fox & Hounds the new spell was cast. One of the coven taking part asked Janice how confident she was that it would work. Janice bit her lip and declined to answer.

Thirty minutes later, Joe and FJ stood at Janice's front door. Janice ushered them inside and told them that they had done their best effort and everything *seemed* to have gone ok. Still, Joe had mixed feelings about the trip. The expanding text seemed to be sapping his positivity.

"It does seem a long way and there's no guarantee it won't just be a waste of time." he said.

"These might be straws that we are clutching at," FJ said in response to Joe, "But they are good straws and they are, quite frankly, the only straws that we have."

Joe nodded.

"Ok. Just the thought of travelling all that way for nothing. I just hope it works."

"You must believe that it will work," Father Jones said as he got into the back of Janice's car and sat alongside Joe. "Or would you rather just sit around and wait for this thing to grow larger and larger?"

Janice sat in the driver's seat, asked if they were all ready and then she set off for the Airport. FJ had booked two seats on a flight to Israel that was leaving in three hours. Janice pulled out into traffic. She drove a ten-year-old SUV. It rarely gave her any trouble, not because she was a witch, but because it was Japanese.

No one said much for the first thirty minutes of the journey. Joe glanced down at the ever-changing mark that had now expanded to the size of a golf ball.

"It's a five-hour flight," FJ said at length, "I might get my head down for a bit," Then he turned to Joe, "Hey, I hope the food is all right." Joe shrugged. He hadn't eaten more than a hundred calories in the last twenty-four hours. Janice couldn't think of anything constructive to say. This escapade was not something you could just make idle chit-chat about and she just drove along the road at a steady pace. She flicked the radio off when the DJ played the song "Devil in Disguise." Whilst not being, by her own admission, the greatest of drivers, she didn't mind the airport run as it was very straightforward; she just had to get there and then turn around and come back. "I wonder what the in-flight film will be?" FJ said, "Do you know the last time..." Then, a van came hurtling out of nowhere and slammed into the driver's side of Janice's car, jolting everyone inside and changing the SUV's trajectory from forwards to sideways. The noise was shockingly loud. The front airbag inflated. The side impact had severely dented both the driver's and passenger's doors. Joe was closest and suffered a few cuts on his arm. The van driver got out and looked in a daze, "Are you alright Janice?" FJ asked. He could see that Joe was pretty much unscathed.

"I am...I think ..." she responded calmly.

"Good." FJ said.

There was no way to get out of the driver's side door, so all three travellers scrambled out of the other side of the car. The van driver stood and scratched his head as though he was baffled about how the collision had happened.

"What were you thinking?" Janice asked him. All he could do was shrug. The steering wheel seemed to have a mind of its own, just for a few wild seconds. It was a rental van and he was already thinking about how to get out of being held responsible for the smash. He didn't even respond to the question. Janice turned to Joe and

FJ, "It looks like the spell didn't do its job."

The police arrived ten minutes later and all the necessary details were exchanged. When all was sorted, including the recovery vehicle that was on-route to tow away Janice's Toyota, Father Jones turned to Joe and suggested that they get a taxi to the airport. They still had plenty of time.

Janice's car insurance company had done its job efficiently and she was already on the trip back home when the airport taxi arrived. FJ and Joe placed their bags in the boot, with no help from the driver, and the journey resumed. The driver was just starting his shift and was a mixture of both energy and melancholy as he had another nine hours of work ahead of him. He didn't speak for twenty minutes as he drove along only slightly faster than Janice had done.

"Where are you going?" he asked. Joe looked at FJ, who answered,

"The airport....and then a sightseeing trip," he said. The driver thought the attempted joke was lame. He didn't care where they were going. Joe wondered why he was non-descriptive with his answer, but he himself felt no inclination to speak at the moment.

They made steady progress. Eventually, the driver asked what time their flight was leaving. He didn't give a toss where they were going. "Five fifteen." FJ answered. The driver knew that the traffic around Heathrow would be at its worst around that time, but thought that they still would get there with time to spare. He edged the speed of the taxi up a tad just to make sure. He didn't speak again until they were thirty minutes away from the airport. He supposed that these two passengers were about the glummest looking ones he'd had in recent memory. They were hardly in holiday mode. Though the older guy with the dog collar at least seemed to be making some effort to be friendly.

The sign for the airport appeared on the motorway. The driver steered the car into the left-hand lane, ready to change lanes and direction. He tuned the radio station into the news station. Just as he did so, a large seagull smashed into the front windscreen. It was such a wallop that the driver momentarily lost control of the taxi and it swerved this way and that. Skillfully, he managed to steer the car onto the hard shoulder. The bird, though broken itself, had managed to fly off. It only got twenty meters and then it dropped to the ground again, where it flapped around.

"Jesus Christ," The driver said, "Where the hell did that come from."

FJ did not reprimand the man for using Jesus's name in vain. Instead, he surveyed the damage to the front window. There was no way that the car could be driven any further. He checked his wristwatch. There was still time to make the flight if they got another vehicle.

The driver got out and placed a triangular warning sign behind the taxi, then he called the windscreen repair company. It would work out cheaper for the taxi owner for them to remove the screen and then fit a new one at a safe location, without going through his insurance.

Joe turned to FJ. FJ looked back at him. This felt like more than just coincidence or double bad luck. Father Jones did not want to ask the driver to order another taxi for them. He didn't want to put anyone else at risk, though he asked, just to weigh up their options.

"*Could* you get someone else to pick us up?"

"I wouldn't bother," The driver said. The radio was still on and he turned the volume up; the news reporter announced that Heathrow Airport was experiencing long delays. The aeroplane scheduled to fly to Tel Aviv had taxied into another plane when its brakes malfunctioned. "*Carnage. The majority of flights are cancelled. Possible suspected terrorist activity*." "You won't be flying anywhere. Not today."

◆◆◆

"Dark forces are at work," FJ said. They'd been driven, thankfully without incident, back home and he and Joe sat in the vestry once again, "The animals and insects have given up on you Joe, but *something* doesn't want us to leave. That is pretty obvious."

"Or arrive in Jerusalem." Joe offered.

"I can't take the chance of us getting on a plane. It would put all the passengers and crew at risk. But, maybe it's a good thing. Maybe this is a sign that we are on the right path. These obstacles are happening because what lies in Jerusalem *will* be the cure for you. The demons have unwittingly given that up in their attempts to stop us from travelling," FJ said. This did make some logical sense and it seemed to strengthen FJ's resolve. He paced up and down the vestry. Then he went out into the church itself and looked at Jesus's statue. He chatted for a few minutes with some of the public that were in there and then he came back and stuck his head around the vestry door, "Stay here. I'll be right back." he said, and then he was gone.

◆ ◆ ◆

Joe passed the next hour or so in an intense state of unease. He repeatedly got up and walked in circles around the table. Time seemed to drag on and on. He resisted the urge to keep checking on the strange circular writing on his right foot every few minutes. There was nothing he could do about it. The horrific idea of taking an axe and lopping it off flashed through his mind. He remembered the rock climber who had become trapped in a crevice and resorted to taking his own arm off. He put that out of his mind and took a deep breath. At the moment, all of his hopes for a cure were in the form of a fifty-something-year-old man he'd never even seen before yesterday. *Why would this man care about his fate?*

Time dragged on and then in the deathly quiet, with just the ticking of the grandfather clock for company, the vestry door opened again. Father Jones had returned.

"Here, come outside," He beckoned for Joe to follow him. Once outside the church, FJ briskly walked to the front iron gates, "What do you think?"

Joe looked around. There was nothing to see.

"What am I looking at?"

"That... this," FJ pointed to a beige-coloured campervan parked on the street, "We are going to get to Jerusalem one way or another!"

This seemed like a very desperate attempt from very desperate men.

"But, won't it just crash or have a bird fly into it or..."

"I know what you are thinking, I've thought of those potential pitfalls as well. Something is aware of our movements, even though the dogs and birds are leaving you alone, for now at least. But, I have an idea. Get your friend Janice on the telephone. Tell her to come here straight away."

Joe called Janice. He was downhearted and

halfway resigned to his fate. FJ's enthusiasm seemed misplaced, *mocking* almost.

Janice had gotten home and then crashed out on the sofa. She hoped that her car wouldn't be written off, even though financially it might be more advantageous for her if it were. After she received the call from Joe, she went and moved all the junk that was on top of her push-bike and then cycled to the church as instructed. When she arrived, very much out of breath, she saw Joe and FJ standing at the gates. She dismounted and the bike toppled over with a *clang*.

"Great. Thank you for coming so quickly," FJ said, "Now, technically we are off the Church premises so I can ask you this; do you think that you could do your thing with this campervan? Make its contents invisible? Just this small space mind you. The world might be too big a place to sustain a spell like that for a long time. As we discovered."

Janice *ummed* and *ahhed*, then said,

"It didn't work before. I don't know. It is a small enough space, so it might be more plausible. It would stand more chance of holding if we *concentrated* the spell on such a small space, then it wouldn't be *thinned out* so much. I would need some help to make the spell stronger," She didn't want to promise anything but secretly felt more confident, "But why?"

"We are still going to Jerusalem, but the long

way around." Joe said.

"You're *driving* all the way?" Janice thought it crazy.

"He who has no choices," FJ said, "Is a poor soul indeed. *We,* on the other hand, have a choice. Just the one mind you. We need to blindside the demons that are intent on destroying this man. They have unwittingly told us, in their actions to prevent us from travelling to the Holy Land, that this action is the answer ...the key to curing him of this affliction. This motorhome needs to be a haven, a sanctuary of sorts, till we arrive where we need to get to."

"We already have the spell, it would just need a little tweaking, but, it still might not hold, even in such a small space." Janice said, she understood FJ's intention and enthusiasm. She did want another crack at it.

"Just until we get to Jerusalem. Until we follow the path his ancestor took."

Janice shrugged.

"Perhaps trying a smoke screen on such a big scale was too ambitious. This *would* stand a much better chance. I'll get on it. Gather some of the ladies. Go to the ley line again."

"Is there anywhere more powerful than the ley line?" FJ asked. Janice thought for a few seconds.

"There is the stone circle at Castlerigg, it is older than those at Stonehenge."

"Where is this?" FJ asked.

"Just at Keswick in Cumbria."

"And that is a more powerful place than the ley line?"

"It's hard to put a number on these things, but the ancients decided to place huge stones there for a reason. There is a lot of untapped natural energy, especially at this time of year. We could be there in just over an hour. I'll get Harriet to take us, she drives very fast."

"Great. Fast but carefully, tell her. Whatever maximises our chances." FJ said.

With that, Janice picked the bike up.

"I'll make the calls. By the way, what is the registration plate? I'll need it for the spell."

She looked and noted down the little campervan's registration plate... *REV 616T.*

17

After an hour's drive, Janice and four of her coven arrived at the stone circle in Cumbria. It was overcast and cloudy but they could still make out the outline of the mountains that surrounded the large naturally occurring plateau that looked as flat as a football pitch. Unlike Stonehenge, the general public could walk up and touch the stones that formed the circle. Unlike Stonehenge, it was relatively obscure. Janice commented that if it was located in the South, that wouldn't be the case. No historian could accurately tell you why this 5,000-year-old circle of stones was constructed, but that didn't matter; the place oozed mystical energy. The echoes of a thousand rituals and meetings reverberated within. Janice walked around the circle and touched each stone in turn. Then they all sat down in the very centre and after another mystical session in the windy outdoors, the spell was cast. Janice had assembled the elite of her most powerful witches (who were available at short notice). One of whom had offered to sacrifice a chicken to add to the potency of the spell. Janice declined the offer. She only ever bought free-range eggs. All of the talented ladies had sat down and had a tipple afterwards in a pub overlooking Lake Windemere. All five were satisfied that the spell-casting had gone as well as they could have hoped for.

Back outside the church, Joe opened the side door of the campervan. Inside, he saw that FJ had also been busy: the interior was decorated with many crucifixes.

"Are we also tackling vampires?" Joe asked him.

"Can't be too careful. Belt and braces. I also sprayed the inside with *holy water*. Blessed it myself this morning."

"That's a useful skill to have in the locker."

"To be perfectly honest, this is the first time I've ever used it."

"Where did you get this?" Joe wondered how he'd returned so swiftly with this new means of transport.

"I know a man who knows a man. He only wanted five thousand for it."

Joe didn't think it was exactly a bargain.

"And you bought it outright?"

"Yeah, sure. We do get paid as well you know. I didn't give him the money straight off the bat, but if you can't trust me, who can you trust. Get your bags and throw them in." FJ also went and got his brown leather suitcase and put it in the back.

"We are setting off now?" Joe asked.

"No time like the present. If Janice and her friends have done their bit, we should be hidden from the forces of evil once inside here."

"And if they haven't?"

"Well," FJ sat down in the driver's seat, "This will be a pretty short trip," He smiled at Joe who strapped himself in for the ride, physically and metaphorically. FJ turned the key and the 2-litre diesel engine fired up, "Here we go!" The twenty-five-year-old campervan set off with an enthusiastic though underprepared lurch forwards.

◆ ◆ ◆

Their plan was simple enough: drive down to the south coast, then through the Channel Tunnel and then carry on driving until they reached the tip of Greece. Then, when they ran out of road, they would get onto a ferry that would take them over to Israel. From there it was a relatively short hike to Jerusalem.

Simple though it was, Joe suggested that it was probably a hopeless task for them to get there on time. He seemed, more and more, to be resigned to his fate, or at least the fate that the demons had lined up for him. Father Jones had insisted that was why they needed to set off as soon as possible. So, within an hour of the spell being cast, the campervan was on its way down the motorway. It maxed out at 70 mph and hogged the left-hand lane like it was the only one in use.

"How long will it take us at this speed?" Joe asked. It was a subtle way of asking FJ to speed up. FJ hadn't worked it out. His plan was very loose. He merely shrugged in response. "Do you think that we will get there before, you know?" Joe looked down at the circular text that was edging its way outwards.

"The answer to that will present itself in due course," FJ said, philosophically. He could see the positivity ebbing out of Joe by the hour, "All we can do is believe that we will."

Joe knew that FJ couldn't possibly know the answer.

"But, aren't we just wasting our time?"

FJ looked to his left at Joe for a couple of seconds. Then he shook his head.

"Certainly not. We have to try. To have faith that something good will happen. If we don't act in good faith and instead resign ourselves to our fate, then we have already lost."

Joe sat back in the seat. He felt more anger than anything else. Possibly it was down to his tiredness, but he now fully resented his ancestor and his *ancient help.* It was he, Joe Briscoe, in

2023, who was carrying the can for something that he hadn't done. Looming ahead was an eternity in hell, and the only thing Joe was guilty of was being an average decent person. He fiddled with the radio and tuned into anything, just to try and take his mind off that resentment.

"Radio works at least," Joe said. The campervan also had air-con. *Dare he try it?* He pushed the button and fairly soon cold air was blowing out of the vents. "Air con works as well."

"I'd say it's cold enough outside. Turn it off till we get to Greece, or at least warmer climates. Plays hell with your miles per gallon."

Joe glanced at the odometer. It had done just over 100,000 miles. That wasn't too bad for the year. Father Jones turned the radio volume down to a nominal level. He needed to concentrate fully on the road ahead as it got a little tricky soon. After an hour of driving, FJ said.

"Have you noticed something?"

"No?"

Then FJ spoke more quietly.

"Me neither. *No accidents*. It looks like the safety precautions we took have worked, touch wood."

"So far."

"So far, so good."

It was starting to slightly irritate Joe: FJ's *always positive tone*. He, on the other hand, was all doom and gloom. He had a knot in the pit of his stomach, which was only to be expected from someone who felt like they were on the brink of falling into hell itself. FJ sensed Joe's growing sense of fear and it pained him. He drove calmly and said the occasional *cliched* phrase every so often. That was all he needed to do. All Joe needed to do was just sit there and at least try to stay positive.

Before too long, a sign appeared declaring that the lanes to the Eurotunnel were fast approaching. At least a chunk of the journey was now ticked off. It was a start. It wasn't a busy time for traffic and the run was steady. As they got closer to the tunnel, they approached a barrier and a man inside a small cabin. They stopped at the barrier and the man in uniform asked them just one question.

"Has this van got an L.P.G. conversion?"

"Err. No." FJ said and then the man told them which direction to go in and which lane to get in. They drove away when the barrier raised.

"What's one of them?" FJ asked Joe.

"L.P.G. It's a conversion to run-on gas. It works out cheaper over long distances. They probably won't be allowed on the tunnel train. Suppose they don't want it blowing up after all that work that they did digging it out."

"Ah. I see. Quite right."

"Has it got one?" Joe asked.

"Haven't the foggiest idea."

Joe found that slightly amusing as they got to within fifty meters of the passport control booth. It was the first time he'd smiled in quite a while.

"You know…I might have a slight problem." Joe said.

"And what is that, you already have a pretty big problem?"

"I left my passport in the vestry."

"Why on earth would you do that?"

"I obviously didn't mean to do it. It all happened a bit fast." Joe said. FJ slowed down.

"Get in the cupboard."

"The cupboard? I'll never fit in."

"The wardrobe then. Hide quickly," Joe clambered into the back and squeezed himself into the built-in wardrobe just as they got to within view of passport control, "Let's hope they trust a man of the cloth."

◆ ◆ ◆

FJ strained and pulled the handle of the door as hard as he could. Joe had trapped the material of his shirt in the wardrobe door in his haste to close it and it had made it jam tight. After much exertion, it flew open to reveal Joe's cramped frame.

"Greetings." FJ said.

"We got through?"

"Yes, we are now in France."

"Have you stopped?"

"Indeed, I have. The Lord would have to be at the wheel if I hadn't."

"I've been asleep, believe it or not." Joe said. He hadn't slept much for days.

"You haven't missed much. The channel tunnel was quite a boring experience all in all." FJ helped Joe out and he immediately stretched out his limbs; as he did so he exposed the mark on his foot, which was now bigger than the size of a tennis ball.

"Can I get out and walk around for a while?"

"Yes. Not for too long: time is of the essence and we don't want to alert anything to our presence."

Joe stepped out of the campervan to see that they were parked at a petrol station in Dunkirk. FJ began filling the tank with diesel. Joe walked around in large circles. He kicked at the layer of sand that covered the tarmacked surface. So far nothing bad had happened. It seemed that they were invisible to whatever forces were trying to harm him ...unless they were waiting for just the right moment to strike.

FJ got some cold drinks from the shop and also a few snacks. Then he went to use the toilets. There was a small toilet in the campervan, but neither of them wanted to use it unless they had to.

"How far into France are we?" Joe asked him

when he returned.

"Dunkirk? Don't you know anything about history? We are right on the coast of France. Very close to Belgium."

"Of course," Joe felt more than a little silly at not remembering, "My head is muggy right now. The beach where all our troops got trapped by the Germans."

"Indeed. Most of the troops got rescued, even though it seemed for all the world like there was no hope. Take courage from that. There is a part of the beach where it all happened that is open to the public. Sadly, this is no sight-seeing trip, we simply don't have the time to spare."

"No, I guess not."

"When we get on the motorway there are no speed limits." FJ said.

"Yeah, I'm not sure that will help us much in this thing. So, this is Dunkirk sand under my feet."

"Yes. A lot of men still died here at the hands of evil, and not that long ago. I didn't plan to come this way, I put the route into my iPhone and I'm going where it tells me to."

"Quite poignant."

"That I have an iPhone? We had a choice of Belgium or just brushing the French border. It's a pretty straight route. Vienna *is* a possibility, if we have the time to visit anywhere on the way, and I always wanted to visit that place. Shall we continue?"

Joe asked FJ to wait a minute whilst he used the facilities. They weren't up to much and perhaps the one in the campervan was superior. No doubt they would find out throughout the course of the journey. His legs stretched, his mind refreshed a little by sleep, Joe sat in the passenger seat and they set off once again.

◆ ◆ ◆

"Flat isn't it." FJ commented as they headed southeast. It was very flat and sparsely populated. Crops and sheep dominated the passing scenery, though never together in the same fields for obvious reasons.

Joe had forgotten his passport, but he'd remembered his phone charger, the type that plugged one end into the cigarette lighter. He charged his phone and then called Ada as she had requested,

"Ada."

"Joe, how is it going?"

"Alright. I had to hide in the back as I forgot my passport, but apart from that. No accidents or rogue seagulls."

"That's good. I sense the passport thing will be ok. How is the Father?"

Joe looked across.

"He's fine. He's driving. The van seems to be

solid enough, though not very fast. He seems to know where he is going."

"As long as you are making steady progress."

"Have you, you know, had any thoughts?"

"On...?"

"On whether I'll make it?"

Ada paused a moment, then,

"No, but that is not necessarily a bad sign."

"No news is good news."

"Well, it's neither good nor bad. What I do feel, quite strongly, is that you need to stay on this path, this road, this journey."

"Ok. I'll check in again further down the line. Tell Janice that the spell is doing well." Joe ended the call. At least there was no negative psychic news. *But would Ada have told him if there was?* She would hardly have said that she had seen into the future and then ...*forget it, you're screwed.* Were they, in fact, just wasting time and diesel? FJ didn't seem to think so. But so far, from what Joe had seen of him, he would probably have been the one on the *Titanic* telling everyone not to worry, and that it would all work out alright. Joe was worried. He found that in some moments, it took all his mental strength to just not lose the plot altogether. The thought of an impending trip to hell might do that to most people. The campervan rolled on.

◆ ◆ ◆

After another four hours of steady driving, they saw the signs for Brussels. They had now made a decent impression on the journey and Joe started to see FJ blinking every now and then.

"Listen, you better take a break and let me drive for a bit." Joe suggested.

"You have a license?"

"Yeah, of course."

"I mean, do you have it with you, just in case we get stopped by enthusiastic Belgian police?"

"It's in my wallet, in my jacket."

"In the vestry?"

"No, thankfully I brought my jacket. I thought my passport was in there as well."

"Ok then. I will pull into the next stop and you can take over until, let us say…Frankfurt." FJ pulled over at the next garage/petrol station and put more fuel in; then he parked up and lifted the hood, which popped up on the third attempt. Joe joined him at the front of the campervan and he checked the engine oil level and also the brake fluid level. Both were fine. He did fill up the water bottle from an outside tap and added some to the windscreen wiper reservoir. "Probably should have checked these *before* we set off. Mitigating circumstances."

"Better late than never. For five grand this isn't bad," Joe said, "Someone has looked after it alright." Just as he said that FJ pulled open the rear door and the handle came off in his hand. He held it up in the air.

"Don't know my own strength."

"Just cosmetic. Will the door still shut?"

"I don't know. I would need to be able to open it first."

"At least it's shut now. You need the bathroom before we set off again?" Joe asked. FJ held up a finger to acknowledge that he did and then he tootled off into the garage. He came back with some more bottled water and walked over to Joe.

"I forgot, I should have done this before we set off." FJ said, just before he sprayed some of the water over the side of the van.

"What are you doing?"

"I'm blessing the van....and all who sail in her." Then he got into the passenger seat and buckled up.

"I hope, now, that we don't end up in the river." Joe said as he sat down in the driver's seat. It pleased FJ that some of Joe's sense of humour had returned. Joe checked the controls. They seemed pretty basic and manageable.

"More likely the Mediterranean Sea. *When*, not *if* we get there." FJ anticipated Joe's possible negative comment.

"Let's keep going then, until we run out of land." Joe started the engine and the campervan set off once more.

18

Ada had met with Janice at her house that morning for coffee and biscuits and a hefty slice of camaraderie. Although neither was actually on the journey physically, they were still very much invested. Ada stroked each cat in turn as they approached and acknowledged her. She had been like a cat on a hot tin roof all morning. Her mind unable to concentrate on anything for long.

"How far ahead are they?" she asked Janice.

"France is only a bit ahead time-wise. A couple of hours," Janice answered, "You look about as jittery as I feel. I wonder how they are getting on?"

Ada closed her eyes and tried to envisage events over in France. After a few minutes, she opened them again.

"Belgium. I saw a lot of tulips."

"Isn't that Amsterdam?" Janice wondered.

"They must have them in Belgium as well." Ada said.

"Unless they've taken a major wrong turn."

"They haven't. They are well on course, though there's still a long way to go."

Janice placed a mug of de-caffeinated coffee down on the table, as well as a plate of homemade biscuits.

"I don't know why you drink this stuff." she said to Ada.

"You know, if I drink more than half a cup of normal coffee, the caffeine makes the psychic messages unbearable."

"When did you figure that out?"

"When I was about seventeen. I was seeing all kinds of stuff. Too much for me to handle, especially at that age. Parents thought I was on drugs or had taken mushrooms or L.S.D. I didn't even know what that was."

"Must've been scary."

"It was more than a little scary."

"And you've not had that since?"

"Nope. But I never drink more than half of it."

"You are fine with alcohol I've noticed. Anyway, do you get anything about how they are?"

"Yes, they are ok. I can tell that. Also, they said they were fine when they called me earlier." Ada reassured.

"So they called you then, but not me. The warding spell must have held up ok then, so far at least. I just wish we could do more to help."

"*Besides* sending positive thoughts. I know. But that *is* all we can do, for now. By the way, what's in the biscuits?" Ada picked one up and noticed it was flecked with what looked like herbs.

"Stinging nettles."

"Stinging nettles? Do you put those things in everything?"

"More or less."

◆ ◆ ◆

Joe had almost come to the end of his four-hour stint behind the wheel. It had gone without incident. He'd kept his right foot down as far as it made a difference and the speedometer needle had hovered around 70-75 mph. The sky was beginning to darken and twilight was steadily coming in. To his left, FJ had closed his eyes and drifted off into a light doze. Joe pulled into the next available service station which was just a little way past the turnoff for Frankfurt. FJ opened his eyes almost as soon as the campervan rolled to a halt.

"You slept a while?" Joe asked.

"A little. Those plates and pans in the back rattling away there didn't help. We should have taken them out before we set off. The drive went ok? They all drive on the wrong side of the road."

"I stayed in the same lane. This thing guzzles

gas for a diesel. We are on half a tank again. Negates the benefit of a cheap holiday if you ask me." Joe was desperately trying to keep things as light-hearted as possible, but when the fear of hell reared its ugly head, it took hold with a firm grip. He felt a shiver all the way down his spine. FJ noticed his facial expression alter.

"Never been my thing, caravans & camping. I like a proper bed and a proper toilet." FJ said as he jumped out of the van. He unscrewed the fuel cap and filled her up once again. When finished, he walked over to the shop to pay. Joe went with him to stretch his legs a little. FJ took a gold-coloured credit card out of a leather wallet. Joe whispered to him.

"Gold card? Don't you have to be super rich to have one of them?"

"No, not at all. But as I said, we do get paid as well you know. Not that much, but working tax credit bumps it up a bit."

"*Working tax credit*?"

"Sure. Why not? We do more than thirty hours per week."

Joe had never thought about a priest claiming working tax credits, but it made perfectly good sense.

This service station differed from the one in France: everything was more ordered and organized with German efficiency, right down to the chocolate bars on display, all lined up and colour coded. As they walked back to the van, FJ asked in a more solemn tone, "How is the mark?" Joe hadn't dared look at it, as though if he didn't, then it might just go away or at least not grow any bigger. He pulled up his right trouser leg. It was still there and it *had* grown in size and now reached up to his calf. From a distance, it shimmered and moved and altered like it contained a thousand solar systems in the dimensions of a football. He didn't say anything. Neither did FJ. They got back into the campervan and set off again, this time with FJ at the wheel. "I'll drive till Nuremberg. Get some shut-eye if you can." he said, in a measured tone. Joe was starting to look extremely jaded.

◆◆◆

Joe didn't or couldn't get any proper rest. With FJ driving again, their speed dropped 5 mph, which seemed a lot under the circumstances. Every other car on the motorway was going faster than they were, most of them a *lot* faster. He did have plenty of time to gaze out of the window at trees, birds and nature. Sometimes large flocks of birds gathered and flew in swarms and abstract patterns. Fortunately, none were interested in him or the beige-coloured campervan that steadily made its way down the motorway.

Around five miles away from Nuremberg, he

tried to work out in his head how long he would have till the steadily growing mark, which was now slightly numb to the touch, would spread and cover his whole body. Halfway through trying to work it out, he realized that this exercise had no point: he would either get there in time or he wouldn't. The man to his right might influence that or he might not and he had no idea which one it would turn out to be. He'd noticed that FJ's general disposition had altered in the last twelve hours or so. Whether or not that was just through tiredness it was hard to gauge, but he was certainly less buoyant and he smiled less frequently. *Perhaps he knew something that Joe didn't.*

The sky above was now dark; the road ahead was illuminated by artificial means. Motorway signs suggesting Munich now started to appear. They planned to swap seats again at the next available stop. Joe didn't feel enthusiastic about having to drive again, but FJ needed another break.

When the stop came and the campervan pulled in, FJ turned to look at Joe and blew out a long breath of air, before getting out and stretching like a cat that had just got up after a long sleep.

"Do you feel up to taking over?" he asked Joe.

"First, I need coffee." Joe said.

The two left the campervan and walked

over to the familiar *M* sign on one of the service station's buildings. FJ had put on his black overcoat. His dog collar was still in place. Perhaps it offered him inspiration or comfort or neither. They didn't waste many words, as though speaking might use up valuable reserves of energy.

"Hungry?" Father Jones nodded towards the menu.

"I should be, but no. My leg is a little numb."

They got two Americano coffees and sat down at a table for five minutes. FJ didn't normally take sugar, but he put three sachets in the drink. Joe followed suit. When the strong coffee was finished, FJ spoke about the journey's progress.

"We are on track to get to the ferry from Athens."

"When does it leave again?"

"4:00 pm tomorrow," The clock on the wall showed 9:04 pm, "We have nineteen hours to get there. Then the ferry takes twelve hours to get to Israel."

Joe watched the second hand of the clock tick its way around. Each second felt like another second wasted. He stood up. FJ quickly darted into the toilets, followed by Joe who splashed his face with cold water. They walked briskly back to the van and Joe readied himself for his stint behind the wheel. They buckled up. FJ gave him a thin-lipped smile and they set off once more.

19

Janice sat down on the sofa. Ada had told her that the spell was still working. Once a spell had been cast, Janice only knew initially at that moment whether it had worked or not; she couldn't track its continued effectiveness and that's where Ada's psychic ability took over. That's all they needed to do, for now. Keep them hidden for as long as possible. The two of her fellow witches who had travelled and performed the spell in the circle of stones had stayed over, just in case they were needed again at short notice. The other two had other commitments and had returned home. All involved knew, only too well, that the spell could break at any moment and there would be no warning signs for this eventuality. They now all sat drinking coffee opposite each other on the comfortable sofas. All three witches felt a certain satisfaction that their skills had worked against such a powerful adversary. All three felt a sense of pride in that being a witch was something useful.

They weren't just a bunch of kooks. All three felt growing unease at the possibility that they had just incurred the wrath of demonic spirits that might come back to them seeking revenge. Julie, in particular, had a little more swagger about her. Next to her sat Lorraine. She had the gentlest personality of the three.

"Shouldn't you call them again and see how they are getting on?" Lorraine suggested. Janice had assumed the, *no news is good news* policy. But she knew that idea was a bit of a cop-out and she nodded as she picked her phone up off the table. In reality, she feared the worst and her face showed it. She called Joe's number. It rang for a while and then went to voicemail.

"No answer." she relayed.

"Oh." Lorraine said.

"That's not necessarily a bad thing. It doesn't mean something bad has happened." Julie said.

"No." Janice said.

"Might be driving." Lorraine suggested.

"Battery might be out." Julie said.

"Might have no signal." Lorraine said.

"They are fine," Ada said, as she walked into the room. She sat down next to Janice, "I've seen the campervan heading towards their goal just a few minutes ago. It was a bit blurred, but it was them for sure."

"What if," Julie said, "What if this going to the Holy Land doesn't work?"

"Do you get anything on that Ada?" Janice asked.

Ada screwed up her face and shrugged.

"I'm unable to read this part or get any insight. Not at the moment."

"Has this happened before?" Lorraine asked. "Where you can't read something?"

"Not for quite a while. Maybe since I was twelve. I've not felt such a block on something."

"You became psychic aged twelve?" Julie asked.

"Yes. That was no barrel of laughs, let me tell you. A dozen voices all at once." Ada said.

"But you came to grips with it." Lorraine said.

"Yes. Took a while mind. I was probably twenty before I *really* got a grip on it and felt like I was the one pulling the strings." Ada added.

"Is the future unwritten or is it all planned out?" Julie asked. Ada didn't answer that one. It was a *no-go* question. No one spoke for a while and then Janice said,

"Come on, let's go and get a drink. Take our minds off, instead of just sitting around waiting."

"I'll drive." Lorraine said. She didn't drink alcohol and hadn't done since her last stint in rehab five years previously. The ladies climbed into her VW SUV and then she drove to the Fox & Hounds.

◆◆◆

Joe found himself in unfamiliar surroundings. He was now on foot, shining a torch to illuminate his path. A noise alerted him to the presence of something to his left and a shadow came and went. Joe followed in that direction. The night sky clouded over very quickly. The moon peeped between clouds. There was something on the ground in front of him. He approached slowly. The beam of his torchlight fell onto the figure of a man, lying face down. Joe took hold of his shoulder and turned him over. He saw his own face. It was rotten with worms and maggots crawling out of it. He woke with a start. FJ was at the wheel.

"You slept, ok?"

"No. Not really." Joe caught his breath as though he'd been exercising heavily.

"We are in Austria."

"How long was I out for?"

"A few hours," FJ informed. Joe lifted his trouser leg. The mysterious mark had shifted and was now above his knee. It wasn't slowing down or speeding up, just relentless in its consistent progress. "How is it?"

"Above the knee."

FJ didn't answer, he kept his eyes fixed on the road. A few minutes passed by and Joe saw *Vienna* on one of the motorway signs.

"Vienna, isn't that the place you wanted to

visit?"

"Well, yes, under different circumstances. There is one place, in particular, I had in mind." FJ replied.

"When does the ferry leave again?"

"Tomorrow at 4:00."

Joe did a quick calculation.

"We have the time, it *is* just off the motorway."

"I don't know if we should risk it. I'm really not sure..."

"No really, we could do. If...if things don't go to plan, then it is somewhere that I always wanted to visit. Though I hated the song," Joe didn't want this trip to be a total waste if things didn't work out, "Just for a couple of hours."

FJ did a quick calculation. Joe was right, they could afford to make a brief detour and there was a possibility that it might be worthwhile.

"Are you sure? Really?"

"Yes. And before I have to get back into the cupboard, I would like to stretch my legs a little."

Partly against his better judgement, FJ took the next turn off the motorway.

◆ ◆ ◆

"You know, I once put a hex on the bloke I wanted." Lorraine said. The four ladies were now sitting around a wooden table at the country pub.

"Did it work?" Ada asked.

"Not really. I ended up marrying him ..."

"Oh, nice." Commented Janice.

"Twelve years of his narcissistic abuse. Right bastard he was." Lorraine added.

"Aren't all exes. But, you know," Janice said, "Some might say that was Karma."

"It was," confirmed Lorraine, "It definitely was. That's what made me change."

"You became a good witch after that?" Ada asked.

"Yes. After that, I only used my skills for good things. Nothing selfish," Lorraine said, "Well ... maybe there was this *one* other time."

"I don't want to know. In fact, I probably already do." Julie said, "That backfired as well, if I remember."

"At least," Janice said, "*This* one seems to have worked."

"As far as we know." Julie said. Everyone looked at Ada for confirmation.

"It is still working. They are unseen." she said.

"And," continued Janice, "I think that calls for a toast." She held out her glass and all four women chinked their glasses in the middle of the table, "To this coven. We have come up against something very dark and very powerful and won."

"We haven't won anything ...yet." Ada said.

◆ ◆ ◆

It had been daylight for an hour. FJ turned off the engine. He'd parked within walking distance of a certain structure that he'd wanted to see above all others.

They got out of the campervan and the doors clunked shut. They were on a tight schedule though, so couldn't dawdle.

"This way." FJ said and then he set off in the direction of a towering spire.

"What is it that you want to see?"

"This building is not too far. I've always wanted to see it. I put it first on the list so we don't miss it." Father Jones had higher hopes invested for this particular visit that he didn't pass on to Joe. They continued on through the side streets of Vienna.

"These buildings look like wedding cakes." Joe commented on the size and shape of some of the smaller structures, then they turned the corner and saw the huge ornate cathedral that was FJ's focus, "Wow. Impressive. How old is this?"

FJ looked up in wonder.

"Saint Stephen's. Twelfth century. Technically the roof is newer than that as it got hit during WW2. Took seven years to rebuild it."

"This has been rebuilt? It doesn't look like it." Joe said.

"The stonemasons did do an amazing job. Even more so seeing it in person."

"They did. Probably aren't many around today that could do what they did."

"Just a handful," FJ commented. They had spoken enough, "Do you want to go inside?"

"Sure."

The two walked over to the cathedral's main entrance. Even at 9:00 am, there was a small queue waiting to go inside. FJ gently took Joe's arm and guided him towards a less obvious entrance, not open to the public. The man given the responsibility of not allowing anyone in through this entrance stepped forward. Father Jones met him with a smile and spoke in a language unknown to Joe. The guard's demeanour softened and he bade the two travellers step inside. They entered a vestibule of sorts.

"What did you say?" Joe asked.

"Something in Latin. I know a few phrases. A fellow priest."

Joe thought this quite a cool trick to have up your sleeve, but that was the first time FJ had smiled in quite some time. They stepped out of the small room and into the body of the cathedral itself. It was huge and lit by a thousand flickering candles. At one end was the high altar. Large statues abounded and lined the ornate walls. Old wooden seats and pews filled much of the floor space. Sections were cordoned off to the public with tasteful barriers.

"Look at all the stained glass. It's amazing." Joe commented. Light poured through intricate multi-coloured panes of glass that depicted many different ancient scenes.

"Mostly replaced in the 1950's," Father Jones whispered, "Hitler again." Then he asked Joe to follow him. They passed an intricate and complex stone pulpit, carved with a myriad of designs and countless figures. One statue was of a man unfortunate enough to have been pierced by multiple arrows. On the far end was a massive painting of the martyr, *St Stephen,* himself, in the act of being stoned to death. The sheer brutality of what was on show was not lost on Joe.

Father Jones stood in the middle of it all on the immaculate squares of the marble floor and breathed it in. Then his eyes fell upon Joe.

"Come and rest your hands upon this," he said and then he stepped over one of the barricades. One of the security staff came walking quickly over and FJ whispered something to him. He immediately turned and left them alone. Joe lifted his leg over the barrier and followed FJ to a marble statue in the form of an angel. He took Joe's left hand and placed it on the cool, smooth texture of the statue. He held it on there for a second and then left Joe to keep contact with it whilst he looked up at the statue's face. Then he nodded to Joe, who slowly took his hand away. "This is the heart of the Church." he whispered.

He offered another thin smile and then they both casually strode back over the barrier, as other visitors began to wander in and gawp at their surroundings as they had done. Some sat at the pews and said prayers. FJ placed his right hand on Joe's shoulder and the two walked slowly towards the exit.

When they were outside in the cool autumn morning air, FJ turned and briefly looked at the cathedral once more.

"Is there anything else you wanted to see?" Joe asked him.

"Not really." FJ looked at his watch, "Time is moving onward. Do you feel anything ...anything different?"

Joe shook his head slowly.

"Not really."

"The mark. Has it grown?"

Joe took a peek down his belt line. He could see that the mark was still working its way upward.

"A little."

FJ nodded. He had hoped for some miracle cure that the cathedral might provide. It was back to plan *a*, such as it was. He didn't tell Joe about his hope for the trip to St Stephen's, though Joe found it damningly obvious what it was. They walked back to the campervan slowly, in silence. The sightseeing trip was over.

20

Ada awoke at 2:15 am. She'd gone to bed at the stroke of midnight and had gotten off to sleep quickly, that process no doubt aided by the three glasses of wine she'd drunk. She woke up in a hurry. The dream she'd had was weirder than normal ...which was saying something. There were ants, lots of ants, that were swarming on a hilltop, looking for something. Then, they weren't ants any longer, just shapes. The shapes formed themselves into columns and then the columns grew in size. Still, they were moving and searching. Then the shapes stopped moving and one in particular formed into a black shape, a black robe. The hood of the robe fell to reveal a human face. The face had an eye etched onto its forehead. It had found the thing that it was looking for.

Ada went downstairs and poured some water into a glass. None of what was happening could be described as good, but this was *not* good, not at all. Ada feared, quite strongly, that the cloaking spell might have been broken. Despite the late hour, she called Janice, who answered within a few seconds. She had stayed up late sipping wine with her friends and she was more than a little tipsy.

"Oh, crap." Janice responded to the news,

"Can you do another?" Ada asked, "If need be?"

Janice placed her glass down on the table.

"I think ...I think we need to rejuvenate our energies first. That last spell took every ounce of our combined power."

"How long will that take?"

Janice looked at her two guests, who had stopped chatting at her request.

"I don't know about the others, but I will need another twenty-four hours...at least. Are you sure that it is broken?"

"Not completely sure, but something is after them and this time it's not ants and dogs."

◆ ◆ ◆

FJ opened his eyes. In front of him was a large shrub. Behind him, Joe fidgeted and moved around on the sofabed.

"I needed that," he said to Joe, "Just to refresh my batteries."

He'd gotten so tired that driving on would

have been a hazard and he'd taken a ninety-minute power nap. Joe was off driving duty for two reasons: partly, because the mark had reached up to his groin and begun to travel down his left leg, making both legs a little numb and also because, passport-less, he needed to stay out of sight and was led down in the back. FJ took a swig of bottled water and then sat upright in the seat. He felt like crap but told Joe that he was feeling refreshed. A glance in the rear-view mirror confirmed his present state; he looked as tired as he felt. "We better press on." FJ said, and then he started the engine once more.

Soon, they rejoined the motorway and the old steady diesel engine did its best to keep the campervan up with the flow of traffic.

Joe had slipped into a melancholy state of disbelief, sadness and acceptance. He watched other cars and vans and trucks flash by and felt the will to fight against this hostile enemy slowly ebbing out of him. He was now almost half engulfed by the beautifully written but deadly text that was slowly consuming him. He wanted to ask where they were or how far was to go, but couldn't summon up the desired energy to speak the words. FJ drove on with a grim expression. His enthusiastic and morale-boosting quips were now totally absent. He needed to keep all his diminishing reserves of energy focused on the task of driving to Athens.

After another four hours of consistent driving, FJ spoke again.

"You can get out soon if you want to risk it. We have just passed the Greek border and left Macedonia." He got no response. "Joe?! …Joe?" He glanced behind into the campervan. Joe was lying on the floor, not moving. FJ couldn't pull over, not for another ten miles. "Joe!" He picked up the bottle of water, took the cap off and tried his best to hit Joe with a splash of water. It worked. Joe stirred and then slowly got up onto his knees, "You had me worried there."

"Where are we?" Joe mumbled the question. FJ saw that his face was still skin coloured and free of writing; the portal hadn't taken him completely.

"Greece," FJ forced a smile, "Not long now."

Joe sat on the sofa bed and took a swig of water. He thought about their simple and one-dimensional plan, largely based on the fact that Joe couldn't leave the sanctuary of the campervan. He would travel, hidden away, in the campervan on the ferry, which would take twelve hours to cross the sea to Israel. It was twelve hours that they couldn't spare but was also the only option available. FJ would get on the plane to Tel Aviv from the airport in Athens and meet the campervan when it arrived on the other side. And, pray that they didn't run out of time.

◆◆◆

Looking to his left, FJ took in the beautiful sight of the Aegean Sea. Sunlight reflected off its surface and also illuminated the tops of the old-looking wooden vessels that floated upon it. It was now hot at 27 degrees and the campervan didn't have air conditioning that worked properly. It had seemed to work back in England, but now it just blew out warm air. FJ had taken off his black jacket whilst driving, quite a contortionist feat in itself and he had the driver's side window wide open. The breeze coming in helped keep him awake as well as cool. Air-con failure aside, the campervan had held up its end of the deal. Apart from that, it hadn't put a foot wrong. As soon as Father Jones had set eyes on it he knew it would do the job for them. Most people would have viewed that as blind, highly optimistic, faith.

He glanced into the back where Joe was sitting. *No change in his position or demeanour.* They would take the coastal route to Athens and, under different circumstances, one of the most amazing scenic trips of a lifetime.

After a few more hours of driving, across to his left, FJ noticed land on the horizon quite a way beyond the blue of the sea. They had reached the *Pagasetic Gulf* and FJ knew that he couldn't drive any longer without taking another break. He pulled off the A75 motorway into a service station and parked up around the back, overlooking the water.

He looked over his left shoulder. Joe looked up at him.

"How are you doing?" FJ asked.

"Splendid."

"I need to rest for a bit. We are on schedule, just a little ahead."

"Ok. Sorry I can't help."

"Do you want to get out and take some air in? It will be a long time on the ferry."

Joe nodded and pulled himself up. He opened the side door and stepped out into the warm air. His short-sleeved shirt was damp with perspiration and his short beard the same. He walked stiffly over to a large rock and sat down overlooking the Gulf. Seagulls and other sea birds were idly going about their daily routines. None felt inclined to attack him.

"Should I be outside of the van?" Joe asked.

"It will be ok for a while, I think. If a pack of dogs comes running up then get back inside."

Joe nodded. FJ wasn't joking.

"The birds aren't interested. It looks like Norman has forgotten about the animals. He doesn't need them now that he has this." Joe looked again at the swirling text.

"That's …" FJ stopped himself from saying

good, "Try not to keep looking at. I'm going to get my head down," FJ stated, "But don't let me go more than two hours, that's important. Got that?"

"Yeah. Two hours."

FJ closed the van door, then lay out on the sofa bed and closed his eyes. The heat permeated everything and made it uncomfortable, but at least the inside of the van was shaded.

Joe lifted his shirt. The mark was just below his ribs.

"Stop looking at it." FJ said from inside the van.

"Halfway. Halfway to hell." Joe muttered to himself.

Such a picturesque view to take in. He might as well have been looking at the local gasworks.

◆ ◆ ◆

Sometime earlier, in a cool stone cellar, a gathering of *unholy* minds took place. At the helm of this meeting was Suleiman, the seer, the prophet, the man who had led the elusive cult of the *Yazidis* for several years, as his father and grandfather had before him. The Yazidis were believed to be a long-abandoned cult. No one outside their exclusive circle had even given them a moment's thought for at least three generations. They were Descendants from the *old Mardi,* an even older cult that worshipped the principle of evil. Only a very few outside of the Yazidis knew of their existence. They had been around since the times of Soloman, and those unfortunate enough to learn of this group and its activities were removed without mercy. So had been the way for decades. Their reward for their service to the dark forces was to hold high office once evil prevailed and held the world in its power. Their members' fanatical allegiance to the cult and to Sulieman held no boundaries.

Suleiman spoke in Arabic rather than his mother tongue. It was the old language of the *Yazidis*.

"I have been given a sign," he said, his arms outstretched. He spoke slowly. His audience of five faces all wore the same solemn almost vacant expression, "There is one travelling to Jerusalem. We are tasked with making sure he does not arrive there. But, he is not to be killed. He must remain alive until the darkness has taken him." This was the first time in several years that they had been called into action.

Suleiman then passed around an old stone vessel. Each of his silent audience used the curved blade of a jewel-hilted dagger to cut their thumbs. They all let a few drops of crimson drip into the vessel. When the process was completed, Suleiman anointed each *soldier* with this mixture with his finger on their foreheads. On each he drew the rough shape of an open eye. The dagger was then placed back into his belt. The six men left the cellar and stepped outside into the dawn mist. Suleiman was the first to straddle a large black and chrome Yamaha motorcycle. The others followed suit on their own bikes. Each one pulled on a black helmet with a snake emblem at the centre. Six powerful engines fired up and revved. Suleiman held up his right hand and then they all set off, kicking up clouds of dust in the early Syrian dawn's light.

◆ ◆ ◆

FJ looked down at the offending object. It wasn't changing or reinflating itself out of sympathy.

"Do we have a spare?" Joe asked from inside the campervan.

"I'll find out," FJ went around to the back, "Shove the door open if you can." Joe put his shoulder against the rear door and heaved it open with the accompanying sound of creaking metal. FJ looked in all the possible places and then he looked underneath the campervan. *No spare wheel.* "Nope. Or if there is one, it is very well hidden."

"How far away from Athens are we?" Joe asked.

The motorway signs had suggested,

"The port at Piraeus is twenty miles.

Just twenty," FJ looked around. From the carriageway's hard shoulder, there were no visible signs of any structures or buildings. Cars vans and trucks all sped past the campervan, kicking up dust as they did so. The available options ran through FJ's mind. He said one of them out loud. "We could hitch a lift perhaps."

"It would mean leaving me exposed; away from the van for longer periods."

"I know, and would place whoever *gave* the lift in jeopardy," He'd already gone off that idea, "I don't have breakdown that covers foreign travel."

"How long till the ferry leaves?" Joe asked.

"Three and a half hours," FJ leant against the side of the camper. He was so hot and tired that trying to come up with a solution was doubly difficult. The next ferry after today was in four days. Joe probably didn't have that long. *That was it. They were done. Out of options.* "We have no other choice but to try and hitch a lift. Then get across somehow. We'll have to be creative."

Joe nodded to himself. *No choice.*

FJ dusted himself down and adjusted his white collar. Perhaps someone would be more likely to help out a priest in distress. After five minutes, that theory proved unsound. Nobody stopped. The relentless and direct heat made FJ feel nauseous and unsteady on his feet. He went back to the campervan and asked Joe to pass him some cool water from the fridge. Joe sighed.

"I'm sorry, I drank it all. I thought we would be able to get more. It feels like I'm burning up from the inside."

FJ opened the bottle from the front, which was now nicely warmed. He leant against the campervan and looked upwards. He wondered whether to say a prayer ...another one. Then, something happened. A 4x4 flatbed truck pulled up alongside them on the hard shoulder. A man in his fifties got out and started talking in his native Greek language. He seemed friendly. FJ managed a smile and then said,

"English." And held his hands out apologetically. This didn't bother the new arrival.

"English. I did not expect," Like most Greeks, he spoke fluent English, "You need some assistance by the looks of it. Flat tire?"

FJ nodded.

"Yep."

The man introduced himself.

"I am more than happy to help you fellows. I am Constantine and I am also a man of the cloth as you are," Then he glanced into the back of the flatbed truck, where a pale blue surfboard lay, "Oh, and also a surfer," He certainly didn't look like a priest or a vicar dressed as he was in an orange and blue Hawaiian shirt and long shorts. He walked around the campervan and then asked the obvious question, "You haven't got a spare then?" FJ shook his head, "No repair kit?" FJ shook his head again, "Hmm. 15-inch rims. Standard tires," He noticed Joe in the back, "You have a passenger."

"Yes. We have a rather urgent...appointment. Father Jones, by the way." FJ said and then he shook his hand. Joe waved with one hand from the back of the vehicle. Constantine took a few steps closer to FJ and asked quietly.

"Is he ill? Not well?"

"He has a rather *unusual* ailment."

"I see." Then the newcomer sounded more positive, "Right, I know a man with a garage about twenty minutes down this road. I will jack your camper up and take the wheel to him. New tire on and then *job done.* You can go on your way."

"That would be excellent. A real lifesaver." FJ sighed. He wasn't exaggerating.

"Why don't you guys come along with me and get out of the heat for a while? I have three seats up front."

FJ looked into the van and then back to Constantine. He had a fleeting image of the 4x4 crashing.

"He doesn't like to leave the van."

"Oh."

"But, hey, could you bring some cold drinks back with you, here's some money." He reached into his trouser pocket.

"Don't be silly. It's on me. Good Samaritan and all that business. I'll be as quick as I can." With that said, he produced a car jack from the back of the truck and quickly pumped the campervan up high enough to get the wheel off. "Don't go anywhere!" he said as he tossed the wheel in the back of the truck. Before long, his truck was like a hazy mirage on the horizon. FJ walked over to Joe, who was sitting on the sofa bed.

"How are you holding up?" he asked him. Joe pulled his shirt up. The ancient text was now halfway up his chest. It spoke for itself. FJ sighed. He knew that words of encouragement would sound hollow, so he offered none. All they could do now was wait and drink the warm water.

Joe dozed as he waited. He'd drifted off into a disturbed half-asleep state that he woke from with a start. FJ had noticed him twitching and grimacing and had nudged his shoulder. He opened his eyes to see Father Jones's troubled-looking face.

"You dreaming?"

"Yes," Joe answered. FJ didn't ask what about, "My legs feel numb." FJ knocked one with his fist.

"Did you feel that?"

"Not much," A few more minutes passed. Still, the surfing priest had not returned, "Why pick me? Is it just the fact that..." Joe sounded very tired.

"Don't speak. Save your strength," FJ placed his hand on Joe's head as the guttural sound of an engine approached. A car door creaked open and then clunked shut, "I think he's back." FJ got up and, sure enough, Constantine was standing there holding a steel wheel, complete with a new tire.

"Howdy," he said, with a smile, "I told you that I wouldn't be too long." Immediately he began placing the wheel over the four bolts and then he tightened up the nuts in order. As he finished the final bolt with one last turn with the wheel brace he asked, "So, where are you fellows going?"

"It's a…journey of a lifetime," FJ answered in a kind of riddle-like tone, "How much do we owe you for the tire?"

"Oh please. Nothing. All the way from England in this?"

"Yep. It's the first thing that's gone wrong. Except for the air conditioning. We must give you some money for your trouble, please."

"No. I insist. They put the tire on for free. Owes me a favour. Now, the air conditioning, I can't help you with that I'm afraid." Constantine looked puzzled as to where these two might be going. He guessed that there was something he wasn't being told. "There was a nail in it. Could've happened to anyone. Is there any other assistance I can give to you?"

"Did you get the drinks?" FJ asked.

"Oh yes!" Constantine went to the truck and got out a silver cool bag with several sodas and bottles of water in it, "They'll keep cool for a while in this."

FJ took two out, walked over to the campervan and handed one to Joe, who opened it and drank it like a man in the desert. FJ did the same. When he'd gulped a good bit down, he wiped his lips.

"Thank you."

Constantine just watched for a few seconds before he said anything else, then.

"Your destination Athens?"

"Yes."

Constantine nodded.

"Well, I'll leave you to it. Safe journey," He got to the truck and then stopped and picked out a business card from the glove compartment. He walked over to FJ, who was already getting ready to set off again, "My number is on here. Just in case you get another nail."

FJ thanked him and then watched the 4x4 flatbed's chunky tires start turning once more as it rejoined the motorway and then headed off in the direction of Athens.

"You ready?" FJ asked Joe, who nodded once in response. FJ climbed back into the driver's seat. He could see Joe, head in his hands, in the rear-view mirror. The campervan moved off once again.

21

Six grim-faced men on large motorcycles hammering down the motorway in formation. They looked like some strange desert-based wing of the *Hell's Angels*...minus the leather jackets.

One by one, at Sulieman's instruction, they pulled into the last service station on the road to Damascus. Each filled their thirsty tanks to the brim. One excited young traveller came out of the shop to look at the bikes. He was particularly interested in Suleiman's right-hand man's black *Harley Davidson 833cc custom cruiser.* When he took out his phone to take a selfie snap next to it, his phone was swiped out of his hand and tossed to the ground. A heavy motorcycle boot trampled unceremoniously on top of it. The boy's protests fell on deaf ears and then the young man saw the dagger in the belt of the rider. He listened to his instincts and took refuge back inside the service station.

The cult members bought cold drinks and

then they sat down on the grass. No one spoke. It looked like the least cheerful picnic outing of all time. Two of the members took out curved daggers and began to sharpen them with stones they picked up off the ground. Some members threw rocks. Some smoked cigarettes. When Suleiman was ready, he gave the nod and walked over to his black Yamaha roadster, closely followed by the others. Six large engines roared into life again and their journey continued. The young motorcycle enthusiast watched them leave from behind the glass of the service station window and then looked down at his phone's broken screen.

◆ ◆ ◆

"We are ten minutes away," FJ said. The words didn't illicit a response of any kind. Joe sat motionless in the back with his head bowed. FJ pulled the campervan over. The hot Grecian sun felt less vicious now that they had cold drinks. FJ took hold of Joe's shoulders. "Joe," Joe looked up at him, "I need you to hang in there. Just a while longer."

"What if..." Joe croaked, "What if this doesn't even work?"

"It will. Believe me, it will," FJ smiled. Of course, he had no guarantee whether or not it would work, just his and Ada's faith, intuition and the knowledge that demonic forces had tried to stop them from boarding the plane to Tel Aviv. "I need you to lay low now," Looking at his condition, this would not be a difficult task, "Passengers aren't supposed to travel on the ferry, but no one will search the van. Anyway, once it's set off, they can't very well kick you off can they," Joe gave a single nod, "It's twelve hours. I won't have any contact with you for twelve hours, but I'll see you in Israel. I'll meet the ferry at Hafia," FJ checked the refrigerator, which had joined the air-con and stopped working properly. "Keep these drinks in the cool bag," FJ stood up, "I'm going to drive into Athens now and then get you and the van onto the ferry. Hang in there. We've come this far." Joe nodded and FJ closed the van's side door behind him. He got behind the wheel again and set off towards the city of Athens at the very tip of the country.

Within half an hour, the campervan had run out of land and FJ had been directed to the spot on the harbour where a giant ferry, painted the same cobalt blue colour as the sea surrounding it, sat waiting. Its monstrous mouth was open and allowing vehicles inside. FJ got out and felt the gentle breeze from the sea caress his face. He asked to speak to the person he'd called the previous day; he wasn't on duty, but the rep from the shipping company that operated the ferry assured FJ that there was easily enough room for the campervan and that he had an hour until the ferry began its *thirty-six-hour* journey.

"Thirty-six hours?" FJ quizzed. The rep spoke good English.

"Yes. That is the standard time to reach Haifa."

"I thought it was twelve?"

"No, no. Thirty-six. You must've made a mistake."

This news came like a bolt out of the blue Aegean Sea. Thirty hours was way too many. Joe probably wouldn't last twenty-four.

"Is there a faster boat?"

"No sir. This is the only one that makes the crossing."

"How long till it leaves?"

"We close the door in," he looked down at his watch, "Fifty-two minutes. You need to have all the paperwork done in thirty minutes."

FJ's mind raced. Options were few. Joe couldn't travel by plane. His condition was too bad and also, he would be away from the magical protection of the van should he need it. If the plane crashed because of Joe's involvement ... *he couldn't take that risk. Thirty-six hours*. The mysterious writing had travelled too far in less time than that. He pulled the business card from his shirt pocket. He was clutching at straws, but he called the number as the light sea breeze cooled his face. It was answered quickly.

"Hi, this is the man who you helped out with the wheel, the one with the camper van."

"Oh hello. How is your journey going?"

"Not great. We are at the ferry and it is going to take a lot longer than we expected to get across."

"Takes around three days, doesn't it?"

"Something like that. The thing is, my friend, the passenger you saw, needs to get to Israel as quickly as possible."

"To see a doctor?"

"Something that will cure him. I know this is a long shot, but is there any way that you know about to get there quicker than that?"

Constantine put out his cigarette and pondered.

"My friend has a boat."

"A boat. A fast boat?"

"Faster than the ferry."

"How long would it take, assuming he would let us rent it?"

"Well. It's at least *four* times faster than the ferry would be."

"And he would take us? If we paid him?"

"All I can do is ask him for you."

"Ok. Please ask and call me back on this number."

"I will do. You take care."

"This ferry leaves in fifty minutes. If we don't get him on, then..."

"Don't worry. Leave it with me."

Constantine ended the call.

Don't worry. That was a little rich. Five minutes passed by quickly. Now FJ had just *twenty-five* to complete the paperwork. He knew in his heart of hearts that Joe wouldn't survive the thirty-odd-hour ferry trip, but it might be their only option.

He waited, leant against the campervan that had got them there in one piece. *Had it all been in vain?* He waited longer. Gulls swooped down and soared back up. Boats both large and small came and went. Then, when the time to sign the paperwork for the ferry had arrived, his phone rang.

"All he requires is that you pay him for the fuel." Constantine said.

"Amazing," FJ exclaimed. Then he realized the risk of taking Joe out of the campervan's protected bubble. He calculated a quick risk assessment. Joe had left the camper for brief periods and had no problems. This man, Constantine, had been sent their way for a reason. He instinctively felt it would be ok, "We are still at the docks."

"Wait there, where the ferry is docked and we will come and find you."

That was it. The decision made. He walked over to the ferry rep and informed him that they would not require their services. Not that he needed to do that, the ferry would leave on schedule with or without them on board.

Time ticked on. The ferry's yawning mouth closed. The required checks were done and then redone. FJ watched as the massive ferry chugged forwards, churning up cool blue water and turning it white. It was about one kilometre away in the distance when the roar of Constantine's flatbed truck signalled his arrival. He jumped out, still in the same Hawaiian shirt. Out of the passenger seat got a stocky middle-aged man with a thick salt & pepper slightly greying beard. *Heracles* wore a similar shirt to Constantine.

"Greetings," Constantine smiled and took in the scene. "This is my good friend Heracles. He doesn't look much like the original, but he is a fine sailor."

FJ took a few steps and shook the new arrival's hand. He had a firm grip and uncommonly large hands.

"Nice shirt and very nice to meet you. You have the boat I'm guessing?"

"Yes," Heracles replied, "And you need to get to Israel, am I right?"

"Yes. Quite urgently."

"You have a sick friend, Constantine tells me?"

"Yes, he's, well, he's in the van. He doesn't like to leave it if he can help it."

The thick-set newcomer took a look at the

campervan.

"Well, the van won't fit in my speed boat, so he will need to."

"Yes, of course. I wasn't sure how big your boat was." FJ said.

"The Standard speedboat size." Heracles confirmed.

"Ok." FJ walked over to the campervan and told Joe the plan.

"We don't really know these people," Joe said, in a weakened voice, "Can we trust them?"

"Yes," FJ replied without hesitance, "We need to get you out of here and over there," He felt it best not to mention the obvious risk involved in doing so; Joe seemed to have forgotten that the campervan was protected under a smoke-screen spell. He nodded and FJ helped him up off the sofa bed. His legs were weakened, partly through lack of use, and partly because of the thing that was consuming him. With one arm around his shoulder, they ventured out into the hot Greek sunshine. Joe sat down on a barrel, as FJ asked Constantine. "Is there somewhere we can put the van?"

Constantine asked Heracles the same question and then he returned to FJ.

"It can be stored at Heracles's place until you come back. You are coming back, aren't you?" FJ nodded, although he wasn't sure, "He runs a small fleet of fishing boats. They often dock in Israel, which is good as he is well-known by the port officials. Though we probably won't be seeing any of them the way we are going."

Heracles had been studying Joe carefully with steely eyes. He ambled over to FJ.

"I don't mean to sound rude, but should your friend be travelling in his condition? I mean, will he survive the journey? I don't need that much … extra paperwork."

FJ assured him that all would be well. He gave some insight into the reason for their trip. He just came out with it.

"He needs the healing power of a holy pilgrimage."

Heracles nodded.

"You are English. Wouldn't Lourdes be nearer?"

"It would my friend, but not as effective," FJ said with a smile, "Now, how much can I give you for the fuel?" FJ asked. Heracles held up his right hand, waved it and shook his head. He had now seen these two needy travellers and changed his mind, "No, I must give you something?"

Heracles just walked towards the campervan and got in the driver's seat.

"He's very well off," Constantine whispered to FJ, "He will be offended if you offer him money *too* often."

FJ shrugged. He didn't look like someone you would want to offend. Heracles got out of the campervan and walked back over. He exchanged a few enthusiastic words with Constantine in Greek and then said,

"I used to have one of these. Lost my, *you know what*, in the back of it, aged seventeen. A long time ago now, but it takes me back in time, it really does. Happy days." Then he asked FJ to drive the campervan the short trip to his two-hundred-foot-square unit. Inside it smelt of fish, but not in a bad way. FJ parked the campervan just inside the doors as instructed as Constantine hooked the speedboat up to the back of the 4x4 flatbed. When Heracles pulled the cover off, it looked immaculate in green, blue and white. "My record is thirteen hours. I think I might be able to break it if I put the hammer down. Conditions are just about perfect. You *are* in a rush, right?"

"That's why he's so keen to help," Constantine whispered to FJ, "He now has an excuse to try and break his record crossing time."

As they drove to the quayside, FJ looked behind at the angular-looking, streamlined beast of a machine; a complete contrast to the hulking ferry. Perhaps the chance meeting with these two locals was the good fortune that they so desperately needed.

22

Janice's friends and fellow witches had returned home. It was now just herself and Ada who were bracing themselves for the latest news from afar. Ada had not been able to shed any light on *anything* that might be happening, which was quite worrying because it suggested that something was blocking her field of vision. She'd worked a half shift at the supermarket and then had been denied leave for the rest of the week as they were so very short-staffed. The waiting game had never been a favourite of hers. Her mini pulled up outside Janice's house and they greeted with a light embrace. On the way there she'd passed Derek who, in turn, was on his way to see his brother. He'd called his mobile twice and gotten no response. He still had a key and he let himself in and looked around. Everything was as it was, though Joe was nowhere to be seen. His car and work van were still parked on the street. Derek was puzzled and felt guilty about telling Joe about his parentage. Perhaps he had gone off on a crusade to find his actual father. All Derek could do was wait until Joe got back in touch.

◆ ◆ ◆

"No news then?" Janice asked Ada.

"No. Nothing."

"I wonder where they are. Do you think they are there by now?"

Ada merely shrugged. Janice offered coffee, but Ada asked for something stronger. Janice poured them each a Gin & tonic ...not too large.

"If I didn't feel so helpless." Ada said.

"I feel exactly the same."

"I don't suppose you have a crystal ball stashed away somewhere?"

Janice shook her head.

"Never even seen one."

"Should we go to the ley line?"

"I think its power is low at the moment. Probably won't do any good." Janice said.

"The stones?"

"Not much point. They won't work like that."

"So, what do we do then? All this sitting around is driving me mad."

"The only thing we can do.... sit and wait a little longer and *be ready*."

"I have this sickening feeling," Ada said, "That Joe might not be the only one in danger."

"What do you mean?"

"Well, don't you think that they might come for you, to try and break the spell?"

That possibility hadn't occurred to Janice.

"Let's bloody hope not." she said and then took another sip of gin.

◆ ◆ ◆

"Are there any sharks in this water?" Joe asked as he was being helped into the rear seat.

"Sharks?" Heracles wondered, "Why are you worried about sharks?"

"Just like to know." Joe said.

"Well, if there are, telos!" Constantine said, "They won't catch us in this thing."

"You're coming with us?" FJ asked Constantine, as the boat gently bobbed around in the water.

"Can you drive the boat?" Constantine asked. FJ looked at all the complicated-looking controls. So many levers, switches and buttons.

"Not without a two-hour lesson and even then..." FJ shrugged.

"Well, I'm coming as well because Heracles will need a break. We will split the helm between the two of us." Constantine added.

"Let's see the sharks chase us in this." Heracles said, and then he made up a little rhyme in Greek, about being chased by sharks. "I once caught a twenty-footer. Reeled it in myself."

Constantine spoke quietly to the two travellers.

"As you can tell, it is his pride and joy. He needed very little persuasion to make this trip. I certainly didn't have to twist his arm. Just keep telling him how nice the boat is. And also, he's my most loyal member of the congregation. Never misses a Sunday sermon. Well ...rarely."

Heracles nodded and smiled at the helm. He was ready.

"Let's get this party started." he said and then he pushed the button that started the powerful twin engines.

"Will we have enough fuel?" FJ wondered. Heracles pointed to an extra couple of fuel tanks at the back of the boat.

"We'll fill up again at the other side. Hang on to your sunglasses." Heracles said. The boat surged forward, accelerated quickly and then sped out of the harbour. FJ looked skywards and smiled.

"This reminds me of that tv show from the '80s," he said.

"Crocket and Tubbs?" Constantine asked. FJ nodded.

The breathtaking speed of the boat was surprising to both Englishmen. Joe put his head back and stared up at the cloudless blue sky. It felt like he was now in the hands of something *other* than fate.

The boat leapt across the water. It almost defied the laws of physics.

"So, you are going to Jerusalem?" Constantine asked.

"Yes, or just outside." FJ answered.

"Your friend is a strong Christian?"

"He...he wants to visit the holy land."

"Have you been before?" Constantine asked Joe.

"No. First time."

"You will feel something special when you get there. I certainly did. That is why I became a priest."

◆ ◆ ◆

On the long road to Damascus, Suleiman signalled to his followers that it was time to make another stop. The six motorbikes again pulled off the motorway and into a service station. Six helmets came off and six pairs of mirrored shades went on. Suleiman walked slowly and deliberately over to the shade of a large palm tree. His followers watched with reverent respect as he knelt on one knee and bowed his head. This was the sign that he was going to slip into his *seer* state. This was how he communicated with the darkest of spirits and demons. This was the reason he was the chosen one. A few minutes later, when he stood up again, he had gained the knowledge that he required, straight from the blackest of sources. His five companions bowed their heads as he walked towards them. Soon after, they resumed their journey west.

◆◆◆

There wasn't much idle chat taking place. The noise of the sea and the speedboat's engines made it difficult to be heard without shouting. Heracles had opened the taps and the boat was going flat out, skimming over the top of the water like a stone thrown across a pond.

Heracles looked to be in his element: at the helm, one hand on the steering wheel, large cigar in the other. They sped past fishing boats and several other small vessels. The crews of many of them recognised the speedboat and waved as they passed by like they were standing still. When they reached thirty miles out from the harbour, there were fewer and fewer other vessels and then, eventually, just open sea in front and behind. FJ looked up into the sky. Thankfully, no birds were getting ready to swoop down and attack and no shark fins were trailing behind them. Luckily, the shielding spell on the campervan was not needed, for now at least, but whether that would remain the case they would find out in due course.

Joe looked over the side of the boat at the

sea rushing past. The vertical rise and fall of the boat became monotonous, if not a little nausea-inducing, but at least they were heading with great speed towards their goal. *They had to believe in it*, FJ had said once again. Believe they would get there in time. Believe it would make a difference.

After a time, Joe fell asleep. The dream he had was not exactly sunshine and roses: he was on a ladder and all around him was pitch black. He tried to climb up, but every time he made a move to place his foot on the next rung, it slipped to the one beneath. He glanced below. Something was waiting down there, in the pitch black. FJ saw him grimace and twitch as he slept but did not disturb him.

After a while, FJ and Constantine also sat down in the comfortable leather seats at the back of the boat. Noticing that Joe was now asleep, Constantine asked,

"So, what exactly is wrong with your friend?" FJ sighed.

"If I told you, you wouldn't believe me."

"I didn't like to stare, but I saw that his skin is discoloured, I thought it was a tattoo at first, just below his collarbone."

"It is."

"I've never seen anything like that before. What would cause that?"

"It's a complicated story."

"We have about ten hours in which for you to tell it."

Father Jones could not think of a valid reason why this man should not be told the truth. These two Greek men had gone above and beyond in helping them and they were hardly going to throw them overboard on knowing the truth.

"He has been targeted by evil spirits. The strange marks and symbols on his body appeared overnight."

Constantine didn't look completely amazed. He took the news in his stride. He nodded and answered,

"Evil spirits," FJ nodded. "What did he do to invoke such a punishment?"

"Nothing. Not himself. It's something from way back in time."

"The sins of the father." Constantine offered.

"Something like that," FJ said, "We need to get him to Jerusalem. We need to follow the path Jesus took on his way to the crucifixion."

"You seem very sure about this."

"I'm doing a good job of believing it, but no, in truth, I'm not sure it will be enough to save him."

"Why such a specific place?" Constantine wondered.

FJ looked directly at him.

"He is the last remaining descendant of Simon of Cyrene, the man who carried the cross for Jesus."

Again, Constantine took this information in his stride. He understood, without any further explanation, that dark forces wanted their revenge for this single act of kindness.

"So that's it. I knew there was more to your story than met the eye. Have you known this man long?"

"Joe," FJ looked at Joe who was sound asleep just a few feet away, "Just a few days."

Constantine nodded.

"Let's see if we can get you to your destination on time." Constantine said as he slapped FJ on the shoulder. Then he got up and spoke to Heracles. It was getting close to the point where he would take over the helm.

Heracles begrudgingly accepted the swap over and he sat down next to FJ, but not before he took a closer look at their sleeping passenger.

"He's not looking too great," he whispered to FJ, who smiled back in response. "Is that a tattoo on his body? I don't remember seeing it earlier."

"Something like that." FJ said. Heracles shrugged and tossed his cigar over the side and then sat back. If anyone could get them to Jerusalem in time, it was him.

23

Four hours had passed by and so had the journey's novelty. Now, it was all about workman-like consistency. Now it was just for the helmsman to focus on the task at hand and point them in the right direction. It would be easy enough for an unskilled person to end up lost in the middle of the Mediterranean Sea.

There were islands off in the distance to both right and left, mostly uninhabited. They passed quite closely to a large island called *Thera* and then it was open sea again. The speed of the boat was constant, relentless and driven with a determination similar to that of an Olympian seeking his first gold medal. The sounds remained constant. The splash of the water, the noise the boat made when it made contact again after rising upwards, and the deep low hum of the twin engines.

Father Jones closed his eyes. He also needed to rest. He felt that he would need more in reserve before this journey was over. His fifty-something-year-old body ached here and there and his neck was stiff with all the driving. He lacked sleep. The sky was now beginning to darken. The moon's silvery reflection was visible on the water. Dusk was fast approaching.

◆ ◆ ◆

The six motorbike riders had reached Damascus. They had stopped just once more, all briefly walking around the petrol station in silence. The cashier had watched them with suspicion from behind the toughened perspex counter. They stretched their limbs one last time before the final push to their destination. Suleiman held his open hand up to signal five minutes. When that time was up, they gathered in a circle, almost like a sports team getting instructions from the coach. Sulieman reinforced their instructions with promises of riches and power. They had been promised a place at the high table, once the world was in darkness. Then they climbed back onto their chrome machines and set off once again, riding two abreast. Each rider clicked on their headlamps as they thundered onwards.

◆ ◆ ◆

"Rhodes is just to our left," Constantine said. Heracles was steering once again. FJ noticed a darker outline, Rhodes, about a mile or two away. It contained many points of light that looked like stars in faraway galaxies. It stayed there on the horizon for a while. FJ had no accurate way of determining how far they were into their journey, but Heracles did shout out the occasional fact as they sped onwards.

"Making good time," and, "The record time is on!"

The sea looked blue and black as the moon shone down upon it and, for the most part, it was just the sound of the water and the engines that could be heard.

Seven hours had passed since they set off from Athens. Joe's eyelids opened. He looked towards the front of the boat. At the wheel was someone thinner than Heracles, yet not Constantine. Then the driver at the helm turned to face him.

"Norman." Joe whispered.

"Greetings. Are you enjoying the trip?" Joe looked around. Both FJ and Constantine were dozing.

"How did..."

"I get onboard? I'm quite resourceful, as indeed *you* have proven to be. Mind you, those women you hang around with ...comical to say the least if not more than a little irritating. Perhaps I'll tire of them and get rid of them, perhaps I won't."

"Just a vision." Joe told himself out loud.

"Indeed. Where am I taking you? You might well ask. You were rather naughty and disobedient in not carrying out your part of the deal that we made and then going into hiding. It clearly stated in the agreement that you signed, in good faith I might add, that non-compliance with the completion of said aforemention tasks would result in a one way trip to, well, you know where. Excetera, excetera. All this wasted time skulking away in a grubby little caravan. What were you thinking?"

"I'm not scared of you." Joe uttered.

"No? You should be. The blackness has almost taken you, I can see it from here."

"Not quite." Joe said.

"It's only a matter of time. No matter how fast this vessel travels, you can't outrun your own destiny my dear dear fellow. I'll be seeing you very soon. Bon voyage!"

Joe blinked a couple of times and then re-focused. It was Heracles at the wheel, stoically and methodically steering the boat towards the docks at Haifa. The strange text was at the base of his neck. His whole body felt numb and disconnected. He tried to keep his eyes open, though the nightmare was right here and now, not in dreamland. Occasionally a splash of water hit his face. It was welcome and refreshing, rather than cold and annoying. His eyes did eventually close again. They opened when he heard the words...

"Joe, Joe, wake up," FJ had a gentle grip on his shoulder as Joe struggled to come to his senses. The first sensation he felt was...the lack of one, the lack of movement. The boat had stopped, "We have reached the shore. Israel."

Joe could scarcely believe it, but there, at the front of the boat, stood Heracles, hitching a large rope to one of the moorings. He was in silhouette as it was dark.

"What time is it?" Joe asked FJ, who consulted his watch. It had stopped dead.

"Darn, the watch is not waterproof. What time is it please?" FJ asked Heracles, who consulted his Rolex and then held both hands in the air as though he'd just scored the winning goal in the world cup final. He said the same phrase in Greek first, then in English.

"Meraki! I did it! A new record! Eleven hours and fifty-seven minutes!"

"It's three am," clarified Constantine, who had been *relieving himself* elsewhere, "We reached Haifa safe and sound. Beat the ferry by a good twenty hours."

"If not more." said Heracles, with more than a hint of pride.

"What are you going to do now?" asked FJ, "Turn back?"

"Turn back?" Heracles answered, "Oh no, that's enough for one day. We'll return tomorrow. I feel a nice cold drink is in order and I know just the place."

"I thought drinking was banned in Israel?" FJ said.

"Controlled drinking is allowed!" Heracles pumped his right fist.

"I'm not sure," Constantine whispered, "How much *control* will be exercised."

"Look," FJ stood up straight, "I want to thank you for getting us here. You really went above and beyond what anyone could have expected."

"No problem," Heracles said, "You coming with us?"

FJ looked down at Joe who was sitting on the small pier with his head in his hands.

"I'm afraid not. We need to get to where we are going."

"Is he going to be alright?" Constantine asked.

"I hope so." FJ said.

"What do you do now then?" Heracles asked.

"Get him into a taxi. Head to Jerusalem." FJ said.

"Go do it," Constantine said, "I will call a taxi for you and set you on your way. Call me later. Hopefully, we can all return together tomorrow."

Constantine called a taxi, which turned up in

just a few minutes. FJ helped Joe into the back and held the door open just long enough for Heracles to wish them good luck. Then the door closed and the taxi set off into the heat of the night.

"Whereabouts in Jerusalem?" the taxi driver asked. He spoke English just as fluently as everyone else in Israel, perhaps a little more so.

"The Church of the Holy Sepulchre," FJ replied, "Please."

"Wonderful building. Why there?"

"We are sort of, on a ...just there, if you please."

The driver said nothing in response for a while. Then,

"You wish to visit Jesus's last place is that it?"

"Yes, the church, or where he walked with the cross. Do you know where that is?" FJ asked.

"The *Via Dolorosa*."

"What is that?"

"The way of sorrow," the weathered-faced driver said, "I'm not sure it's the same place as some say it is. The way they have it signed."

"What do you mean?"

"It is a subject of some debate and no one really knows for sure," He turned and glanced into the back, "Where Christ's last steps were. Where he carried the cross."

"Did he carry it far?" FJ asked.

"Well, no. Supposedly, someone carried it for him when he fell down," The driver maintained a steady pace on the ninety-minute journey. He wasn't rushing. On the late shift, there never was much of a backlog of jobs waiting. "Yes, no one knows the exact route he took on that terrible day. They are more sure about his destination, where they nailed him to the cross. The Golgotha."

FJ sighed. They were so close. The yellow glow of the streetlights illuminated the route, which blended modern buildings with ancient.

"Where do you think the path that he took is …*was*?" FJ asked.

"Me? I'm no authority on the subject. Wouldn't it be better to visit later during the day? Some parts are closed to the public until 9:00 am. Though the Church opens its doors at 5:00, I believe," The driver then glanced into the back seat towards Joe, "Is your friend sick? Is that why you want to visit this place?"

FJ nodded.

"He is. I thought that if we re-traced the steps, it might help…"

"Hmm. Well, stranger things have happened. If you want, I will take you to the *Via Dolorosa*. But if you want to visit someplace on holy ground, the Church of the Holy Sepulchre contains at least some of the stations of the cross and is the place where the crucifixion took place. Did you know that Golgotha means skull shaped?"

"Is it authentic? Is it the right place?"

"I have no reason to doubt it. Though it was

decided over a hundred years after his death that these were the places."

FJ looked to his right at Joe. The swirling text was just under his nose. The taxi driver had noticed his two-tone face and assumed he must've either had a really bad tattoo or been in shadow.

"Where would you take him, if you had to?" FJ deferred the decision to the driver, partly through exhaustion.

"Me myself? I don't know. Perhaps if..." the driver was distracted by two bright motorcycle headlight beams that suddenly appeared in his rear-view mirror. He squinted and had to flip up the mirror. He cursed their lack of consideration.

◆ ◆ ◆

In Heracles's favourite bar, he was already halfway through his first beer. It was his favourite bar for several reasons, but he praised the quality of the draft beers everytime he visited. The place was quiet, as you might expect at 4: 20 am.

"Always better on draught. Perfect temperature." he said to Constantine. Who had joined him to celebrate his new *Aegean Sea crossing* record.

"It's the same thing as the bottles. It's just psychological that you think it tastes better."

"Whatever. I will take a couple of bottles with

me for the return trip and let you know."

"You know, technically, we have entered the country illegally ...again." Constantine said.

"No one cares. As long as we cause no trouble. We leave the same way tomorrow and no one is the wiser." He took an extra long drink and then wiped his mouth, "Do you think those two travellers will find what they are looking for?"

Constantine shrugged.

"I don't know old friend. I'm not sure it will be up to them. Even if they find it."

Heracles chugged the last of his beer and then ordered another.

"I guess we will find out tomorrow." he said.

◆ ◆ ◆

FJ saw smoke rising from the crumpled hood of the taxi. It had collided with an old white stone wall and had come to a dead stop. He'd been unconscious momentarily. The noise of motorbike engines faded into the distance. The driver was either out cold or dead, sprawled across the steering wheel. If his car had an airbag, it hadn't deployed. Joe was laid out on the seat next to him. A frantic voice shouted. FJ didn't have a clue what they were saying. He gently slapped Joe's face and he came back to consciousness.

"What happened?" Joe asked.

"We took a wrong turn," FJ said and then he got out of the car and opened the driver's door. The car was on fire under the bonnet. The driver was moving slightly. He had cuts on his arms and forehead. "Are you ok?" FJ asked him. The driver opened his eyes and exclaimed something in Hebrew. The source of the frantic voice, the owner of the house wall that the car had struck, became quieter as they called the emergency services to the scene. Luckily, the driver didn't appear to have any life-threatening injuries. FJ didn't want to move him but needed to drag him away from the burning vehicle. He pulled him twenty feet away to the side and then he went back for Joe. The text now covered his nose.

"Come on. We must move." FJ advised. Joe stirred and tried to get out of the car.

"I don't think I can walk. My leg feels busted." he said. The house owner came over and gestured and advised in broken English that they must stay for the ambulance. They hadn't the time to spare. FJ looked around in a circle. Over in the house's garden were a couple of handcarts full of produce. He strode over and tipped all the contents out of one of them. Oranges spilled out and rolled off in different directions, much to the annoyance of the owner. FJ then wheeled it over to Joe and manoeuvred him into it, legs dangling over the front. The man shouted more things at them as FJ began to push Joe away from the scene with as much effort as he could muster. When he'd gotten twenty meters, he had to stop and catch his breath. The sound of sirens could be heard in the distance and a column of smoke rose into the air. He didn't have a clue where he was or which direction to go in. *So close.* He pulled his phone out of his pocket.

◆ ◆ ◆

Ada had ended up staying over at Janice's house. She had drunk more than her allotted glass of white wine ...quite a lot more. The spare room was cosy and she shared it with one of Janice's cats, which was startled when her phone rang and jumped off the bed. Ada answered quickly.

"Father Jones?"

"Yes, it's me."

"Where are you?"

"Close to where we need to be. In Israel. I don't know where ...some motorbikes ran us off the road. I need your help ..."

"Yes." Ada got up and wrapped her cardigan around her shoulders.

"Janice, I need you to reach out. Do what you do. Tell me which way to go. Can you do that?"

Ada ignored the fact that he had called her *Janice* by mistake.

She took a deep breath.

"Ok. The phone will go quiet. Don't hang up, I'm still here," she said and then she closed her eyes. She reached out, as she had done a thousand times before. Within thirty seconds she started to feel something and see things, "Is there a large tree in front of you? With yellow things on it?"

FJ looked ahead. Indeed, there was a large tree with yellow flowers.

"Yes."

"It's dark."

"It *is* dark." FJ replied.

"Head left. You will see a pathway between two houses, one white and one more of grey colour. Go through there."

FJ moved the handcart forward and to the left. About ten meters up ahead, there was the gap. He pushed onwards. When he'd gone through the space, he saw that there were lots of similar-looking stone dwellings all closely packed together. Off to his right, he saw the beams of headlamps and heard the guttural, threatening roar of motorbike engines.

"Where to now, the houses all look the same?"

"Hang on..."

"Quickly Ada, we are being hunted."

Ada had nothing and then a knock on her door further distracted her concentration. Janice was awake and wanted to know who had called. Ada ushered her out and she stood outside the door and waited. A beam of light illuminated a man and a wheelbarrow. A motorbike engine revved not far away.

"Forwards and then a sharp right," Ada said, all at once. FJ pushed forwards and then turned sharply to find himself in an alleyway at the back of some more dwellings. A light shone down the alleyway. Voices shouted out in the dark. "Quickly go right and then left." FJ followed her instructions as the shouting got louder. He emerged into an open space that was overgrown with tall shoulder-high grass. Ada desperately tried not to break concentration, but nothing else was coming to her.

"Ada....Ada.?" FJ heard angry voices and loud engines and saw lights shining from several directions. Suleiman signalled to his henchmen, one of whom started spraying petrol onto the ground from a can. Suleiman waved him back and the riders retreated to the tarmacked surface to their rear. Suleiman held up a finger to check that the breeze was behind them and then he took out an old flint wheel lighter and lit a cigar with it. After taking just a few puffs, he tossed it ten feet in front of him onto the bone-dry petrol-doused grass. The petrol burst into flames and the surrounding grass caught fire. Within seconds a raging wall of fire started heading towards FJ and the wheeled cart. Thick smoke filled the air. The smell of burning filled the nostrils. It wasn't pitch black now; dawn was beginning to break and a soft mist had filled the air. FJ started to cough. Suleiman dismounted from his machine and smiled at the carnage he had unleashed. His right hand rested on the hilt of the curved dagger in his belt. “Ada..?” Ada tried not to *over-*focus. The phone connection was still active, but her psychic link had been lost, “Ada, if you have anything else, now would be a great time to let me in on it.” He coughed and covered his mouth. The wall of flames was looming closer by the second. Suleiman waved two of his men forward across the scorched earth. To their right, the other three were edging closer, their bikes purring and growling.

“They came this way. They will burn, but not die. This area is surrounded by a wall. There is no escape.” Suleiman rasped. His followers never doubted his vision or wisdom. They had already proven that they were more than willing to kill for the cause. The fire left nothing but open ground in its wake. They edged closer, their bikes’ tyres warmed by the smouldering ground. The smoke from the fire billowed upwards, pushed in the FJ’s direction by a firm breeze. Then, the smoke rose upwards for a few seconds, before it slowly started to waft in the opposite direction. The breeze had changed. The wall of burning grass turned on a dime and began to bear down on three of Suleiman’s men, two of whom turned the handlebars of their bikes hard to the right and roared off, just barely ahead of the flames. The third rider had stalled his engine and just as he restarted it, the fire caught him. The petrol can he held exploded with a boom and rained down fragments and flames that lit up the sky like a firework display. Within minutes, the fire had run out of grass to burn. The beams of headlights from the surviving riders on either side met in the middle of a patch of land. There was a six-foot-high wall running in between and that is where the wasteland ended. Suleiman walked slowly over to the wall. He pulled the dagger from his belt and the sharp blade glistened. One bike moved its beam to shine down one side of the wall, from the opposite side another did the same. Suleiman walked over to a smouldering stack of rubble, boxes and sacks that were the only thing visible and pulled them over. They toppled to the ground. There was nothing else to see. No charred bodies. He held his hand in the air and with a pointed finger, he drew a circle and then he went back to his bike to resume the search.

"You cut that fine," FJ whispered. Ada had directed FJ to a hole in the wall that was just about large enough to push the barrow through.

"Go left twice, then right when you can," Ada advised. FJ made a left turn, "No, the next left. Not this left," FJ complied. He pushed on as the sun broke free of the horizon. Then he looked down and noticed that his feet were on a path.

The path led between houses and palm trees and it was quite concealed. "Keep going until, until… just keep going for now."

The cart felt heavier all of a sudden because the path was fairly uneven and unkempt. The noise of the motorcycles had faded. There was a little traffic noise off in the distance, but that could have been anyone in any vehicle. Then FJ heard a siren wailing away in the distance.

As the darkness lifted, taller buildings showed themselves. Ada had told him to head in their direction. His hands had suffered several scrapes and cuts from the handles of the wheelbarrow. Ignoring the pain, he pushed onwards. He put Ada on the phone's speaker and she guided him, *left* or *right*, every so often. She'd gotten herself into a *flow-state* just at the right time and managed to keep it going longer than she ever had previously. The tension and pressure were immense, but Ada managed to ignore it. When Janice thought about attempting to ask for an update on the situation, Ada held up a single hand to squash it.

"The Church of the Holy Sepulchre," FJ said. He'd noticed his phone's battery was only at 10%, "Which direction?"

Ada tried to get that last vital piece of the puzzle. She'd drained most of her resources and had gone on in the trance-like state for much longer than was comfortable. She began to feel the connection slowly slipping away.

"I...I can't get it. I'm losing you. Good luck..."

The next moment, she was gone. Their phone connection had ended at the same time as her psychic one. FJ looked up. It was now daylight, just about. He typed the church's name into the Google search bar. His phone was losing its energy almost as fast as Joe was losing his and he was now almost completely covered with the mysterious text that was a portal to another dimension. Only the tip of his forehead showed his natural colour. FJ pushed onwards.

Google Maps placed them on Jaffa Street, just outside the city hall. The church was not too far away. He shoved onwards. Passers-by gave them the strangest looks. A dishevelled-looking, dust-covered man wearing a dog collar pushed around an even more dishevelled-looking man in a handcart. They had their fair quota of beggars in the city, but these two were something different.

The city was waking up. FJ asked a woman what time the Church opened its doors and was ignored. *Did the taxi driver say 5:00 am?* He was sure that he had. Inspired, he pushed onwards, through the new gate. Off to his left was the national park. He shoved and shoved and they passed the St Joseph souvenir shop. *He hadn't the time to judge.* A church bell in the distance chimed five times. He was close now ...very close. Joe looked up at him wearily.

"We are nearly there," FJ panted, as he pushed the cart. They passed Zak's, antique shop and then further along, whoever Zak was, it looked like he also had a *Jerusalem gifts shop*. "Maybe they are two different Zaks," FJ muttered in-between breaths, almost delirious with exhaustion and the knowledge that they were within touching distance of their seemingly impossible goal.

A large dome with a cross on it. This building was big and built from stone that looked as old as the pyramids. There it was, the entrance to the church. FJ didn't have time to gawp at its beauty. He pushed on towards the entrance. A church employee who was standing at the entrance took one glance at the pair of them and then held up his hand. He spoke in a mean-spirited tone of voice, though FJ had no idea what his words meant.

"English. In English, if you please." FJ said. The employee sneered for a split second. He didn't want to be up at this hour on this particular day, dealing with tattoed beggars and strays.

"You cannot enter in this state." he said. He pointed to their clothing and then to the cart. FJ gave himself and Joe a quick glance and then wheeled the handcart off to the side. Then he pulled Joe up, using whatever strength he had left in him. Soil, dust, earth and soot covered their clothes and faces. FJ looked down and saw that the sole of his leather shoe had lost its stitching and was flapping about as he walked. With Joe's left arm over his shoulder and FJ supporting him around the waist, they hobbled towards the entrance again. Several other church-goers and early-rising tourists were already filing inside the church grounds. The employee at the entrance had called over a fellow member of staff. Now they both stood barring the path inside. They allowed two more locals inside, both of whom gave disparaging looks to the motley-looking duo as they passed by.

"Go and clean yourselves up." One of the men barring the way said.

"Take a bath." The other suggested.

"We need to get inside ..." FJ said.

"Not a chance, looking like that."

FJ tried to steady himself and sound more coherent.

"This man needs the healing power of this place."

His plea fell on deaf ears.

"You are not coming in here until you clean yourselves up."

More visitors looked the dishevelled pair up and down as they passed inside. They didn't smell great either, as one visitor openly commented. Another said that they smelt like *shit* and held her nose as she walked past them.

Father Jones summoned up every ounce of the energy that he had left and tried to burst forward in between the two makeshift doormen. It was futile. Between them, they shoved both Englishman backwards, away from the door and FJ and Joe fell to the ground in a crumpled heap.

"So close. So close..." FJ panted as he started to try and pull Joe up. He was spent. He had no further strength left. Nothing to mount another assault with. He was about to let Joe fall back to the ground when a passerby appeared at Joe's other side and steadied the ship.

"Over here," he said. "Just walk with me for a little while."

All of a sudden, to FJ, Joe felt weightless. It seemed like this man was carrying the vast majority of the burden. They walked twenty meters or so to a rough patch of ground. Underfoot were scattered stone cobbles and gravel. An unkempt path of sorts.

"Here," The stranger suggested. They lowered Joe down to the ground, "Rest a while in this place."

Joe's eyelids flickered.

"I'm sorry Joe," FJ lamented, "I tried, I really did. It wasn't meant to be. It just wasn't meant to be." Then he thanked the stranger for his help.

The stranger looked at FJ with brown eyes through a long fringe of hair. He spoke once again.

"Just one act of kindness."

FJ sat down next to Joe and closed his eyes

for just a few seconds. When he opened them, the stranger was nowhere to be seen. The sun seemed to shine just a little brighter for a moment. He'd done all he could, but they were out of time. FJ slowly stood up and asked out loud.

"Why. Why all this way for this?"

He heard a voice respond.

"What are you shouting at?" There was no one else nearby. Perhaps he was so exhausted that he was hearing things. Then he heard the same voice again, "It's gone."

FJ turned to see Joe picking himself off the ground. His face ...clear. His strength returning with every heartbeat. FJ just watched for a time. Joe lifted his shirt. His body was clear. FJ looked down at the ground they were sitting on. He placed his fingers through the dust and rocks. The cuts in his hands were gone. Twenty meters away, running almost parallel, was the *Via Dolorosa, the path of suffering*; the route believed to have been walked by Jesus on his way to his crucifixion.

"Looks like they were a bit out." FJ said.

"Who?" Joe asked.

"They got the path a bit wrong. It's here ..." He let dust and dirt fall through his open fingers.

"It worked then. Your idea." Joe said.

"It did. It really did. Miraculously."

"How did you know that it would?"

"I don't have an answer to that, but the demons did give it away when they tried to stop us from getting here. Those motorcyclists were something else altogether." FJ said.

"Which motorcyclists?"

"They tried to stop us from getting here ... doesn't matter."

"They gave up?"

"I don't know. I hope to never see them again."

"Just don't cut it so fine next time. Please." Joe said.

"Next time?"

"There won't be one. It's all over," This time, Joe helped FJ to his feet, "Come on, let's go," They walked slowly past the church. "Who was that man, the one who helped us?" Joe asked.

"He didn't say his name."

They found a man washing the front of his store with a hosepipe and asked him to aim the water at them to clean themselves up a bit. He took surprising little persuasion. Luckily it was a very warm morning and their clothes dried quickly.

Zak, whether or not that was his real name or even his own shop, let FJ charge his phone on the condition that he bought a gift. He ended up with a miniature model of the church, which he gave to Joe as a memento of the trip.

"That's nice," Joe happily accepted the gift, "But most of it was a complete blur."

"You were pretty out of it, especially towards the end."

"But we did it. Somehow you did it. You realise now that I owe you more than I can ever repay you. I escaped a trip to hell."

"Just doing my job. It was a team effort," FJ insisted, "Also, a drink will suffice." FJ called Constantine, who was still in the same bar with Heracles. He told him the good news.

"Wonderful." Constantine said in response. He in turn passed the news on to Heracles who raised his glass of beer to toast their success.

FJ had four missed calls, three from Ada and one from Janice. All roughly twenty minutes apart. He called Ada and she almost knocked the phone off the table in her haste to pick it up.

"Ada, we did it." That is all he said.

"You're ok, Joe is ok?"

"Yes. We are both safe and sound. The plan worked. Now, we are going for a little celebration."

Ada asked what had happened, FJ told her that the tale was too long and at present, he didn't have the energy left to tell it. He was running on fumes. He promised her the full story on their return. Then they jumped in a taxi and gave the driver directions to Heracle's favourite bar.

When they entered the bar, Constantine greeted them both warmly. He looked at Joe and then made a sweeping gesture with his hand from head to toe.

"All one colour, the tattoo has gone!" he said.

"I have heard the term *off colour*, but you took it a little too far." he smiled. Heracles nodded.

"You did look pretty ...unusual." FJ said. Both Constantine and Heracles slapped Joe on the back. They had both seemed to accept his supernatural tangle with demonic forces as if it was a fairly normal everyday occurrence and they even had a giggle about it all.

Joe stopped laughing and then he went to sit at a table by himself. The rawness of what had just happened came over him all at once. The sheer undiluted terror he'd felt about being so close to falling into hell itself. *So close that he could almost smell it ...taste it.* That feeling wasn't going to disappear into thin air overnight. But, for now, it was time to celebrate that Norman had lost the struggle and he had survived by a razor-thin margin. When, in between joking with their Greek allies, FJ noticed Joe had moved to the quieter area of the bar, he went and sat down with him. He didn't speak for a few moments, and then he said,

"I can't begin to imagine how it's been for you," Joe smiled back thinly, "But I want you to remember that there are other forces at work out there besides the forces of evil. Look across at those two. Do you think it was a mere chance that they crossed our path? Remember the fire that suddenly changed direction?"

"Fire? When was that?"

FJ placed a hand on his shoulder,

"And, Ada and Janice, plus those other ladies I'm not supposed to talk to."

"You know, you're right," Joe said, "I wasn't sure at first why I got singled out, but, being descended from whoever or whatever. I get it now. There is a bigger plan. I'm just glad it's over. I saw a glimpse of where I was going and it was worse than anything I could have imagined. I want to thank you, Father. You really went out on a limb."

"As I said, just doing my job." Father Jones said. His mind drifted back to the unfortunate monk back in the middle ages, who had been left to suffer his fate.

◆ ◆ ◆

After the desire to drink anything else had left him, and with no intention of getting behind the wheel of his beloved speedboat *that drunk*, Heracles decided to take off his ship's captain hat. It was more of a decision made by his legs, which had become a little unsteady underneath his solid frame.

"That's the cue to turn in. Get our heads down for some much-needed rest." Constantine said. It had gone past 8:00 am and was not before time.

They were staying in a small hotel that belonged to a friend of Heracles. He and his employees very often stayed there overnight, mostly when in Israel on fishing business.

All four unlikely comrades single-filed through the white hotel doorway. Constantine urged Heracles to turn the volume down on his singing and described him as an *early morning alarm call.*

Joe's blemish-free body fell in between white sheets and he got the best six hours of sleep that he'd had in a week; especially considering he was so tired that he forgot about switching on the room's air-con. He awoke the next morning feeling hot and sticky, but well-rested.

He hopped into the shower and let the water run cool. He stayed there for ten minutes, letting the water wash away all the dust, soil, sweat and trauma. Then he turned the dial up and let the water run warm. He washed his entire body with the smallest bar of soap he'd ever seen. When he'd finished and dried himself off on an oversized white cotton towel, he nipped across the corridor to the door FJ had disappeared behind. He knocked, but no one answered. Joe pushed the door open and saw FJ led flat out, still asleep. He quietly closed the door again and left him to it. *It was no wonder he was exhausted.*

Joe walked down to the small dining room. Constantine and Heracles were both sitting at a table drinking coffee. Heracles looked remarkably un-hungover. Joe joined them and poured himself some coffee. Constantine slapped him on the back once again.

"Good man. Did you sleep ok?" he asked.

"I did." Joe answered.

"Where is the Father?" Heracles asked.

"Still sleeping. Like a baby. I didn't want to wake him."

"He is a very good man," Constantine added. Then he looked at Joe's grubby clothes. *He* was clean, but his clothes were showing the signs of battle, "We need to get you some new clothes. You look like a beggar ...no offence."

"I know a good little place around the corner." Heracles said, with a nod.

They drank their coffee and ate some croissants. Heracles may have looked ok from the outside, but croissants were all he dared eat for the time being.

When they'd finished breakfast, Heracles led Joe to the clothing store that he had mentioned. He looked at some of the items himself and ended up buying a t-shirt with the words *The Holy Land* across the front. He planned to wear it at Constantine's next service.

Joe picked out some lightweight cotton shorts, that were smart rather than sporty. He also bought a pair of boxer shorts and a T-shirt, along with a pale blue short-sleeved shirt. The material seemed good quality and the prices reflected that. When it came time to pay, Joe pulled out a rather dirty-looking wallet and brushed the soil from it. Luckily, his bank card was still in there. Then, before he paid, he realized that FJ was in a similar wardrobe situation. They had some spare clothes back in the campervan in Athens, but Joe did his best to guess FJ's dimensions and he bought him something clean to change into. Except for socks, which he forgot altogether.

"I got you size medium," Joe said as FJ woke up. He took a look and then thanked Joe for the gifts; not what he would have chosen, but not covered in dirt either. He had a quick shower and then got changed into his newly acquired pastel-coloured clothes. No socks. The sole on his right shoe was still flapping around and they needed a second trip to the clothing shop, where FJ bought some deck shoes. They all got a decent discount on the advertised prices, thanks to Heracles.

"Now I really do feel like I'm in an episode of *Miami Vice*." FJ said.

"You look cool. Maybe *Miami Vicar*." Heracles commented. He had his toes poking out of leather sandals so, in truth, he wasn't the best judge of coolness.

When all four were ready, changed and rested, Heracles gave the signal that it was time to head back down to the coast. The speedboat awaited.

24

Suleiman and his band of stone-faced followers felt the bitter taste of failure. One of their number had been put out of action by the fire, daggers had not tasted blood and a trip to hell was averted at the last second. But, instead of heading back to Syria to lick their wounds, they stuck around in Jerusalem. Their leader had been *blessed* with another message. Suleiman had known better than to try and follow their prey to the holy church of Sepulchre, but he didn't say anything about this latest vision and his followers knew better than to ask. At his instruction, they rode out to a remote part of the city and then parked their bikes in the ruins of an old stone dwelling. They gathered together in silence, forming a square shape, with Suleiman semi-delirious in a trance-like state sitting cross-legged in its centre. His dagger was unsheathed and ready to draw the blood of a goat that had been unfortunate enough to cross their path. The ancient ritual began.

◆◆◆

"If you need to pee you can do it over the side." Heracles said.

"What if we fall in whilst we're doing that?" FJ asked.

"I can turn this on a dime and go then back and fish you out. If, the sharks don't get you first." He winked at Joe.

FJ was in no doubt that Heracles could do that, and after all, it wasn't exactly a long drop to the water. None of them had worn life vests on the way to Israel. Now that all were safe and well and there was no need for haste, it seemed more prudent to wear one. It would have been ironic to succeed in a seemingly impossible mission and then come a cropper on the return journey.

"You did say there were no sharks." Joe said. Heracles sniggered.

"Not very big ones." he replied.

When everyone was in position, the engines started and they set off back to Athens. This time there was no big hurry. No records to break or people to save. Joe would have some time to reflect on his near-death experience. FJ would have time to relax and regain some of the energy he had expelled over the last couple of days. His whole body felt like he'd just undergone a week of commando training. Constantine and Heracles looked exactly the same as before: two chilled-out Greeks just enjoying life.

An hour in, Heracles called Joe to the front and asked him if he would like to steer the boat. He showed him some of the controls, but not all. Joe did steer for a time and followed the GPS for directions. It seemed a lot easier than expected, though he was only doing the basics. FJ also had a turn at the helm and thought it very exciting for the first fifteen minutes and then he was more than happy to relinquish the captaincy back to the big man with the beard. Each passenger sat back and relaxed. It had been a tiring couple of days for all involved. After four hours of steering, Constantine gave the seemingly infatigable Heracles an extended break. He made himself comfortable and got some shut-eye. Just an hour later, when Heracles was refreshed and back steering the speedboat, he suddenly turned to the others and said loudly,

"Are you ready for a detour?"

"Detour?" Constantine asked.

"Unless anyone has anything against the idea, I'm going to take a right turn," FJ and Joe looked at each other and wondered what the hell he was talking about, "Boys it is Friday and we are going to spend it in Rhodes! It's party time!" It obviously hadn't taken him long to recover from the previous night.

FJ looked at Joe and shrugged; neither felt like

they had the required energy to party, but it was his boat, his rules.

"Let's just go with the flow," FJ said to Joe, "It might be fun. What's one extra day."

"Shouldn't we get these boys back?" Constantine shouted above the engine noise. Heracles held one hand to his ear and shouted,

"I can't hear you, it's too noisy." Further attempts to talk him out of this idea would have failed miserably, so no one tried. Also, he looked so happy about having the freedom to act this spontaneously, that it would have been a crime to interfere with it. Hence, two hours later, they docked the speedboat on the southern tip of Rhodes at a place called *Agios Georgios* beach. That's where they would be staying the night, at one of the beachfront villas that were owned by a cousin of Heracles. Off-season, he let him have a key to one of them, in return Heracles let him eat for free at his fish-themed restaurant in Athens.

It seemed like heaven on earth to Joe and FJ. Though most of the locals didn't know any different, this was just *normal* to them. Heracles had worked *at least* a sixty-hour week in his twenties and thirties and that's why he liked to party in his forties.

"This is pretty amazing." Joe said as he walked through the door of the three-bedroom apartment. It was tastefully decorated and immaculately clean. That was down to the cleaners who came twice a month, rather than Heracles.

"You two will have to share a room," Heracles said to FJ and Joe, "Twin beds though, so you won't have to bunk in together. I'm not sharing with Constantine. The man snores like an ox."

Constantine whispered to FJ and Joe,

"It's not uncommon for him to be found sound asleep on the beach." Both chuckled in response.

Heracles opened the fridge and offered up a choice of different beers. They all sat on the balcony overlooking the sea, watching the waves gently lap up on the crystal-clear sand of the beach.

Two more beers each later, Heracles asked,

"Who's hungry?" It was a good question; besides the croissants, none of them had eaten much in the last twenty-four hours. Heracles's fridge contained only beer. Like children being offered ice cream, Joe and FJ raised their hands, "Ok then gentlemen, freshen up because we are going to hit the big town!"

"Big town, where is that?" FJ asked.

"Faliraki." Heracles clarified.

"Oh, I think that might be just a bit too wild for me." FJ said.

"Don't worry, it's off-season. It's not like what you might have seen on television." Constantine reassured.

"There are still some good bars open," Heracles said, "And, the best kebab place in all of Greece. I'll call the cab."

Heracles seemed to be providing the energy for the rest of the group. There is a theory that certain people, like narcissists, drain your energy, this man was like a shining beacon. A human battery. Enough of his energy radiated into FJ, who now felt more enthusiastic about the planned experience; though priests weren't particularly well known for their road trip adventures. Constantine seemed to read his mind.

"Don't worry," he said in the cab, "This isn't a road trip. We are just going there and then coming back."

Joe felt like everything from now onwards was a new experience to be grateful for; though that may have been the effect of the several beers he'd already drunk.

Soon, the fifty-minute drive was almost completed and the quartet of *revellers* began seeing neon bar lights scattered here and there in the distance. Heracles rubbed his hands together with excitement. He did visit Faliraki during mid-season on at least one occasion per year and usually ended up tagging on to a group of younger part-goers, boasting that no one could drink him under the table and no one ever did. By comparison, tonight would be a heavily scaled-down affair.

"We have two hours," Heracles informed them, "Then the kebab place closes."

To the others, two hours seemed more than enough time to take in the few bars that were still open, sample this delightful cuisine and then head on back. In truth, FJ was already thinking about the comfortable-looking white-sheeted bed he'd sat on back at the apartment. Nevertheless, he felt a couple more cold beers in a lively setting would be a tonic for the troops.

The first bar they ventured into was full of young locals and late-season holidaymakers. The thud, thud of the booming bass soon became annoying, even to Heracles, who suggested they move on after just one drink. The next bar was empty, save for two rather sullen-looking and over-tanned late-deal-takers, who probably wouldn't have known a good time if it bit them in the ass. They passed by that bar altogether and moved on to the third bar, which was about half full and pulsated with better music. Like Goldilocks, they had found the right balance and they made themselves comfortable at a table near the bar.

Heracles had an extended inhibition-less dance. Constantine joined in for one song, with Joe and FJ clapping with enthusiasm from the table. *They'd done it.* The time for reflection would be later; for tonight, they would kick back and do their best to expel any remaining remnants of built-up tension and trauma.

◆ ◆ ◆

When it got to midnight, Heracles realised that the group was done for the night and the time had come to return to the seafront apartment. The other three were flagging and, though he'd never have admitted it, so was he. It was kebab and then home time.

"You all ready for the best kebab on the island?" he asked. He got two affirmations, "Ok, let go." As they all got up from their seats, FJ asked,

"Where is Joe?"

"He went to the toilets I think." Constantine said.

"I'll go and get him. Let him know we are leaving," FJ said and then he walked around to the other side of the bar where the toilets were situated. He wasn't at the urinal. He tried the stalls. There were just two of them and both were empty. He walked back to the others, "He's not in there."

"You sure?" Constantine asked.

"Yes."

"Can't you call him?" Heracles asked.

"I can't. His phone is back in the campervan in Athens."

"Where did he go to then?" Constantine

asked.

“I don’t know. When was the last time you saw him?” FJ asked. All three tried to sober up quickly, though thinking logically through a cloud of several beers was not the easiest of tasks.

“About…come to think of it, about two songs ago.” Constantine replied.

“Come on,” Heracles decided, “Let’s spread out and go and look for him.”

They formed a three-man search party and spread out about twelve feet apart. They made a sweep of the dance floor and then the outside. It was now eerily quiet. Most of the other punters had left in the last ten minutes when the DJ announced that there were only three songs left to play.

“Maybe he has gone off to be sick somewhere.” Constantine suggested.

“I don’t think he’d go too far.” FJ said.

“Then where on earth is he?” Heracles wondered.

◆ ◆ ◆

Joe’s eyes opened. He was in the back seat of a car and his hands were tied together with a piece of rope. The back of his head throbbed. He sat up. There was just him and someone driving. When he looked out of the window, he didn’t see any buildings or houses.

"What's going on?" he asked. The driver answered without breaking his gaze from the road.

"You are awake then."

Joe didn't recognize the accent. It wasn't English or Greek, though he thought he'd heard it before.

"What the hell is going on?"

"We are going on a little trip," The driver said, "Fun fun fun." Then he turned around and smiled.

"Norman..."

"Yes. Happy to see me?" His teeth were sharp and triangular.

"What do you want? It's over, the marks are gone."

"No, no no, it's not over. Not by a long chalk."

"How are you driving?"

"You are a special case and special cases require special measures. Now, sit tight, we have almost reached our destination."

◆◆◆

Without any other way of finding Joe, who had just seemed to vanish into thin air, FJ called Ada, who had been having her own low-key celebration of sorts along with Janice. They had sipped a nice bottle of wine between them and Ada had been preparing to spend the night in

Janice's spare room again. She was pleased to hear FJ's voice …at first.

"What do you mean he's gone missing?"

"We went to a bar and now he's just gone. Vanished into thin air."

"Where are you?"

"Faliraki."

"Faliraki, did you say?"

"Yes, we took a detour on the way back. Ada … can you shed any light on this please?"

Ada took a deep breath. She had used up most of her psychic energy several hours earlier.

"Wait. Give me a moment. My reserves are very low but not *quite* empty. Hold the line …"

She held up a hand as a signal for Janice to keep quiet and then closed her eyes. She gathered whatever psychic energy she had left and reached out into the void once again. She saw shapes moving forwards and backwards. It was all muddy. Unclear. It dawned on her that she might be spent and would need to recuperate, but she didn't stop trying. Then, like a long-distance runner who suddenly breaks free of the wall and gets a second wind from out of nowhere, the shapes started taking form and tuning in, becoming clearer and clearer. She opened her eyes again.

"You still there Ada?" FJ asked.

"I am. I think I know what has happened. The demon that Joe called Norman. He's become corporeal."

"Co... what? What does that mean?"

"It means that he's become solid. Taken human form."

"Can he do that?"

"Well, yes it looks like he can."

"Why would he do that if he's immortal as a demon?"

"Demons are like any other narcissists. They hate to lose at anything."

"And if he's human, where is he?"

"That's the problem," Ada said, "He's on the same island you are on."

"Oh God, no!" FJ exclaimed.

"That's not the worst bit. He has Joe."

"He has him? Where, where is he? What does he plan to do?"

"It's not good."

"Can you direct us to him?"

"I'm afraid not. I'm out of the loop now for a while. I've used up all I had left and then some. Feeling quite light-headed actually."

"We'll never find him then. It's impossible on an island this size."

"Perhaps not, there is something I saw just before everything faded out."

"What did you see?"

"White arches and a tower. Oh, and a very old tree in a circle."

"That's it?"

"I'm afraid I can't give you any more. I'm sorry I just can't. That's all I have."

"Ok. Ada, don't worry. We *will* find him," FJ ended the call and turned to the others, "He's been kidnapped."

◆ ◆ ◆

The car came to a standstill.

"This driving business is quite fun," Norman said, "It's *crazy* good fun. That's what I like about you lot, you are resourceful if nothing else. If there is something that you haven't got, one of you invents it," Norman turned into the back and smiled, "What I don't like about your lot is ... well, apart from the smell, when you don't know your place in the bigger scheme. You've pissed me off Joseph. You have rather pissed me off. Does it show in my expression?" He got out of the car and went around to the passenger door. He opened it quickly and then just stood there. Joe looked at him.

"You made yourself human?"

"Hmm. How astute. A relatively straightforward procedure, but not a permanent arrangement. Like I say, smelly creatures. Too many bodily functions. Too many big ideas. I remember when you were little more than apes. Less fun, but much easier to deal with. Anyway, if you want something done properly, better do it yourself," Norman smiled, "Well come on, I'm waiting."

Joe shuffled across the seat and then slowly got out of the car. He felt drunk and tired. If he set off running, he probably wouldn't get far.

"Norman, can't you see that it's over."

"It's over, *it's*? No no, it is *you* that is over."

"Come on man. Please just let it go."

"There you go again. *Man.* You don't know what you are dealing with, do you? Even now right at the end."

Joe looked around. By the looks of it, Norman had parked up at the local church.

"So, what do you want from me? I'm not the same guy as the one from the past. Whatever he did, that was nothing to do with me."

Norman smiled again and revealed his triangular teeth. He held out his hand and opened it. In his palm were several large nails.

◆ ◆ ◆

Heracles and Constantine couldn't believe their ears.

"Kidnapped?" Constantine said, "Who by?"

"The demon that had cursed him. The reason we had to visit Jerusalem."

Heracles's jolly face fell deadly serious. This warm evening had just taken a major swerve in atmosphere.

"Where would they take him?" he wondered.

"My friend said that she saw some arches and an old tree. She is psychic and sees things from afar. But, that's all she had." FJ said. Constantine had an idea why she might have seen arches and an old tree.

"Sounds like Saint Nectarios. It is the main church on the island. I've visited it many times."

"Come on then," Heracles said, "Unless anyone has a better idea, let's go there."

Most of the taxis had stopped operating for the night. There was one that was en route to pick up some other punters from the bar, and the trio managed to convince the driver that they were the ones who had booked it.

"The walk will do them good," Constantine whispered as they got in, "To the church please, as fast as you can." It was the cab driver's last run of his shift. He didn't ask why they wanted to go to the church after midnight, he just set off and put his foot down.

◆ ◆ ◆

"Ok," Norman said, "Seeing as you like helping people so much, I think it is only right and proper that you experience what they did. You know, so you get the full effect. So you can *empathise* more accurately."

"*I* like helping people? This was someone else

a very long time ago." Joe said. He had no plan of escape other than to keep Norman talking until he thought of one.

"Yes. Meddlers. Do-gooders. Insects that don't know their place. Once again, a big big mistake giving some of you humans empathy. I have gotten along without any at all perfectly well all these years."

"I'm a telecoms repair man. I fix telephone lines."

"I am not concerned with what you are now," Norman said with a shrug. Then, "See that tree behind you?" Joe turned around and saw a thick old tree within the grounds of the church, "Interestingly enough, that tree is over two thousand years old. The oldest tree on the island. That is where *you* are going to share the fate of the one you carried the cross for. Fitting isn't it? I do like a fitting ending, don't you?" He jiggled the nails around in his hand. In his other hand, he held a rusty hammer. The smile left his angular face, "Now then, let's get to it. This whole *being human* thing is beginning to bore me a little."

"Wait a second."

"Wait, for what?"

"You wish to crucify me on that tree. Why aren't you making me suffer first? You know, carry something or..."

"Hmmm. Perhaps I *am* rushing things a little. It's not often I get to play around as one of you lot. Details, details. What could I get you to carry around for a while?" Norman looked around in a circle but couldn't see anything suitable, "Oh well, nothing here. Back to plan *a*. Ironically, you will have a good view of the church cross from where you are situated."

"What about a suitable crown? You are missing a trick here, aren't you? You've waited two thousand years and are wasting opportunities."

Norman stopped his forward motion and his eyes lit up.

"Now there is a genuinely good idea. Well done you," Norman again looked around in a circle and spotted a rose bush off to the side, "Perfect," He started to walk towards it. Joe started to edge away slowly, "Don't bother trying to run. I made myself human and also made myself three times as strong as the best of you," He muttered to himself, "Actually I had some help with the becoming human thing. Those dim-witted idiots don't realise I hate them just as much as the rest of you. They actually believe they are getting some kind of reward." He walked over to the rose bush and began to fashion a crown of thorns from its branches. With his back turned, Joe started to edge away. "I said not to move. You will only make it worse for yourself," Joe stopped. "Worse!" Norman chuckled. *How worse could it be.* Joe's tired and alcohol-influenced brain frantically tried to think of a way out of this predicament. He picked a direction and ran; rather clumsily as his hands were still bound together. Norman didn't move for a time and Joe managed to get thirty meters away before he appeared next to him. He placed a crown of rosebush thorns on Joe's head in one quick, fluid movement. "There you go," he said, proud of his handiwork. Blood started to run down Joe's forehead from the thorn cuts, "Now you are looking the part. I must say this is fun. I should try being human a bit more often, instead of every thousand years or so. Not *too* often mind. Like I was saying …smelly creatures." He dragged Joe over to the tree by his outstretched arms. Then he positioned him so that he would face the church's cross. When he was perfectly in line, he pushed him up against the trunk. The old tree had thick branches coming out at right angles. Norman then produced a curved knife. Joe looked at the blade as he held it aloft. Norman lowered it and then sliced through his bonds. Joe immediately took a swing at Norman's smirking head. He made decent contact, but there was virtually no effect, except that it increased the size of his grin. "Spirited. I must say. Now, which arm first," With a vice-like grip, he took hold of Joe's left hand and raised it to shoulder height. Joe did his best to struggle and Norman punched him in the jaw, knocking him out cold, "You will come around before long. Probably when the first nail hammers in."

At the entrance to the church, the taxi stopped. FJ got out of the front and Heracles and Constantine out of the back.

"Look!" FJ spotted two figures in the taxi's headlights around twenty-five meters away, over by the great old tree.

"That is your friend and someone else with his back to us," Constantine said, "It looks like he's about to…"

"What is in the trunk?" Heracles asked the taxi driver.

"Just an oil can, a boat hook and some other junk. Why?"

Heracles went around the back and opened the car's boot. He picked out the boat hook, which was four feet long, made of wood, with a metal hook on one end for gathering boat moorings. He held it in his right hand.

Norman raised the hammer. The fingers of his left hand held a flat-headed nail over Joe's open palm. Joe's eyes flickered open. Norman smiled.

"Good. You are awake again. No time for sleeping on the job. This is something that you really didn't want to miss," He pulled the hammer back. Joe waited for the impact and the pain.

"Hey, hey, over there!" Constantine shouted. Norman stopped and lowered the hammer. He turned to see three people moving quickly towards him.

"Oh. How touching. Your friends have come to join the party," Norman rasped, "Perhaps I will crucify them as well. What do you think? Would you like to have your friends keep you company? Would that be thoughtful of me?" FJ slowed as he got a little closer. Heracles had hurriedly flanked to his left and Constantine was a step away to FJ's right.

"Let's just talk this through can we?" FJ said. The taxi driver had no idea what was going on. His shift had ended and he set off for home.

"Men of the cloth. How laughable you lot are. Talk what through? What would you like to talk about? I have a lifetime to chew the fat. However, let's not. I have pressing matters to attend to." He focused his attention back on delivering the first nail. FJ grabbed the hammer just as it was about to connect. Norman swatted FJ backwards ten feet. He lay on his back, blood pouring from a busted nose. Then he appeared right beside Constantine. "Next," he said and then he grabbed the Greek priest and threw him six feet into the air. He hit the ground with a thud. Then Norman swiftly ducked under the arc of a swing of the boat hook. He turned to face Heracles, who had never seen anyone move that fast before. "Now then, what are you?" Norman asked, "You have a different *vibe* to the other sheep. Could it be that you are part.....” then he stopped, a look of surprise etched across his face. He looked down. Protruding out of his chest was the wooden shaft of the boat hook, “This is a little ...unexpected...” he said, as he dropped the hammer. Then he fell to his knees, as the bloodied FJ and the bruised Constantine came ambling over.

“Good shot!” Constantine said to Heracles.

“Not really, I was aiming for his head, but close enough.” All four looked down at Norman who had flopped onto his back like a beached turtle. He held out an outstretched hand and tried to say one last thing but ran out of life before the words could form.

“He’s dead,” FJ panted, “He made himself human and now he’s dead.”

“I won’t ask for the full story,” Constantine said, “For now, let’s just get Joe and go back to the apartment.”

“I just killed someone,” Heracles said, “I could go to jail.”

“I doubt that,” FJ said, as the four watched the body of Norman dissolve into what looked like a mummified corpse, “Come on. Let’s go,” he said and then he put an arm around Joe for support, “Are you ok?” he asked Joe, who nodded.

“I will be.”

The taxi had gone. The four set off walking slowly back to the apartment.

“You see that throw?” Heracles said, “I used to

be an ace with the javelin."

"Just one of your many talents," Constantine said, "Just one. Now call us a cab or one of your many friends. I'm not walking all the way back."

◆ ◆ ◆

It was 2:15 am when all four men arrived back at the apartment.

"I still don't believe what I just witnessed with my own eyes," exclaimed Constantine, "I knew evil existed but that was something else altogether. The way that weird fellow shrivelled up at the end."

"Do you think that we should have kept the remains?" Heracles wondered.

"No. I do not," FJ said flatly, as he manoeuvred Joe down onto the sofa, "Is there anything you want Joe?"

"Yes," Joe answered wearily, "Get me another beer please."

"Have something a little stronger," Heracles said. He produced a bottle of Metaxa from a cupboard and poured him a small glass of brandy, "This will do you some good."

They sat around the table overlooking the beach for another half hour, with the eternal sound of the waves in the background. Each periodically sighing or blowing out air. Each was too tired to say much. FJ called Ada and told her the latest update about Norman and Heracles's amazing throw that pierced his body and killed him. Both Ada and Janice went to sleep that night with their minds exhausted but at rest.

When the time came for FJ to turn in, he again asked Joe how he was.

"I'm ok ...strangely," He held up the hand with a slight puncture in the centre, where Norman had lined up the nail. "There is one thing I've realised though."

"What's that?" FJ asked.

"My climbing up telegraph pole days are well and truly ...over."

◆ ◆ ◆

The next day, they each awoke at their own pace. Heracles stirred first and sat facing the sea with a strong coffee an hour before the others surfaced. One by one the others joined him. When everyone was present he made a large omelette, because all he had were eggs and frozen bread, and they all ate some with toast.

The morning unfolded like any other off-season morning. Several locals and a handful of visitors walked across the beach in front of them. Sticks were thrown for dogs to chase. A couple of jet skis meandered in and out just off the shore. None of the recently formed four companions spoke much. When it got to midday, despite the idyllic setting being the perfect place to recuperate, Heracles suggested that they head on back to Athens, as he had things to do. No one argued. The island *was* beautiful but had been the scene of something quite horrific. Each of them wanted to return to normal as soon as possible.

It was another several-hour stint in the speedboat that passed quickly and without incident. The waters were calm and smooth. During the journey, Joe dozed in one of the comfy seats. He occasionally relived moments from the previous night and decided to let his mind think about it, rather than trying to block it out. Heracles, again, did most of the steering. He, as usual, looked the least fatigued of the quartet. He did wonder, though, what Norman had meant when he'd asked him *what* he was. He was just a regular person, *wasn't he?* He found that an odd statement to make. But, as his mind was equally as strong as his body, he put it out of his thoughts. FJ dozed for a few more hours on the seat next to Joe. He hadn't become a priest to indulge in this sort of crazy adventure. Sadly, it was one story that he couldn't really tell during the Sunday sermon. Though it might have been the catalyst for increasing attendance numbers if he were to do so. Constantine took a brief turn navigating the boat. He stayed up at the front for most of the return journey, happy to let refreshing sprays of water hit his face.

When the speed boat was being hitched up to the flatbed truck back on Grecian dry land, all four island hoppers stopped and took a moment. They would soon part ways. With Norman now gone, FJ and Joe planned to get a flight back to the U.K, with Joe simply explaining that he had *lost* his passport. Heracles would go back to running his business and Constantine would resume his pastoral duties.

FJ spoke first,

"The campervan. I'm leaving it to you Heracles as a reminder of this adventure," Heracles shook FJ's hand. He might never use it, but that wasn't the point. "Constantine, thanks for all your help, whether you are a man of the cloth or not, you are a true gentleman." FJ shook Constantine's hand and in return, he slapped him on the back.

"May you both have a safe journey home," Constantine said, "And hopefully, our lives will be a bit duller from now onwards."

"I hope so," echoed Joe, "That was enough excitement for one lifetime."

Heracles didn't agree with the *duller life* sentiment, but even he was relieved to get back to normality.

They did what people making holiday friendships tend to do and agreed to keep in touch. This time they all meant it. Constantine dropped the two Englishmen off outside the police station to report the *lost*, passport and obtain the required documentation so that Joe could fly home.

"Expensive trip this." Joe said. FJ nodded,

"Don't worry, you can halve me the cost when we are settled back at home. Not that I've been keeping tabs ..."

"Really, I insist on paying *at least* half. After all, we didn't come all this way for any other reason but me. Plus the cost of the campervan."

"Yes, well, the Church funded most of it. Don't leave town though." FJ said with a smile.

After much form-filling and *white lies*, Joe had the necessary requirements needed to board the plane home.

"You sure you didn't want to drive back in the van?" Joe asked FJ as they left the police station.

"Err no. Would you want to spend more than an hour in the back of that thing again? All those plates rattling around." FJ stated. Joe shook his head.

"I threw the plates into a bush somewhere along the way. But, nope. It played its part though."

"We would not be here talking without it. Perhaps one day we might go back for it."

They had retrieved their sparse belongings from the campervan and, during a spot of lunch in a local café, FJ booked the flights back to the U.K. using his mobile phone.

"Amazing what you can do with just a phone isn't it," FJ stated. Joe agreed with a nod, "Shame the young ones are glued to them all day long, but they certainly do have their uses."

Joe called Ada and told her their flight's arrival time, which was 7:10 pm that evening. Ada said that she would bring Janice with her and collect them from the airport. Joe didn't 100% trust the mini to get there, but he thanked her all the same.

"It's a shame we don't see more of the city," Joe said, "You know, whilst we are here."

"I guess so, but do you have the energy? I know I certainly don't."

"True. That can be for another time. I do just want to get back now."

"Agreed."

The airport was just a short taxi drive away. Joe and FJ stepped out into the warm air and saw the airport's main doors in front of them. Then, out of nowhere, the raucous noise of a motorbike engine filled the air. FJ looked around sharply. A local Greek man in a t-shirt pulled up on a small scooter and parked near the doors. Joe looked at FJ and smiled.

Once inside the modern airport, they hopped onto a conveyer belt that took them to the correct gate and then they sat and waited an hour until it was time to board the Airbus 320. Joe sipped a lager and FJ a double brandy …for medicinal purposes. Then, right on schedule, the notice board showed that it was time to make a move and get on the plane.

"£79 each," FJ said as they stepped on board, "Extremely good value. I don't know how they do it."

"We probably, well actually, *you* probably spent three times that on diesel getting there."

They had seats next to each other on the right, near the wing.

Joe thought again about his brother. He had called him when he'd retrieved his phone from the campervan and Derek's sense of relief was audible. He'd bent the truth and told him that he'd gone on an impromptu break and then lost his phone, which was kind of true. Apart from Derek, no one else seemed to know that he'd been away. The respect that had been lost seemed quite insignificant now. It would not be long before their relationship was watertight again.

The Airbus taxied into position and then took off. It was just a four-hour haul. Both Joe and FJ put their heads back and closed their eyes.

"What a trip. What a trip." FJ said, as the plane reached its ceiling height and levelled out.

Joe tried to get some more sleep but found that he couldn't drift off. He dozed, his eyelids half closed and gazed out of the window into the blue sky. After half an hour, he looked to his left and saw that FJ was dozing, and then he turned back and watched the clouds again. In contrast to the previous few days, life seemed to be passing by in slow motion.

They were an hour into the journey when, suddenly, out of nowhere, Joe heard a bang and then he saw smoke emanating from the jet engine under the right wing. There was a noise like the churning of metal. Joe looked at FJ again, whose eyes immediately opened. He then followed the trail of smoke visible through the window. The two looked at each other. Other passengers had seen it too and there was a growing murmur of unrest. The captain thought it best to make an announcement through the tannoy,

"This is your captain speaking. We have sustained a malfunction of the right jet engine. That engine has now been shut down. Please do not be too alarmed, we still have one fully functional engine and will land at the first opportunity to effect repairs and arrange alternative transportation. Thank you for your co-operation. Captain out."

The two flight attendants walked down both aisles and reassured all the passengers that there was no need for alarm, but advised that there would be unavoidable delays. *Everyone would get home as soon as possible.* When the attendant reached FJ, he asked her what had happened. She whispered back,

"A bird flew into one of the engines. It is

extremely rare, a chance in a million and nothing to be unduly worried about. We are been diverted to Belgrade airport." Then she moved on down the aisle. FJ and Joe looked at each other again.

"In a million," Joe said, "I don't like this. What's a bird doing flying this high up." FJ looked around. There must have been at least a hundred passengers. Men, women and children. He looked back at Joe.

"Norman was dead, wasn't he?" FJ said.

Joe looked out of the window at the smoking engine.

"We took a big chance getting onboard," He turned and looked at all the worried faces. Then he sat back, "It's me they want."

"What do you mean?"

"It's me they want, not all these innocent people."

"It could be a complete coincidence." FJ offered.

"You know that it's not. It's only a matter of time before the other one goes. Remember the taxi? There's no protection on here."

"You don't know that. Anyway, what could you do to prevent that from happening?"

"I don't know, I don't know. What if I make a deal with them."

"You're not making sense."

"None of this makes any sense," Joe said. "What if I agreed to their demands?"

"Joe, they wanted you in hell."

"What if I did a deal and saved all of these people?"

"A deal? What are you thinking? You can't exactly open the door and jump out. Did you bring a parachute with you?"

The sky lit up with a bright fork of lightning. Then another.

"No," said Joe, "But they will be listening. If I agreed to their terms."

FJ looked around the plane once again.

"That goes against God's wishes. In thirty minutes, we will land at Belgrade airport."

"Will we though? Or will we crash-land into the sea?"

"We will. Never make a pact with demons."

"But look at all these people. They are all innocent."

"So are you Joe, *so are you.*"

Joe sat back. *Thirty minutes.*

Father Jones looked upwards. Joe's hands gripped the seat. He gritted his teeth and waited …

BOOKS BY THIS AUTHOR

Midas (Author Peter Birkett)

Separated and betrayed. Andrew Gold is in the worst place. It couldn't get any worse, could it? When he stands to lose his kids as well as everything else, a special gift is bestowed upon him. This gift has some unwritten rules. The first one is: don't use it for selfish reasons. That is easier said than done when the cause of all your misery is just within touching distance.

Chiller (Author Peter Birkett)

After gaining and losing the power to heal, Andrew Gold started settling back into everyday life. He'd started a new business and even had a new love interest. Things were starting to look up, but that was before digging on a construction site on the edge of town unearthed something evil from the past. Angry protestors got more than they bargained for when they chained themselves to the machinery overnight. Signs in the night sky heralded the return of an ancient race with selfish designs on planet Earth. With these invaders thriving in freezing conditions, everywhere was about to get a lot colder.

Viral (Author Peter Birkett)

"Just the one train journey." The psychic told him. "Yes, but the the Siberian Express?" Andy replied. Still, they all knew that they couldn't fly to the coldest city on earth, not with the ancient alien weapon packed away in their luggage. And what was waiting for the small band of travellers at the end of this journey? "You will know it when you see it." The psychic said. Not much to go on, but what choice did they have? If they refused, the world was doomed.

Printed in Great Britain
by Amazon

27918564R00190